By Emma Donoghue

STIR-FRY

A NOVEL

EMMA DONOGHUE

HarperPerennial
A Division of HarperCollins*Publishers*

A hardcover edition of this book was published in 1994 by HarperCollins Publishers.

HarperCollins books may be purchased for educational, business, or sales promotional use. For information please write: Special Markets Department, HarperCollins Publishers, Inc., 10 East 53rd Street, New York, NY 10022.

First HarperPerennial edition published 1995.

Designed by C. Linda Dingler

The Library of Congress has catalogued the hardcover edition as follows:

Donoghue, Emma, 1969–
    Stir-fry : a novel / Emma Donoghue. — 1st ed.
        p.   cm.
    ISBN 0-06-017109-X
    1. Women college students—Ireland—Dublin—Fiction. 2. Teenage girls—Ireland—Dublin—Fiction. 3. Dublin (Ireland)—Fiction. I. Title.
    PR6054.O547S75   1994
    823.914—dc20   93-40267

ISBN 0-06-092624-4 (pbk.)

95 96 97 98 99 ❖/RRD 10 9 8 7 6 5 4 3 2 1

I want to thank Siobhan Harding, Daniel Levine, Una Ní Dhubhghaill, Lene Rubenstein, Margaret Lonergan, Jenna Roberts, Cris Townley, Debra West-gate, my agent Caroline Davidson and my editors Terry Karten and Alexandra Pringle, for their most constructive criticism.

This book is for Anne

CONTENTS

1

PICKING

"2 ♀ SEEK FLATMATE." Two diamonds of masking tape held the card to the notice board. "OWN ROOM. Wow! NO BIGOTS."

It was all in red ink except the Wow!, which must have been scrawled on by a passerby. A thumb had smudged the top of the 2, giving it the shape of a swan with its beak held up to the wind. Maria leaned against the wall, getting out of the way of a passing stream of hockey players, and rummaged for a biro.

She copied the ad onto the first page of her refill pad, which looked, she realised with a surge of irritation, as blank and virginal as the homework notebooks the nuns always sold on the first day back to school. She drew a jagged line below the number. Chances were the room would be filled by now, since the card's top two corners were dog-eared. Still, it was worth a bash, better than anything else on offer. Maria wasn't sure how many more weeks she could stand with the aunt and her footstools. Her eyes slid down the notice board. It was leprous with peeling paper, scraps offering everything from "Grinds In Anglo-Saxon By A Fluent Speaker" to "heavyduty bikelock for sale." All the propositions in the accommodation section sounded equally sinister. "V. low rent" had to mean squalor, and "informal atmos." hinted at blue mould in the bread bin.

Returning her biro to her shirt pocket, Maria stood back against a pillar papered with flyers. She clasped her hands loosely over her refill pad, holding it against her belly. The corners of her mouth tilted up just a little, enough to give the impression that she was waiting for someone, she hoped, but not so much as to look inane. She hugged the refill pad tighter against her hips; it felt as comfortable as old armour. Her eyes stayed low, watching the crowd that had over-flowed every bench and table in the Students' Union.

A knot of black-leather lads were kicking a coffee machine; she looked away at once, in case one of them might accost her with some witticism she would be unable to invent a retort for. Behind the layer of grit on the window, her eye caught a flat diamond of silver. The lake had looked so much bluer in the college prospectus. Her grip on the pad was too tight; she loosened her fingers and thought of being a pike. Steely and plump, nosing round the lake's cache of oilcans, black branches, the odd dropped sandal mouldering to green. A great patient fish, waiting for summer to dip the first unsuspecting toe within an inch of her bite. Maria swal-lowed a smile.

Bending her knees, she let herself down until she was sit-ting on the top step. Something tickled her on the side of the neck, and she jolted, but it was only a stray corner from one of the orange freshers'-ball posters. She read the details over her shoulder, noting that *committee* was missing a few conso-nants. Then she told herself not to be so damn negative on the first day and turned her face forward again. In the far corner, under a brown-spattered mural of Mother Ireland, she spotted a slight acquaintance from home. His corduroy knees were drawn up to his chin, an Ecology Society pamphlet barricading his face. No, she would not go and say hello, she was not that desperate.

🔄

Trigonometry was a stuffy mousetrap on the fourth floor. She counted twenty-four heads and squeezed her leg an inch farther onto the back bench. The girl beside her seemed to be asleep, streaked hair hanging round her face like ivy; her padded hip was warm against Maria's. When the tutor asked for their names, there was a sort of tremor along the bench, and the girl's head swung up.

Maria was reading the ad one more time; she could feel her mouth going limp with indecision. As the registration list was being passed around, she gave a tentative nudge to her neighbor and held up the refill pad at an angle. "Sorry, but would you have any idea what exactly the wee symbol stands for?"

Salmon-pink fingernails covered a small yawn. "Just means women," the girl murmured, "but they'd be fairly feministy, you know the sort."

Her glance was speculative, but Maria whispered "Many thanks" and bent her head. She was far from sure which sort she was meant to know the sort of. In the library at home she had found *The Female Eunuch*, a tattered copy with Nelly the Nutter's observations scrawled in the margins. She had richly enjoyed it—especially the bits Nelly had done zigzags on with her crayon—but could not imagine flatmates who'd go around quoting it all day. Still, Maria reminded herself as the tutorial dragged to a close, it was not familiarity she had come here for. If Dublin was going to feel so odd—so windy, littered with crisp packets, never quiet—then the odder the better, really.

It was five past twelve before she could slide round the cluster of elbows and out of the office. A knot of lecturers emerged from their tearoom behind her, their Anglophile accents filling the corridor. She hurried down the steps in search of a phone. Catching her reflection in a dusty staircase window, Maria paused to poke at the shoulder pads on her black jacket. Damn the things, they were meant to give an air of assurance, but they made her look humpbacked. She pushed back her fringe and gave her peaky chin an encouraging look.

"Yoohoo, Maria!"

She ignored that, because nobody knew her name.

The shriek went higher. She peered under the handrail to find the streaky blonde from the tutorial waving from a huddle of trench coats. To reach them she had to weave between an abstract bronze and the Archaeology Club's papier-mâché dolmen.

"It is Maria, isn't it?" The girl wore an enamel badge that read MATERIAL GIRL.

"Yeah, only it's a hard *i*," she explained.

The voice rolled past her. "Hard? Godawful. I'm dropping out of maths right away, life's too short. I heard the trig man read out your name, and I thought, well she looks like she knows what he's burbling on about, which is more than I do."

"I sort of like maths," Maria said reluctantly.

"Perv." Her eyes were straying to a mark on the thigh of her pale rose trousers; she picked at it with one nail. "Personally I'm switching to philosophy, they say it's a guaranteed honour." She glanced up. "Oh, I'm Yvonne, did I say? Sorry, I should have said."

Maria let her face lift in the first grin of the day. Not wanting it to last a second too long, she looked away and mentioned that she needed a pay phone.

"Over in the far corner, past the chaplaincy. Is it about that flat share?"

"Well, probably." Too defensive. "I haven't really made up my mind."

"Personally," Yvonne confided, "I wouldn't trust anything advertised in that hole of a Students' Union. A cousin of mine had a bad experience with a secondhand microwave oven."

Maria's mouth twisted. "What did it do to her, exactly?"

"I never got the full details," Yvonne admitted. "Well, listen, if the Libbers don't suit you, I have an uncle who's leasing terribly nice flats, apartments really, just outside Dublin—"

"Actually, I want something fairly low-budget," Maria told her. "Got to make the money stretch."

Yvonne nodded, her hoop earrings bobbing. "God, I know, don't talk to me, where does it go? I'm already up to my eyes in debt to Mum for my ball gown. How are we going to make it to Christmas, Maria, tell me that?"

🄴

"Yeah."

"Eh, hello, sorry, is that oh three six nine four two?"

"Far as I know."

"Oh. Well, it's just about your ad."

"Me wha'?"

"Wasn't it you?"

"Not that I know of."

"Your ad. Your ad on the notice board in the Students' Union."

"I haven't a notion what you're talking about."

"But, sorry, but I saw it there just this morning."

"What did it say?"

"Well it starts 'two' and then a sort of symbol thing—"

"Hang on. Ruth? Ruth, turn off that bloody hair dryer. Listen, have you taken to advertising our services in the S.U.? What? No, I amn't being thick. Oh, the flat, all right, well why didn't you tell me? Yo, are you still there? Nobody tells me anything."

"It's just I was hoping, maybe I could come and have a look, if it's not too inconvenient? Unless you have someone already?"

"For all I know she could have sublet the entire building to the Jehovah's."

"Maybe I should ring back later."

"Ah, no, it's grand. Why don't you come over for eats?"

"Tonight?"

"Tomorrow we die."

"You what?"

"Seize the day, for tomorrow we die. Sorry, just being pretentious. Make it eightish."

"Are you sure? That'd be wonderful. Bye so."

"Hang on, what's your name? Just so we don't invite some passing stranger in for dinner."

"Sorry. It's Maria."

"Well I'm Jael. By the way, was our address on the ad?"

"I don't think so, no."

"I suppose I'd better give it to you, then, unless you'd prefer to use your imagination?"

"Do I get the feeling you're taking the piss out of me?"

"You bet your bottom I am. OK, seriously, folks, it's sixty-nine Beldam Square, the top flat. Get the number seven bus from college, and ask the conductor to let you off after the Little Sisters of the Poor. Right?"

"I think so."

"Be hungry."

She loved the double-decker buses, every last lumbering dragon. One Christmas her Mam had brought the kids up to Dublin for a skite. Maria was only small, seven or so, but she dropped her mother's hand halfway up the spiral steps of the bus and ran to the front seat. Sketching a giant wheel between her mittens, she steered round each corner, casting disdainful glances at cyclists who disappeared under the shadow of the bus as if the ground had gulped them down. As she revved up O'Connell Street the afternoon was darkening. When the bus stopped at Henry Street, she had to be prised away; she gave up her hand and followed her mother's stubby heels into the crowd. Looking back over her shoulder, she saw the Christmas lights coming on all down the street, white bulbs filling each tree in turn and turning the sky navy blue. Maria tried asking her mother why the light made things darker, but by then they were on Moore Street, and her voice was lost in the yelps of *wrappinpaypa fifatwenty*.

This was not the same route but a much quieter journey, or perhaps a decade had dulled her perceptions. The bus chugged round Georgian squares, past the absentminded windows of office blocks. Gone half seven, and not a soul abroad; only the occasional newsagent spilled its light at a corner. Maria got off at the right stop but, dreading to be early, walked back to the last shop and loitered among the magazines for twenty minutes. The girl behind the counter had a hollow cough that kept doubling her over on her high stool. As the time ticked away Maria began to feel so uncomfortable that she finally bought *Her* magazine and a bag of crisps.

She was licking the salt off her fingers as she rounded the third corner of Beldam Square. Number 69 edged a narrow street; the digits were engraved on the fanlight. Maria knocked twice on the side door's scuffed paintwork before discovering that it was on the latch. Inside, she fumbled for the switch; a light came on ten feet above her, round and pearly as the one in the dentist's that she always focussed on during drilling. Halfway up the first flight of carpeted stairs, she remembered the glossy under her arm. She unrolled it and scanned the slippery cover. "Boss Giving You Grief?" That was fine, and not even the most fervid feminist could

object to "Living with Breast Cancer." She had her doubts
about "Why Nice Men Aren't Sexy," and when her eye
caught "Ten Weeks to Trim Those Bulges for Christmas!" she
rolled up the magazine and left it at the base of the stairs. She
could collect it on her way out. She might not even like them.

Between two steps Maria found herself in darkness. Damn
light must be on a timer. At arm's length she reached the bannister; it was a cool snake of wood drawing her hand
upward. Not a whiff of lentils, she thought, as she was
guided round a bend and up another flight of stairs. How
many feminists does it take to screw in a light bulb? One to
screw in the bulb, one to stir the lentil casserole, and one to
object to the use of the word *screw*. Her obnoxious little
brother it was who'd told her that, when she was complaining about something sexist on the telly one evening. She'd
got him for it with a dishcloth later.

Grey light knifed the top steps. The clean, unvarnished
door hung several inches open; Maria watched it shift a little
in the draught. She buttoned up her jacket, then undid it
again. The savor of garlic was tantalising. Her first tap made
almost no sound; she summoned her nerve and thumped on
the wood.

"Hi, hang on, dinner's burning," came a yelp. A long
pause. "I mean, you can come on in."

Maria was standing in the shadowy hall, fingering half a
peanut at the bottom of her jeans pocket, when the woman
elbowed through a bead curtain. Stuffing wisps of hair into
her black cap, she smiled, warm as toast. "I'm Ruth, the other
one." She brushed the beads out of the way and guided
Maria in. Clearing a place on the tartan blanket that draped
the sofa, she murmured, "Just hang on there while I have a
serious conversation with the stir-fry. Oh, goddess, what a
mess."

Maria cleared her throat. "It's not that bad," she commented, fitting herself on the sofa between a dictionary and a small box of blackberries.

"See, I meant to come home early and tidy up so as I could play the suave hostess, but I was queueing for the library photocopier and my watch stopped, so anyway, I'm just in." Ruth turned back to the wok and gave it a shake that made the hob clang. "And this cursed onion keeps sticking to my nonstick surface."

Maria watched her swerve between the stove and the table, carrying wine glasses and earthenware plates. Ruth's narrow face, framed in brief dark curls, swung round the kitchen. From the sink she pulled a heap of wet branches, stood them in an empty milk bottle, and placed it grandly in the center of the table. Maria's eyes waited for a drip from the rusty tip of a leaf to fall onto the wood.

Ruth subsided onto the sofa. Her eyes rested on her over-sized black watch, then lifted; they were wary and chocolate-brown. "Typical, I bust a gut getting everything ready for ten past, and her ladyship isn't home yet."

"I was meaning to ask, is it spelt with a *Y*?"

"Is what?"

"Her name. As in *Yale lock*."

"No no, it's a *J*. Jael from the Book of Judges. In the Bible, you know? Sorry, I shouldn't assume. Anyway, this Jael killed an enemy general by hammering a tent peg into his brain, if I remember rightly."

"Oh." After a pause, Maria tried raising her voice again. "And she's at college too?"

Ruth let her breath out in a yawn before answering. "In a long-term sense, yes, but right now she's probably moseying round town buying purple socks and drinking cappuccinos." She leaned back into the cushions and rolled her head from side to side.

"She does that often?"

"Every few weeks. Only sometimes shoelaces rather than socks. It's her hormones, you know."

They were beginning to giggle when the front door banged open and feet clumped down the passage.

Ruth's narrow face opened. "Jaelo," she sang. "Come here and entertain our guest."

A pause, and then a pale, freckled face broke through the beads. She was very tall, with very ostentatious ruddy hair. An unsettling laugh as she tossed her plastic bags onto the sofa, just missing the blackberries. "Hello there, new person, I'd forgotten all about you. It's Maria, right?"

"Yeah, but with a hard *i*—Mar-iy-a," she explained. "But it doesn't really matter, everyone tends to pronounce it wrong anyway." God, how seventeen.

"Did you deliberately pick it to rhyme with *pariah*?" asked Jael, her chair scraping the bare board floor.

"Eh, no, actually." Go on, don't cop out. "What does it mean?"

Struggling with a bootlace, Jael paused, one foot in the air. "D'you know, I couldn't tell you. Some sort of deviant. It's one of those words you throw around all your life until someone asks you what it means and you realise you've been talking through your rectum."

Maria cleared her throat.

"Outcast," murmured Ruth as she carried the wok to the table, her face averted from the steam. "Pariah is the lowest of the Indian castes."

"And knowall is the second lowest." Jael slid her hand into the crocodile oven glove and lunged at Ruth, who dipped out of the way.

The nearest seat was taken by a red-socked foot. "Sorry, Maria, my size tens need a throne of their own. Sit up there at the head of the table," commanded Jael. "Only don't lean back too far, or the chair might collapse."

Maria slid onto the chair and accepted a smoking plateful. She tackled a mushroom.

"Don't mind the woman," said Ruth, unrolling her denim sleeves and passing the basket of garlic bread. "She broke it herself last summer; we had a few people in for dinner, and she got carried away in the middle of an impromptu guitar recital."

"All my guitar recitals are impromptu," said Jael in a depressed tone. She wrenched the corkscrew from the wine bottle gripped between her knees and bent toward Maria.

Automatically Maria covered the glass. "None for me, thanks."

Jael trickled the wine through Maria's fingers. Maria snatched her hand away. Red drips scattered on the table; one ran along a crack in the wood. "I said I—"

"I heard what you said." The round-bellied glass was two thirds full. "But you can't insult Ruth's cooking by drinking water, especially not plague-ridden Dublin tap water."

Maria sucked her fingers dry one by one as the conversation slid away from her. The wine tasted as rich as the over-priced bottles her Da kept in the back of the shop for the occasional blow-ins from Dublin on their way to a holiday cottage. They often chose her town square to stop in, to stretch their legs and fill up the boot of the car with ginger cake and firelighters. How many years before she would become a foreigner like them? She reached for her glass and took a noiseless sip. Three years of the uni, that's if she had the luck to pass everything first time. Then some kind of a job for which her statistics classes would in no way have qualified her. Or maybe she could cling on and do an M.A. in art history. Go on the dole and help kids paint murals on crumbling city walls. On what day in what month of this queue of years would she find that she had become a rootless stranger, a speck in the urban sprawl? The accent was wavering already; her "good night" to the bus driver this evening featured vowels she never knew she had.

There was something glinting on the window behind Ruth's bobbing head; a hawk shape, a giant butterfly? Maria didn't want to interrupt their argument, which seemed to be about the future (or lack of it) of the Irish language. She could look more closely at the window in daylight. If she was ever here in daylight. If she didn't catch the train home tonight and start sorting potatoes in the shop on Monday morning. At least in a small town people knew how to pronounce your name.

By the time Maria had forked down her cooling dinner, Jael was boasting of her twenty years' experience of fine wine.

"They put it in your baby bottle?" suggested Maria.

She turned, big-eyed. "You mean you didn't warn her?"

Ruth was staring at the fridge with an air of abstraction. "I knew I'd forget to add the bean sprouts. Sorry, warn what?"

"That we're old fogeys. That dreaded breed who lurk under the euphemism of Mature Students." Jael lifted a curl away to point out invisible crows' feet round her eyes. "Your charming hostess is twenty-four, and I, loath though I am to admit it, am twenty-nine."

"You're not." Maria's eyes shifted from one to the other. She took another sip of wine. "Neither of you look it. I don't mean you look young, exactly, but not nearly thirty."

Jael cackled, balancing her last mushroom on a forkful of broccoli. "I retain my youthful appearance by sucking the blood of virginal freshers by night."

"You look much more aged than me," Ruth reflected. "Doesn't she, Maria?"

"I'm not taking sides, I'm just a visitor."

Ruth reached past Jael for the wine. "If her hair wasn't red, the grey would be much more obvious. And you should see the cellulite on her hips."

Jael made a face of outrage and flicked a pea at Ruth; Ruth retreated to the sink to fill the kettle.

"So what about you?" Jael asked.

Maria jumped; she had been engrossed in making a swirl of wine with her fork on the table. "What about me?"

"Oh, the usual things," said Jael, tugging her frayed, multicolored jumper over her head and tossing it just short of the sofa. "Place of origin, college subjects, vital statistics, bad habits, thoughts on the meaning of life."

Maria considered, the fork tasting metallic in her mouth. "I don't like listing myself," she said, smiling slightly to cushion the words.

Was that respect in Jael's salty blue eyes, or amusement?

Maria edged her glazed mug over to be filled from the cafetière.

"But then," Jael went on, "how are we meant to know whether you have all the necessary attributes of a good flatmate?"

"Guess."

Her mother would slap her hand for being rude, but then, her mother was more than a hundred miles away. And they never had cream in coffee at home. She took the jug from the outstretched hand of Ruth, whose eyes rested on her. "Tell us this much—how did you come to answer our ad? I'd have thought you'd have friends from home coming up to college with you."

"Oh, I have. Well, school friends, not real friends. They're mostly doing commerce or agriculture. They're nice, there's nothing wrong with them," she added uncomfortably. "It's just that I've had enough of pretending to be equally nice."

Ruth nodded. "I used to have some friends I could only describe as nice. Life is too short."

"Besides," Maria went on, taking a scalding mouthful of coffee, "I can just imagine what sharing a flat with school friends would be like. Borrowing stamps and comparing bra sizes, you know the way."

Jael coughed so hard she had to put her cup down. "There was none of that in my day. Support girdles we wore, back then."

"Oh and also," said Maria, turning back to Ruth's gaze, "why I noticed your ad was the bit about no bigots."

Hunched over her mug, Jael sniggered, for no reason that Maria could see.

"That was my idea," Ruth murmured. "It simplifies things."

"It was eye-catching," Maria assured her.

Another snort.

Had she said something stupid? Was she showing her youth again? She leapt into speech. "I was once stuck in a Gaeltacht in Mayo learning to speak Irish for three entire weeks with a pair of bitches who supported apartheid. I don't think I could stick a flat unless everyone in it was basically liberal."

"We Dubliners are very liberal altogether, you'll find," Jael commented, shovelling the coarse curls back from her forehead. "Life, liberty, and the pursuit of Guinness."

"I'm the only Dub here," commented Ruth.

"Ah, Kildare's only a county away. Besides, I've been soaking up the metropolitan atmosphere for a fair while now; I'm as much a true Dub as a snobby Southsider like you anyway." Jael ducked to avoid the tea towel. "Listen, why don't we start showing this bogtrotter round our bijou residence?"

In the half-light of the corridor Maria glimpsed black-and-white posters of a cityscape. Something brushed her ear; she put up one hand and found an asparagus fern hanging overhead, its points sharp against her palm. They had no plants at home; her dad claimed they gave him hay fever.

"This room's a bit bare, I'm afraid." Ruth's voice reverberated in a narrow doorway. As the light snapped on, Maria narrowed her eyes, taking in pale orange walls and flame-striped curtains. "If you really loathe the colour . . . I mean, we keep meaning to get around to repainting it."

"It's distinctive," said Maria warily.

"Ruthie babe," came a bellow. "I'm off to the off-license. Don't suppose you'd have a tenner on you?"

She was gone, fumbling in her jeans pocket. Maria's palms bounced on the bed tentatively. The nut-brown chest of drawers looked antique; when she tugged at the top drawer, the wrought iron handle came off in her hand, so she stuck it back in hastily and sat on the edge of the bed.

Their voices trickled down the passage. It occurred to her to cover her ears, but that seemed juvenile. She concentrated on the old calendar hanging from a nail beside her. *Ireland's Underwater Kingdom,* it read; the picture for October was a crab that seemed to be signalling frantically at her with a strip of seaweed.

"So she's gone at last." That was Jael, husky.

Maria held her breath.

"Really?"

"Her flight was at eleven this morning. Unless she missed it, which is unlikely."

"Well." Ruth again, distant. "Hope she finds a job all right. There's not much for her in Dublin."

Jael's voice lifted to a call as she clattered down the stairs. "See you later, ladies. Be good."

Cold air was coming off the bare window. Maria pulled the sleeves of her jumper down to cover her fingers and leaned on the sill. Her breath made a circle of glittering condensation; she touched her little finger to its chill, and made a small *m* in the center. When she heard steps in the passage, her hand poised to rub out the mark, but instead she reached for the curtains and drew them across. The room was safer now, but smaller. "Couldn't see anything but roofs," she told Ruth.

"Yes, but this room faces west; it's glorious in the late afternoons. Come and see the rest?"

It would be strange to live up so many steps, without a garden to wander into. The elegant and the shabby met in every corner of this flat. She craned her neck to examine the moulding around a bare light bulb.

"Georgian," Ruth explained. "Gorgeous fanlight over the front door, did you notice? Three floors of the building got converted into offices in the fifties, but the penthouse was too oddly shaped for anything but a flat. A bugger to heat in the winter, but I love these high ceilings. They elevate the mind, don't they?"

Maria nodded, rapt. The highest ceiling she had ever slept under, she remembered now, was in Uncle Malachy's smelly barn one night when she'd gotten locked out by mistake; she hadn't wanted to throw a stone and wake Mam, who was still weak after the operation. "So who's down below?"

"You're unlikely to meet them; they use the front staircase. There's a firm of chartered surveyors, an optician, and the Girl Guides HQ. In the basement there's what purports to be a baldness clinic, but we suspect it's a brothel for businessmen. Is there a brothel in your town, Maria?"

"I wouldn't know," she answered, after a puzzled moment. "I've lived there all my life, but I've no idea. There've been rumours about the flashy cars outside Mrs. Keogh's, but I'll bet that's because she's a redhead."

Ruth chuckled under her breath. "Must tell Jael about that."

The bathroom was lined with white tiles, clean but cracked in places. Opening the hot press, Ruth prodded a folded towel into line. When she turned, her face looked tired in the hard fluorescent light. "I'd better be honest with you, Maria, you might find it a bit isolated here."

"Isolated from what?"

A disconcerted pause. "Depends what you're looking for." Ruth bent to fish an empty shampoo bottle out of the bathtub. "I'm not wildly sociable, myself; I do things at college, debating and stuff, but when the day's over I like to curl up with tea and a book."

"Me too."

"Really?" Ruth's mouth softened. "You could get somewhere nearer the university with a younger crowd, for the same money. But on the other hand, this place can be a sort of home. On good days."

"It seems very nice," said Maria.

"Do you think so? It all depends on . . . what do you do, Maria?"

"Maths and art."

Her hand flapped that away. "No, I mean what do you really like to do?"

She sat on the rim of the tub and let the question hang in the air. Her eyes paused on a ceramic mermaid, old toothbrushes poking up from her breasts.

"I know, isn't it the pits?" said Ruth. "I've tried all sorts of arguments, but Jael is such a stubborn Scorpio. Apparently it's got sentimental value because she got it from an old friend in Denmark. I think she keeps it to annoy me."

Maria traced the yellow hair with one finger. "Why haven't you accidentally knocked it off the windowsill?"

"Do you know, I've never thought of that." Ruth's expression was oddly respectful. "Not sure I could go through with it; what if it decapitated a passerby? Maybe if you came to live here, you could do the deed."

Maria was reminded that she still had to prove herself.

"About what you were asking—I can't really say what I like to do."

"Ah, forget it, you don't like questions."

"No, it's not that." Her fingers rested on the cold ceramic. "It's just that I've never lived away before, so I don't know what I'll be like. At home I draw and watch wildlife documentaries and stuff. I sit round nattering to Mam while she cooks, and keep my brothers away from breakable objects."

"Every house needs someone like that." Ruth's smile vanished as she turned off the light. "And this is our room," she said as she opened the door to a larger, darker bedroom, with a purplish hanging on the wall. "It's north-facing, so we don't sit around in it much."

"But you don't even have proper beds," protested Maria. "Could you not ask the landlord—"

"We like the futon, really. It's great for Jael's bad back, and there's plenty of space."

"Just seems a bit unfair that whoever moves in gets a room of her own."

"Ah, don't worry about it," said Ruth, bending to straighten a corner of the duvet. "We're used to each other by now. I've trained Jael not to snore."

Halfway through a tour of the cupboards, Maria's eye was caught by a moth flapping against the ceiling; she looked up and noticed a skylight. "Can you get out onto the roof? The view over Dublin must be amazing."

"To tell you the truth, I've never got around to it."

"Suppose not," said Maria, regretting her enthusiasm.

"But I must ask the landlord," Ruth added as she pushed an obstinate door shut on a stack of blankets. "Though the mean bastard would probably put another fiver on the rent 'for use of rooftop recreational space.'" Her fingers slid to the switch, and they were standing in darkness.

Maria stood still. Small ads, that was always how psycho killers lured victims to their flats.

"Look," said Ruth.

"What?"

"Up. Have your eyes adjusted?" Directly below the skylight, Ruth's finger was raised. "That must be the Seven Sisters."

"I didn't think Dublin had stars. I mean, with the smog and all." She peered up, open-mouthed.

The front door lurched open.

"What are you two playing at in the dark?" Jael asked, as they came up the corridor to help her with her splitting bags. "Hey," she went on, "some good fairy left me this month's *Her* on the stairs, and it's got twenty gorgeous pages of lingerie. I have my suspicions," she went on, putting the tip of the wine bottle to Ruth's temple.

"It's mine." Maria's cheeks were scorching. "I must have dropped it and not noticed."

"Ah, too bad."

"No, no, take it. I've read it already. On the bus," she insisted. "Speaking of which, I'd better be getting back before my Aunt Thelma rings the police."

They turned on the light in the stairwell for her as she said her goodbyes. They would ring. She would take care. As she reached the first landing, she heard one of them begin to hum, one of those slow fifties croonings you could never get out of your head.

🔄

Maria pretended not to see the youth in a bicycle helmet who was shifting round the phone box, rubbing his hands and peering at his watch in the streetlight.

"Yeah, they'll let me know by the end of the week. I hope so, Mam. I think being a nonsmoker was a plus.

"The rent's not too scarifying. If I got a job on top of my grant, it should be grand. Central heating, and an open fire as well. I didn't check the fridge. Should I have? Ah, Mam, it's very civilised, not like a squalid bedsit at all. You can stop fretting. OK, I didn't mean fretting—being concerned.

"Yes, I'm eating very well, Thelma cooks everything in a cream sauce. Mam, she specifically asked me to call her that, it makes her feel younger. Yeah, she's still at the upholstery. All right. Night-night now. Ta for letting me ring reverse-charges. Say hi to Dad and the lads, will you? God bless."

She swung the glass door wide and darted out, with a quick "Sorry for keeping you." Halfway down the street, hands bunched in her duffel-coat pockets for warmth, she remembered her fountain pen sitting on the directory and loped back.

His helmet bent over the receiver, he was agitated in conversation. Maria knocked timidly on the glass and got a glare in return. "Sorry," she mouthed. "Pen." Her hand made a writing motion, then pointed at the ledge. Dark eyes stared through the glass. "Forget it," she mouthed, her hands flapping; she turned her hot face away and headed down the narrow street.

The door of the phone box crashed open. "What? What is it?"

"It doesn't matter," she called, her voice unsteady.

"Hey, come back here, I'm through with my call." He lowered his voice as she neared him. "I guess I was rude. I was in a hurry."

"It was just my fountain pen," Maria said, clearing her throat. "I think I left it on the shelf." She took it from his hand. Up close, he was skinny and no older than she was.

"I'm sorry I wouldn't open the door, but you know, you could have had a knife or something."

She stared.

"So you're not the most likely of muggers," he admitted, tugging off his helmet and running a bony hand through tufts of hair. "But in Brooklyn we take no chances."

"You're from New York, really?" Then she heard her own voice talking to a male stranger on an empty street. "Sorry to have bothered you. Good night." And she strode off, not giving him a chance to do more than nod.

Safe on the top deck of the meandering bus to Dun Laoghaire, she let her shoulders uncurl, shedding the weight of a long day. Twenty minutes of dreamtime now, as floodlit city corners flared into black suburban avenues. The knobbled branches of overhanging horse chestnut trees cracked against the windows, on and off, pulling her back to consciousness. Glinting on the glass she could see the first spatter of rain.

Her aunt's house was the last in a cul-de-sac of opulent hedges. Maria let herself in noiselessly and was halfway up the stairs when she remembered the no-shoes rule. Damn it to hell, who ever heard of having a magnolia carpet? She was wrenching off her second sneaker when the kitchen door opened.

"Welcome back. You'll join me for cocoa?"

"Surely," said Maria, stuffing her sneakers into her coat pockets. She padded down the stairs and into the gleaming kitchen. "Could I have a glass of water as well?"

Gathering her beige satin dressing gown round her neck, Thelma smiled at the anxious tone. "I'm sure that could be arranged."

"Sorry to be in so late."

"Oh, I got accustomed to it with Alexandra. She was always staying out till five in the morning; university life brought out the vagabond in her."

"Where is it that she is now?" asked Maria politely, stifling a grimace as she sipped the urban water.

"Bucharest. At least that's where the last postcard was from. Live it up while you're young, or you'll regret it later, I always say."

She angled her glass, watching the water catch white ovals of light.

Thelma took a sip of cocoa without wetting her lips. "I've always said to her, 'Darling, make your own decisions and I will respect them.' Especially during her bad patch after her father passed away, I thought she needed to know that."

Maria nodded and reached for her cocoa. She was suddenly weary in every muscle.

"What about you, do you often clash with Caitríona? Battles over boys?"

Maria's lips tightened. "Mam and I get along fine, actually."

"You're not still calling her that, are you? Mam, it sounds so nineteen-forties." Thelma spooned up the last drip of cocoa.

"She prefers it."

"I see." A meditative pause. "Caitríona was never the radical of the family."

"How's the stool coming along?" asked Maria, on the verge of rudeness. She bent her face to catch the steam from the cocoa.

"Very nicely. French polishing's all done, and I start on the seat tomorrow. It's for my dentist's sitting room; he's taking it as payment for that broken crown on my molar." Thelma's face looked girlish with satisfaction. "Would you like to see it?"

The molar or the footstool? Maria wondered, and felt fatigue and repentance tugging her two ways. "In the morning, I'd love to."

"Good night so. There's a hot water bottle in your bed."

🔄

Maria watched the knot of limbs struggle toward the edge of the lake. All round her, students lay draped on the concrete steps, white-faced in the autumn sun. Only at the third scream from the girl at the hub of the group did people begin to look up. "Engineers are at it again," said a lazy voice just behind Maria. "I heard they're aiming to beat last year's total of ten girls in the pond by the end of Freshers' Week."

"At least it's sunny this year," commented another.

Maria could see the woman now; she bucked and shoved, making vain attempts with one free hand to keep her billowing peachy skirt between her knees while a dozen boys towed her, head first, down the steps. The odd giggle escaped from the watchers. With a shriek and a violent kick one leg leaped free, but the sandal dropped off, and four hands caught the ankle again. "Heave! Heave!" They swung her twice over the water, their chant drowning her out. And then the body dropped with a splash.

Almost at once a sleek black head emerged over the lip of concrete, dripping and laughing, calling for a helping hand. Maria gathered her belongings to go. At the top of the steps she turned, staring until one of the engineers retrieved the woman's sandal and another wrapped her in his laboratory coat.

Heading blindly up the peopled steps, Maria careered into a sharp shoulder.

"We must stop meeting like this."

For a long moment she couldn't place the face, then embarrassment flooded her as she recalled the New Yorker. "Sorry, hello. I'm sorry."

"And I'm Galway. Were you watching the ritual witch-dunking?" He jerked his eyes toward the lake.

"She's no witch, she's a bimbo," retorted Maria, more viciously than she meant.

One bushy eyebrow lifted. "Do you know her?"

"She was laughing, for god's sake. How could she let them toss her into all that oil and sludge, and then laugh?"

"Maybe she didn't have much of a choice. If she's going to be in their class for four years, she won't want a reputation for not being able to take a joke."

"Well, I think it's sick."

"Of course it's sick, I was taking that for granted." Galway readjusted the faded rucksack on his shoulders. "Adolescent macho thuggery. That's why I never joined a fraternity back home in my freshman year; I just couldn't see the thrill in walking backward along a roof ridge in my boxer shorts."

She eased into a smile as they began drifting toward the long grey buildings. "Do you want to, I mean, I was just going for a cup of tea."

🔄

Fourth time tonight, thought Maria, gritting her teeth as she recognised the song. It drew squeals of enthusiasm, and another chain of dancers sewed its way into the crowd. She scanned the flushed faces. Nuala, her friend back in fourth year, would have reduced them to *sweaty proles*, or *the twitterati*. It would be handy to despise these fellow freshers; then she could give up the bother of getting to know them and go back to Thelma's to read an early edition of the Sunday papers. But the fact was that half of these people seemed more intelligent than she was, and the other half were better-looking.

A painful prod between the shoulder blades; she turned and found Yvonne's pink nails. "Been queueing long? You could get me a vodka and Coke while you're there. Try the barman with the earring, he's a sweetie."

Maria leaned against the wall. The condensation soaked through her thin sleeve, and she recoiled. "Having a good time?" she asked.

"Of course."

There was no answering that.

"Bet you're glad now that I made you come along."

They inserted themselves in a gap at the bar. Lager and stout mingled in tinted pools along the wood.

"Those harem pants are dead sexy on you," Yvonne said.

"They are not, they make me look bandy-legged." She caught Yvonne's eye. "Sorry, I mean, I'm grateful for the loan. I just hadn't realised they'd have so much gold braid on them; I feel like I've escaped from a circus."

"Mmm, that's why I never wore that outfit myself. But you've got the slimness to carry if off," Yvonne added hastily.

"You look rather luscious," Maria told her, stifling a yawn.

"Salmon has always done things for me," Yvonne agreed. "Nearly fell out of it when I was doing the lambada, though," she added; "that guy Pete's eyes were popping."

The barman noticed Maria's limp wave at last, and hurried them their drinks.

"So tell us, have you found a flat yet?"

"I've rung around a bit, and seen one total dive. I thought I'd have heard from that first place by the end of last week."

Yvonne's attention was wandering. She pointed discreetly, at hip level: "She's the one that got dumped in the lake, wasn't it gas? Looks a bit goosepimply still."

To avoid replying, Maria touched her lips to the creamy head of her half pint. "Anyway, if I don't get that flat, I'll try a few more on Monday."

"Do. So tell us," Yvonne said, turning her pale blue eyes, "you been asked up yet?"

Maria considered lying but hadn't the heart for it. "I jived to a fifties remix with a spotty theology student and got a violent stitch in the ribs."

"Bad luck."

"He was no loss; all he talked about was how many points he won in his matriculation."

Yvonne was smoothing out a crease in her skirt. "You have to start somewhere, Maria."

"Not with him, I don't."

She gave a theatrical sigh. "Your problem is, your standards are too high."

"That's what my mother says."

But Yvonne had drifted a few feet away in response to a wave from a boy in a wing collar.

Now that she came to think of it, Maria could only remember her mother telling her that once. She must have been about nine, that time she was allowed sit up late to watch the Eurovision Song Contest and had kept commenting how yucky the men were, with their big ears or furry chests. Mam remarked that Maria might end up an old maid, being too picky to be satisfied with any one man. Marriage was about give and take and a fair bit of giving up too. It occurred to Maria to suggest polygamy, which she had read about in her history book's brief section on "Our Tribal Ancestors," but her mother was probably too Catholic to find that funny. As her dad took her up to bed he told her not to fret, she'd be the career woman of the family. She laughed and threw a rolled-up sock at him as he turned off the light.

In the dark, she parted the curtains and leaned her elbows on the chilly windowsill. Counting the lights of the small town nestling round her house, she realised that all the women she knew were wives and mothers. Except for the young ones heading for the uni, and that librarian with the hay fever, and a couple of teachers. And of course Nelly the Nutter, who sat on the steps of the town hall, scratching her ankles. That night Maria slid down and tucked the quilt over her head and could not sleep for worrying what she would turn out to be.

And how much farther had she gotten with that question in eight years, she asked herself wryly, as she picked her way through the bar to a spare chair by the window. The music had changed to a slow set, without her noticing; a cover version of a sixties lament inched the couples across the dance floor. Maria leaned back in the crooked plastic chair and turned her eyes to the window. She traced the lasso of lights around the campus buildings until the music and voices blurred into the background. She imagined herself up and away, gliding over the dark lake, gaining height as she zoomed toward the city. Black air between her legs, the office windows glinting as she skimmed by.

Yvonne dropped heavily into the next seat. Then she heaved up again, felt her buttock, and sniffed her finger. "Damn it to hell, I'm sitting in a puddle of cider."

Maria's hand patted the windowsill beside her, but Yvonne let herself down onto the floor and rested her sagging curls on her pink satin knees.

"Still having fun?"

"Yeah. It's just cramps." Yvonne's voice was rigid.

"Ah, you creature. Want an aspirin?"

"Better not, on top of three vodkas it'd probably make me pass out."

It occurred to Maria to reach down and stroke the bent head, but she thought better of it.

They sat wordlessly for two songs, then Yvonne asked, "So where's that skinny guy I spotted with you, all pally in the canteen queue?"

"Galway's not here, and he's not my type."

"Terribly weedy name, Gary."

Maria heaved her voice over the level of the music. "No, Galway, after the county. Yankee nostalgia."

"Even worse!"

"It's not his fault," argued Maria, putting her sore feet up on an ash-powdered bench. "Apparently his granny was postmistress in Oughterard until she emigrated in 1934; she bullied Galway into spending his junior year over here studying Anglo-Irish drama and discovering his roots."

"He might discover your roots while he's at it," replied Yvonne mechanically. "So why isn't he here tonight?"

"Apparently it's a puerile mating ritual. Besides, he can't afford it."

Yvonne stretched and pulled herself onto her high heels. "This one's Madonna. Let's get on down."

"I'm grand here."

Her eyes were hard. "I know it's not easy to make friends at a hundred decibels, but we've got to try."

"I do talk to people after classes."

Yvonne waited, hands supporting the small of her back. "You're only making it more difficult for yourself in the long run, Maria."

"Oh, all right, don't nag."

They squeezed into the crowd.

⑤

The little *m* was still there, a faint mark on the pane.

"I'll leave you to, well, whatever one leaves people in bedrooms to do!"

Maria turned from the window and grinned widely. "I'm ready for bed anyway. Hauling all my worldly goods up four flights of stairs has taken it out of me."

Ruth hovered at the door. "You're sure there's nothing you need, like a nailbrush or something?"

"There's nothing to brush," said Maria, holding out her trimmed nails for inspection. "I'll be grand, don't worry about me." She put the last of her neatly balled socks into the back of the drawer, rattled it shut, and bent to slide her suitcase under the bed. Straightening up, she found Ruth still there, her hand on the door handle, her face almost apprehensive.

"I'm really glad you wanted me, actually." Keep the tone

casual; sit down on the brown candlewick bedspread. "I'd nearly given up expecting you to ring."

"I know, I'm sorry about that," said Ruth in a rush. "There were a few others interested, and we thought we should wait just to be on the safe side."

The safe side of what?

"Sweet dreams, Maria." Her light steps faded down the passage.

She could never sleep the first night in a strange place. The flat was warm, still smelling faintly of garlic. She stretched out on her creaky bed and tracked faces in the damp-marked ceiling. That one was definitely her father, with the big eyebrows and pointy chin. The brothers could be those two blobs in the corner, their features moving too fast to be distinguishable. And who was that with one wide eye and her hair blowing over her face?

Before she could scare herself, Maria turned her nose into the coverlet. There was nothing imaginary about its soft ridges. She ran her fingers over them, counting the rises and falls; she was a giantess, fondling a countryside of motorways.

It occurred to her that she had forgotten to brush her teeth. She yawned, fumbled for her toilet bag on the chest of drawers, and set out for the bathroom. Turning the wrong way down the pitch-black corridor, she felt her hand brush against the bead curtain; she was about to retreat when she heard low voices from the fireside. She jerked, but her feet refused to turn.

When she was about six, Maria had gone through an insecure phase. If she shut her eyes now, she could see her child self, rumpled in brushed cotton pyjamas, creeping down to the living room door and pressing her ear against it as her parents swapped domestic trivia over supper. Just in case they would mention her, let fall some secret praise or sarcasm. They never did, and the child tiptoed coldly back to bed. Eventually she had broken herself of the eavesdropping habit. But on occasion, on nights like tonight, the old curiosity gripped her. Her feet were going numb as she stood in the corridor, her face almost touching the beads. Only half a minute, she promised herself.

Ruth's voice was the softer one. "Yes, but she's only seventeen."

Maria shut her eyes.

"Ageist," commented Jael with satisfaction. "She seems good crack; I'd rather her than that humorless social scientist anytime."

"It's not that. I think she'll be lovely to have around."

"Then what's your problem?"

"It's not my problem, it's ours." A hurt edge to the words. "Just, it occurred to me tonight when we were hauling her suitcases upstairs, she may not have copped on yet."

Maria strained to hear, her ear almost touching the beads.

After a pause, the lazy voice said, "Does it matter that much?"

"It does to me. I'm worried that the wording of the ad was too subtle."

Jael chuckled. "That's your idea of subtlety, pet?"

Then came a phrase too low for her to catch. The curtain was shifting slightly in the draught; would a crack of firelight slip between the beads and light her up? Her knees were locked.

Ruth again, straining. "All I mean is, we don't want another melodramatic exit, do we? I thought we agreed to be honest this time."

"There's honest and there's boringly obvious. I think you should give the girl a chance," Jael went on. Was her voice growing, moving toward the curtain?

Maria swerved away. Her feet carried her silently down

the corridor and into her room. She pushed the door delicately shut before crawling under the quilt. Staring at the ceiling in confusion, she wondered what on earth she had not "copped on" about. All she could think of was a drug ring. She heaved herself over and immersed her face in the pillow.

2

MIXING

Regards to Dad and the lads. I'll be home for the weekend soon. All the best, Maria.

She licked the flap of the envelope, wincing slightly at the taste, and stuck it down. Pausing outside the other bedroom, her fingers played an arpeggio on the door. "Anyone want anything down the shops?" No answer. Odd, surely she'd have heard them going out. Walking down the corridor, she slapped at the fern's lowest tendril, and it bobbed in its hanging basket.

Dirty blue clouds were scudding over slate roofs. A good cold smell in the air and the whiff of turfsmoke as she turned the corner made her think of home. The dusk lasted much longer in the country; nothing to get in its way, she supposed. In Dublin there was only half an hour of grey, then the street lamps blinked on and all the shoppers hustled home in the dark.

The post office was in the back of a newsagent's on the bottom floor of a narrow townhouse; its fanlight seemed to have been shattered by a stone. After practising silently in the stamp queue, Maria managed to ask for "Three 30p's please" without spitting. She dawdled at the candy counter until the boy behind it began to whistle "Why Are We Waiting?" "One of those," she told him, with a minimal point of the finger.

She could tell he was not going to let her away with it. "Mum," he bawled, "how much's the Fizzie Kolapops?"

Maria took it from his oversized fingers and slid out through the crowd. A year ago she would have claimed it was for her little sister. Real maturity would be hers, she decided as she tore the thin plastic with her teeth, when she found herself able to ask for Jelly Tots in a ringing voice.

It tasted as wild as she remembered. Ten years ago at least; Sister Miriam used to dole them out as prizes for good conduct. The breeze snatched the crinkly plastic from her fingers as she turned down the street. Getting nippy now. Maria unzipped her anorak and let the wind shake through her, flapping her long black skirt and tossing strands of pale hair in her face. At home the wind had always seemed horizontal, dulling her ears as she plodded the mile and a half home from school, looking out for a lift from the butcher's van. But here it gusted in spirals, exciting her skirts. If she had a big enough umbrella now, she could lift away from the earth like Mary Poppins, her neat feet spurning the chimneys.

As she turned onto Beldam Square, running her fingers along the scaly railings, someone came hurtling down the footpath. She stepped out of the way, then recognised the bounce of Jael's coppery hair. Whipping the lollipop from her cheek, Maria dropped it into a clump of dandelions.

"Whoah," she called as the red face panted up to her. "What's the race?"

Jael grabbed her by the sleeve of her anorak and dragged her along. "Offy," she gasped, "nearly six." Her voice was harsh as a gull's.

Maria, tripping over her skirt, had no breath to answer.

They made it to the door of the off-licence just as the manager was about to lock it, and though he seemed unconvinced by Jael's saga of an aunt who'd had a car crash, he did reopen the till to sell them a bottle of whisky.

They ambled back, swapping giggled details of Aunt Bridie and her late lamented Citröen Diane. Jael pulled up the collar of her battered leather jacket, wrenching loose hair out of the way. She looked wan behind her freckles.

"But I knocked at your door, I could have bought it for you."

"Did you really?" said Jael. "We must have had our headphones on. Oh, well, my back was aching, I needed the exercise."

Maria staggered up the stairs after her.

A bus ticket, curled on the kitchen table, read "Off with women's group to deface offensive billboard, see yez later, Ruth. P.S. plenty chili left in pot."

Jael scanned it with a groan. "She's going to get herself arrested again."

"She what?"

"The only reason the beer manufacturers didn't press charges last time was because the police rounded the lassies up before they'd finished painting the first syllable of *Objectification*."

"What are they like, this women's group?" asked Maria, rereading the note. "Ruth invited me to go along, but I forgot."

"A clatter of middle-class neurotics whining on about how oppressed they are."

Maria gave her a thoughtful glance and went to heat up the chili.

Hot tea and hot whisky, and the fire scalding their foreheads. Maria wriggled back in the rocking chair, tucking her moccasins under her skirt. She would just finish her crossword before tackling the worksheet of stats problems. Cross-words counted as mental exercise. She struggled with an ana-gram, half-aware of the faint twangs of Jael tuning her guitar on the hearth rug. The night was wrapping round them; an occasional blast of wind shook the navy-blue windowpanes. Once Maria glanced down at the bent head and realised that this was the first time they had ever been in the same room without talking. Twelve across, a Tibetan snow monster.

"My god." Jael tossed back her fringe. "I've just realised I don't know your surname."

"Almighty." Maria sucked the top of her pen.

"I beg your pardon?"

She sighed, doodling a ship in the frayed margin of the newspaper. "Your god's surname."

After a moment, Jael strummed a major chord. "Aha, I get it. A rare but tasty witticism from the Virgin Maria."

Maria stuck her tongue out without raising her eyes. "I should never have told you I was a virgin. Next time we play Truth or Dare I'm going to lie."

"You're learning."

Five notes, rising in jerks like washing on a stormy line. Maria reached down for her tea.

"What was I asking you?"

Maria filled in a clue.

"Classy pen you've got there."

"From my parents, for getting honours in the leaving cert." She looked at the words engraved on the silver side. How many teabags, carrots, six A.M. starts had paid for that? For this?

"They must like you."

"Expect so." Something in the tone made her look down at Jael. "Don't parents usually?"

"Not mine."

Maria waited, stretching one leg and folding it under her again. "Why not?"

"Oh, lots of reasons. No reason, really." A minor chord, a major, a deeper minor. "But what was it I was on about before?"

"Surnames," murmured Maria, engrossed in thirteen down.

"Yes, how come I don't know yours?"

"Murphy."

"I don't want to know it, I want to know why I didn't know it already. Murphy, really? How disappointing."

"Mmm."

Jael laid the guitar in her lap and leaned across it menacingly. "Maria bloody Murphy, either you pay me some attention or you'll get a plectrum somewhere painful."

She stared over the rim of the paper. "It just never came up in conversation, all right? It's not that unique as names go; you could have guessed it."

"The point is, you never tell me anything."

Maria was trying to be reasonable. She still felt like a visitor here. "What do you want to know?"

Jael leaned back against the sofa and snarled softly. "What do you tell Ruth? I bet she knew your surname weeks ago."

"Nothing. Just things," said Maria. Her finger picked at a rough bit of wicker on the chair arm.

"When I came in from the pub the other night, you were gossiping about nuns who used to teach you macramé."

"That was one sentence. Mostly we hadn't been talking about anything. It's nice to just sit, sometimes," she finished pointedly.

The plectrum Jael was aiming at the handle of the fireguard fell in the coal scuttle. "I promise to sit quietly like a good girl if you'll talk a bit first."

Maria's eyes had strayed to twenty-seven across; the fountain pen bobbed in her hand. "Does *separate* have an *a* or an *e* in the middle?"

"If I tell you, will you tell me something really intimate?"

"Oh, don't be silly." Their eyes locked bullishly. "Like what?"

Jael smiled greedily and folded her arms. "Like . . . your worst nightmare."

"I don't really have nightmares," protested Maria, snapping open the newspaper. Then she laid it across her knees. "Every now and then, though, I dream I've chopped my mother's hands off with an axe."

"Glory be." Jael cleared her throat.

"But I'm so used to it, I wouldn't consider it a nightmare," added Maria, lifting her pen again. "I think it comes from the time she was chopping tomatoes, and I jumped out from behind the fridge door to say Boo!, and she cut the top off her finger."

"Well, don't tell Ruth about it."

"Why, is she squeamish?"

Jael started picking out the notes of "Jingle Bells." "No. I just like to know some things she doesn't."

"You're pathetic."

"That's me." The tune sped up, Jael stumbling over the high notes.

"Anyway, is it an *e* or an *a* in *separate*?"

"Haven't a clue."

⑤

Somehow it was the middle of October. Two weeks too late to start introducing herself to all her fellow students in the canteen. Yvonne talked to her sometimes, and so did Galway, and that was it. There was a lively threesome in her sculpture tutorial that she wouldn't have minded talking to, but every time she saw them she buried her head in her notebook, having forgotten the names they told her last time and the time before. Besides, what had she to offer them, or them her? It was the same as every guide camp, Gaeltacht, or class party:

Maria found herself sitting in the corner, with folded arms and a slightly amused expression, trying to remember if she had chosen to be there. Despite all her resolutions to try a little bit harder this time, hang round the bar more, not let the smile slide off her face, she had ended up more isolated than ever.

Head cushioned on her arms at a library desk, Maria considered the possibility that she was just not a friendly person. No matter how warm she felt on the inside, her skin stayed cool.

No getting maudlin before noon. She stared over the edge of the beige partition. Was that Ruth over in the history shelves, crouched under a leaning tower of hardbacks?

"You can't be going to read all these by lunchtime," protested Maria as she relieved her of the top half of the pile.

Ruth scratched her scalp through her black velvet cap. "I'll just fret over their indexes and take down a few conflicting hypotheses about the causes of the Great Famine. I never seem to actually read books anymore, I just consult them."

"And carry them," Maria reminded her, thumping down her load and resting against the sharp edge of the desk. "Better than weight training."

Ruth put one small desert boot up on the chair to strike a pose, showing off an invisible biceps. "With a body like mine," she asked in a husky bass, "who needs a history degree?"

"Do you mind?" A pair of steel glasses loomed over the partition. "Some of us are trying to work."

Ruth's face shut down. "Sorry," she said, and the head disappeared.

"I've been meaning to ask you," whispered Maria, "why didn't you come to college till now?"

"Don't spread it round," said Ruth, sheepish, "but I was a civil servant."

"Not one of those drones who spells surnames wrong on envelopes?"

"I was that drone." She began scribbling to get her pen to work. "Three years of earnest dedication to the Irish state."

Maria sat on the edge of the desk and put her shoe tips up on Ruth's plastic chair. "Had you, like, a pension and all?"

Ruth leaned back and laughed softly. "God, they breed them right where you come from. The pension was the whole point. My mother nearly had a canary when I told her I was packing in the job. I kept insisting it was a dead end, and all she'd say was, 'But your pension!'"

"So then you came here."

"To wake myself up. It was a sort of . . . quest, you know?" The pen was still dry; she put it down.

"Never been on one myself. And did it work?"

Ruth wrinkled her forehead. "Only sort of. Not the way I had expected, but other ways. All I found out was some people stuff; nothing I could get a grip on."

"Well, so long as you're awake, does it matter how you were woken?"

The dark eyes lifted and crinkled at the corners. "I suppose not." But the books drew her lashes down again. "I'd rather it was a way that would win me a first this June, that's all."

"Is that a hint? Should I leave you in peace?"

Ruth leaned her head on her hand briefly; when she looked up, the lines were smoothed away. "Please don't. In fact, while the sun's out, why don't we stack these tomes of wisdom up here—no one's likely to steal them—and go soak up some vitamin D by the lake."

Their voices lifted as they moved away from the desks. "I didn't expect you to be so easily corruptible," Maria reproached her, holding open the swinging door. "You're meant to be a scholarly role model for me, as well as mother figure and general mentor."

Ruth made a loud retching noise, startling a librarian just below them on the escalator. "Why me? Jael's older, she can be your mother figure."

"Nah, she can't cook."

A heavy sigh from Ruth, as they crossed through the grimy glass tunnel into the arts block. "Everyone could cook if they wanted to, only they pretend it's a special gift so a few poor suckers have to do it all the time."

"I honestly can't. Food doesn't like me."

Ruth's eyes lit up. "Wouldn't it be gas if you went home for Christmas and dazzled your entire family with pineapple curry and crème caramel!"

But Maria had dropped back to peer at a typewritten notice on the wall. "Hey, do you think I have the makings of a part-time library administrative assistant? Sorry, I missed that last bit."

"I was saying I bet I could teach you to cook."

"I swear, my mother's been trying for years, and I'm a culinary cretin. All I ever liked doing were cake mixes, because you can blame them if anything goes wrong."

"What could go wrong?" Ruth held the heavy door open for Maria to walk into the sun. It dazzled them, held them on the spot a moment. Then the students following behind jostled them; they shaded their eyes and moved across the courtyard.

"Well, once I did a sponge cake," continued Maria, "only I forgot the egg, so it came out all pale. I was too mortified to admit my mistake, so my father thought it was the fault of the manufacturers and got Mam to write them an outraged letter."

"Did you get your money back?"

"Worse," said Maria. "They sent us twelve packets of the cursed stuff by return post."

The lake glittered sharply in the afternoon light; they

headed for the wooded east side, away from the sprawled couples on the southern bank.

For five or ten minutes they soaked in the white sunshine, without a word. Maria kept waiting for it to feel awkward, but it never did. She sat cross-legged on the concrete edge of the lake and watched an ant haul a piece of crisp into a crack. Red leaves were scattered all along the concrete footpath; as they dried, their sides arched backward, making them sharp as arrows.

"Hey, I've thought of another reason why Jael couldn't be my mentor," Maria said at last. "She intimidates me." She threw a handful of the leaves at a nearby duck; they fell short and basked on the surface of the water.

Ruth was leaning against a tree trunk. She nodded, without opening her eyes. "She used to intimidate me too, until I learned how to get under her skin."

"How's it done? Will you teach me that instead of cookery?"

"Sure you'd really want to?" asked Ruth lightly. "Under Jael's skin is not the most comfortable place to be."

"I thought age was meant to calm people down, but she's so over the top," said Maria, crushing a rusty leaf to fragments in her palm. "I mean the other day, right, I found myself snared in some kind of intense ambiguity when as far as I knew we'd been discussing the price of teabags."

Ruth's mouth twisted up at one corner. Her eyes were closed against the sunshine.

"You won't tell her I said any of this, will you?" asked Maria, brushing her hands clean. "She probably thinks I'm a moron anyway."

White lines made a delicate tracery around Ruth's eyes. "Don't mind her slagging," she murmured. "She only mocks people she thinks highly of."

"Really?"

"Like I only give cookery lessons to people I think highly of."

Maria sat up and wrapped her arms around her knees. If there was one thing she could not bear, it was the suspicion that someone might think she had been fishing for compliments. There is nothing more juvenile, she told herself. And few things more pathetic than sucking up to a flatmate because you can't make friends your own age.

"Has Jael been giving you a hard time?" Ruth was watching; her voice was suddenly concerned.

"No, no. I'm sure she just takes a while to get used to."

"Listen, if she's ever really—if she makes you feel uncomfortable, tell me."

"And what'll you do?" asked Maria cheekily.

"Oh, probably beat her to death with the shower attachment."

Maria's hands, suddenly warm, scooped a pile of leaves together on the concrete. "I'm sure I'll grow out of being scared of her. Suppose you've known each other for decades?"

"We only met the spring before last, and we've had the flat just over a year."

"But I presumed you were at school together."

"No way," said Ruth in amusement. "Madam went to a posh boarding school. And I haven't kept any of my pals from the convent. The good girls were boring, and the baddies got pregnant and left early."

Maria nodded eagerly. "But the baddies were more fun, weren't they? In primary school I was a good girl. We swapped *Chalet School* books and went ahead with our mitten patterns during lunch break."

"Don't remind me!"

"But then these twins—I can't remember their names," Maria began, her forehead creased with effort. "Never mind what they were called, all that matters is that they were cool. They stayed back to repeat sixth class, and claimed me for their gang. They wore their socks down around their ankles, and they could roll their tongues into the shape of brandy snaps."

Ruth sat up, coughing. "You have a lurid imagination, Maria."

"But it's true."

"A lurid memory, then. But why did they want you, what strange anatomical feat could you perform?"

"I think it was because I pretended to know all about what we called the Facts."

"Mmm, I remember them. Should have been called the Wild Guesses."

"The Stabs in the Dark," Maria contributed, then winced and said, "that's literally what we thought it was. Anyway, these twins dared me to chalk 'Father Malone has a ginormous willy' on the back wall of the bike shed, and I did."

"And had he?"

"It was a rough estimate, based on the size of his ego."

"Well, good for you anyway, you wee vandal." Ruth smoothed her black wool tights and picked a tiny twig off one knee. "So you became a bad girl?"

"Not for long. Sister Miriam—the head nun—she tried to break us up. She called me over one lunch break and said she didn't think my mammy would like me to be friends with those twins, they weren't my sort, and why didn't I have a chat with Baby Jesus about it and tell him what she said?"

Ruth slapped the concrete. "That's *exactly* what our nuns used to say. They must teach it in the novitiate."

"Thing was, she needn't have bothered. The gang dumped me after Christmas when they discovered I didn't know what an erection was."

"So you palled up with the knitters again?"

"Yeah, except from then on I wore my socks down around my ankles."

"Speaking of ankles," murmured Ruth, leaning over, "is that a shaved leg I see before me?"

Maria pulled her sock up to meet the trouser leg. "Just a trick of the light."

"I wouldn't like to have to report you to my Wimmin's Anti-Depilatory Committee for cruelty to poor dumb hairs."

"I'm a, what is the word, a postfeminist," Maria told her, pouting. "I can shave any part of my body I choose."

"You're not choosing, you're conforming to male expectations."

"Ruth, the nearest male is about two hundred feet away across a pond and can't even see my ankles. Now, piss off and let me sunbathe."

🔲

She clung to the central pole as the bus chugged its way up the avenue. From time to time, overhanging horse chestnuts rapped their jewelled fingers against the roof. A heavy-jowled labrador cantered alongside, barking irritably.

Yvonne licked the edge of her pink-glossed lip. "Is something bothering you?"

"I'm all right." Maria pulled her head round slowly. "Apart from having spent the morning being humiliated by a personnel manager called Eugene."

"Oh, the job interview? I forgot all about it. How did it go?"

"It was my fault entirely. I put 'typing skills' on the bottom of my resumé, just to fill up a line, really, and the bastard gave me a test on his computer."

Yvonne let out a small moan.

"It's only filing and reshelving they want library assistants for, so I fail to see what the test was for."

"But you told me you could type."

"Yeah, but I learned on the manual at school and had a few goes on the electric in my uncle's office." Maria leaned her heavy head against the pole. "This monster in the library has all sorts of strange buttons, and the keys go into spasm as soon as you put your fingers on them. Do you know, I managed to type *system* with five *S*'s."

Yvonne pursed her lips. "Did the Eugene guy tear stripes out of you?"

"No, he was horribly chummy. Breathed down my neck while I was struggling with the delete button, then stopped me halfway and murmured, 'That's fine now, Maria, we'll let you know.' The bus jolted, cracking her head against the pole, and she straightened up. "I hate authority figures who keep calling you by your first name and pronouncing it wrong."

"Oh, stuff him," said Yvonne. "Don't see why you're letting a silly job interview get you down."

"Maybe that's because you're not the one who needs a job."

They lapsed into a stiff silence. After a minute, Yvonne ducked to peer out the window and sketched a cross on her scarf. "At least the traffic's not too heavy. We're past the church already."

"Which church?"

"A tall one. Tell me, Maria, do you still go to mass?"

Maria stooped toward the window, then reached above her for the bell. "We should have got off two stops ago, I'm sorry, it's not my day." They squeezed toward the side door, then realised that the driver was going to open only the front one and thrashed through the double line of bodies. "Bugger Irish busmen," Maria muttered, "they never bloody well open the bloody exit door."

Her stride gradually slowed and shortened as they neared Beldam Square. "Tantrum's over," she announced, turning. "Though why you'd still want to visit me I do not know."

"Christian duty," Yvonne told her with a theatrical sigh. "But listen, about mass. Do you still go?"

"Of course. I mean, yes," she went on more warily. She dipped to pick up a squashed can.

"No, I just wondered, because so many people seem to stop as soon as they get to college."

Maria found an overflowing bin and tucked the can into a corner, while she considered. "Do you go?"

"God, yes, but then, I'm living at home," said Yvonne defensively. "My mother would have a coronary on the spot if I refused."

"I sort of like it, especially if there's a good folk choir. It's peaceful."

"Yeah, but are you very into the religious part of it? Do you actually believe in, what's the *T* word, the bread turning into his body?"

"Transubstantiation?"

"That's the one. I never could spell it."

"I suppose I do." Maria's voice was suddenly uncertain. "Nobody's asked me that since I was seven and wearing my First Holy Communion veil."

Yvonne nodded. "I made sixty-three pounds off my relations that day. And Mum let me use her clear nail varnish."

"I sicked up carrots on my dress."

"Oh, Maria, you make up these gross little stories for effect."

"It's god's truth. Come home with me some weekend, and I'll show you the stain."

Yvonne shoved her into a bristly hedge.

As she was brushing the tiny leaves off her jumper, she sobered. "I'm still not sure about the believing business. I suppose if you believe any of it, you might as well swallow the lot."

"Like Madonna," said Yvonne, nodding.

"Is it?"

"You see, I don't actually like *all* her songs, only the fast ones. But it makes it simpler to have all the albums and be able to sing along to all the lyrics and be known as someone who likes Madonna. Guys remember, you know? They tease me about it."

Maria gave her a wondering look. "It does sound very like Catholicism. But it'll be gone in two generations, you know," she added grimly.

"What, transubstantiation?"

"The whole caboodle. Most of our generation aren't bothering with it, are they?"

Yvonne counted the damp cracks on the pavement.

"Don't worry about it, I could be wrong. Come on, let me buy you an ice cream."

"But it's winter," Yvonne protested, following her into the corner shop. "And it's about to rain."

"So the ice cream will feel warm by comparison," said Maria, and asked for two large cones.

They strolled through Beldam Square, their tongues keeping the overflowing cones just under control. On the grass a toddler was hitting something repeatedly with a yellow spade; the shivering mother sat on the edge of a nearby park bench, the collar of her raincoat turned up.

"I'm getting to like Dublin," said Maria. "All greys and dark greens, and so much grittier than suburbia."

The blustering wind slapped a bleached curl into Yvonne's eyes. She cast a dubious glance upward and said, "I felt a drop. At least in suburbia we have umbrellas."

"Probably just birdshit."

"Maria, for interest's sake, where's the nearest way out?"

"Over there, by the bust of Saint Oliver Plunkett."

"Because I get the impression it's about to—"

The skies split. They raced for the wrought iron gate but

found it locked; Maria let out a roar of laughter, tossed her ice cream cone into a wire basket, and led Yvonne off down the path. The woman jogged in the other direction, her protesting child hoisted over her shoulder. They found the entrance gate at last, its spikes silvery with rainfall. They rounded the perimeter in short bursts, snatching shelter under bulging hedges.

"Slow down," panted Yvonne. "I'd rather drown than suffocate." She peered between dripping lashes at the front door, reading the number on the streaked fanlight.

"Not that way, it's a brothel." Maria beckoned her round the side.

Hanging on to the bannister, Yvonne heaved a breath. "Did you say what I thought you said?"

"Well, it's a probable brothel."

"I don't think I want to know. Come on, I'd kill for a cup of tea and a mirror."

As they marked the last flight of stairs with their muddy shoes, Yvonne asked hoarsely, "Do I get to meet your wonderful flatmates?"

"They mightn't be in." Maria struggled with the key. "Yoohoo?" She collected an envelope from the radiator and headed for the kettle while Yvonne collapsed into the rocking chair.

"I feel old."

"Wunderbar!"

"Sorry?"

"It's a check, my grant's come in." Maria kissed the page. "Oh, glory be. I'll be able to pay my fees and buy one and a half protractors now."

"Are you on a grant? That's nice. How much do you get, if it's not rude to ask?"

Maria tossed over the letter and pulled two red mugs off their hooks.

"Is this per term?"

"No, twice a year."

Yvonne slid it back into the jagged envelope. "Not very much, is it?"

"You're damn right it's not. If my folks' grocery shop wasn't paying my rent, I wouldn't be here."

"The government should do something," said Yvonne. She fingered her mascara for signs of damage. "Grocery, did you say? That must be nice. Fresh fruit and all."

"It's not like the Southside supermarkets, if that's what you're imagining. No gleaming pyramids of nectarines."

Yvonne stuck out her tongue and asked for the bathroom. By the time she emerged, makeup restored, Maria had wetted the tea.

"That's a strange picture."

"Which, the one over the fireplace? It's just two women." Maria held the jug and sugar bowl in one hand, the two mugs in the other; she hissed as her fingers began to scald.

"Were they somebody famous's sisters or something?"

"No idea," said Maria, setting the mugs down by the hearth and sucking her hand. "Ruth found it in a market in Marseilles."

Yvonne rocked herself gently. "Ghastly rug, if you don't mind my saying so."

"Jael calls it the hide of the malnourished mammoth. Nice on bare feet, though."

After a few sips of tea, Yvonne leapt up. "If the film's not till ten past five, I've time for a full tour."

"Well, here we have the common-or-garden hall."

"Whose room is this?" said Yvonne, her fingers on the door handle.

"Theirs."

"Could I take a peek?"

"I'd rather you didn't," said Maria awkwardly. "I mean, as

they're not here. They're, we're quite into privacy."

"OK, sure." Yvonne folded her arms. "I just had the impression that you were all one happy family."

"We are when it's communal space. But bedrooms are different."

"Tell that to my mother," said Yvonne, lightening her tone. "If she walks in on me and Pete snogging one more time—"

"She doesn't!"

"She does it deliberately. Vicarious thrills for the menopause, that's my theory."

Maria opened her door. "And this is my room; better shade your eyes against the stripes. I have tried to dull the impact with posters."

Yvonne rotated, examining the faces. "Bogie's rather hung over. Is this Garbo? She looks so different when she's smiling."

"Don't we all?"

Smirking at herself in the mirror, she picked up a green eye shadow. "I've never seen you in this."

"Haven't got around to wearing it yet." Maria sat on the edge of her bed and let her back go limp.

"So tell me, how's the little Yank?"

"You never give up, do you?"

"Well, you did say you've been exchanging poetry," murmured Yvonne as she smoothed olive green below her eyebrow.

"He needed to borrow *The Complete W. B. Yeats* for an essay."

"Sounds like a lame excuse to me."

"Galway can't afford to buy books."

"Ah, da poor wee diddums," Yvonne muttered under her breath as she shaded the other eye.

Maria lined up the hangers in her wardrobe with a clang. "Look, he's not trying to worm his way into my affections.

He's a nice guy, and the most unsexual person I've ever met."

Yvonne tutted as she put the cap back on the eye shadow. "Don't be bitchy. He'd be quite cute if he put on some weight and spruced up a little."

"I don't care whether he's cute or not, he's just a friend."

"I don't think women and men can be friends." Her tone had flattened, as she stared out the window across the slates.

"Why not?"

"I can only speak from personal experience, but it certainly never works for me. Either I fall for them or they fancy me or we just never get closer than the first friendliness. There's so much stuff I'd never tell a guy."

Maria joined her at the windowsill and drew a wave in its thin layer of dust. "How are they ever going to understand us if we don't tell them stuff?"

"Dunno." Glancing at her watch, Yvonne remarked, "You know, we should head. There might be a queue, it's got Robert Redford in it. Don't you just melt when he walks onscreen?"

"Does nothing for me." Maria carried the mugs back to the sink.

"Blasphemy! That's nice, on the kitchen window. Is it an eagle?"

"No, an axe. From ancient Crete, no less; Ruth painted it on."

"My mother would like that. She's a bit of a culture vulture," commented Yvonne, shaking the raindrops off her coat and slipping it on. "Personally I've never seen the thrill in old things."

"Then why are you in art history?"

"Beats me," said Yvonne, following Maria out the front door. "I should have done physics, the male-to-female ratio is out of this world."

⑸

Having nothing else to do on Tuesday evening, Maria let Ruth drag her along to the women's group.

She felt almost conservative in her neat grey jeans and Aran jumper, since the first two women in the door were wearing layers of tie-dye over black leggings, topped off with home-made jewelry. Maria decided that it was a feminist uniform and was disconcerted when a junior lecturer turned up in a grey suit. After the kettle had boiled and somebody's bag of late windfalls had been shared out, a woman in faded jeans and brown braids wheeled in. Maria had seen her around in the maths corridor. She smiled briefly, then dropped her eyes, in case the woman stared back without recognition.

"Hey, Pat," said Ruth softly. She unwrapped a plastic bag and handed round wedges of banana bread, still warm.

Maria filled her mouth with its sweetness, so no one could expect her to talk. The scaly apple rested in her lap like a cannonball. She wanted to sit at the back, but she was drawn into the circle of chairs and shaky desks.

They began with a round of names and reasons for coming along; the first three were imaginative, then came a chorus of "I just wondered what it would be like" and "I agree with, sorry can't remember your name, the woman with the plaits." When the circle was completed, Maria took an unobtrusive bite of banana bread.

A bronzed woman from the States—Maria's mind had dropped her name already—got the ball rolling by announcing that her sociology professor wasn't exactly harassing her, but he did make funny remarks whenever she asked a question in class.

"Funny how?"

"Sort of suggestive. I can't describe it, but I bet he wouldn't look at a male student that way."

"Would if he was gay," Pat mumbled through her ploughman's.

"That's hardly the same power differential."

Nods all round. They swapped gossip on which tutors to avoid, which deans were worth complaining to. Was it fair to scrawl unsubstantiated rumours on toilet walls? The talk drifted to the ethics of tearing down the Feed the World Society's Fundraising Ball posters, which featured a Kenyan girl wearing only a grass skirt. "So what if it's an authentic tribal costume," Ruth broke in, "they're selling black breasts to white boys all over again." Her agitated hand swept a crust off the desk. Maria looked away, oddly embarrassed, and bit into her apple. It was old and sharp, grainy under the tongue. An Australian asked whether it was true the university had no support group for incest survivors, and would anyone like to help her set one up?

Maria leaned out of her corner of the fractured circle and tucked the apple behind a chair leg. She had nothing to report, and if she had, she wouldn't know the right words. Perhaps if she kept her face attentive, like in history class with old Sister Michael, no one would notice her. The debate heated up over the issue of abortion information in the Students' Union handbook, when Pat, her braids scattering, started referring to knock-kneed liberals and a red-haired Belfaster said that personally, when she called herself a feminist, that didn't mean she was into killing unborn babies.

Ten minutes later they had grudgingly agreed to disagree, and the others shifted the talk to relationships and how arrogant men (in general but of course not inevitably) were. Maria noticed Ruth drawing her knees up under her chin and listening in silence to an English woman's saga of bad communication and good sex. She considered the small, dark-curled head, sunk into the billows of a cream jumper. Maybe Ruth was too dedicated to her studies for any of that?

A porter put his greying head in the door to comment that

they'd have to be out in five minutes, girls, this room was booked for the Archeologists' Cheese 'n' Wine.

"Got to run," said Pat, deftly reversing her wheelchair down a zigzag aisle between desks.

The flame-haired woman from the North turned back into the circle and surveyed it impatiently. "Maria. What does all this say to you?"

"Well," she began, then trailed off. A ring of benevolent faces angled toward her. "I wouldn't like to generalise."

"But isn't your own experience all you've got to go on?" asked a pale woman, pushing strands of hair behind her ears.

"I haven't had much. Of that kind of experience that would be relevant."

She was saved by the Northerner who broke in warmly: "Isn't all experience relevant, Maria? I think the group should value the special insights of celibacy. In fact, why don't we make that our discussion topic for next week?"

Shivering at the bus stop, Maria and Ruth kept quoting "the special insights of celibacy" in a Belfast accent and relapsing into mirth.

"I made such a fool of myself."

"You did not, celibacy's very trendy," said Ruth.

"I just can't stand having to talk and everybody watching me."

Ruth leaned out into the wind, looking for any sign of a bus in the darkness. "Don't worry, it's always like that for the first few sessions. After a few good bust-ups, people relax."

She chewed her lip. "But I'm not sure I want to label myself a feminist or an anything."

"Grand." Ruth yawned, leaning her head against the bus shelter. "All you have to be for this group is a woman. We don't frisk for your opinions at the door."

"But what's so wonderful about women?" It sounded more sullen than Maria meant; that was her cold nose talking. But now that she'd said it, she had to go on. "I mean, we're not actually sisters, we don't really know each other even," she stumbled. "Why would it be any different if a few guys were let in to speak for themselves?"

"Listen, I've worked in mixed groups. Take my word for it, they're a waste of time."

The hint of condescension set Maria's teeth on edge. Would the bloody bus ever come? "I just don't see what's so wrong with men that we have to sit around whining about them."

"Is that what it sounds like?" Ruth's glance was puzzled.

She was too far in to retreat. "I suppose I just don't have a problem with men as such."

"Well, bully for you."

Her throat hurt. "All I meant was—"

The eyes turned on her looked black in the shadow of the bus shelter. "Of course you wouldn't see anything wrong with the little dotes, Maria, if you haven't been raped, denied a job, or battered by one yet."

"Neither have you." Had she? Stupid, stupid thing to say.

The answer was reluctant. "I know plenty who have."

Maria was flailing in deep water. There was no light but the white glare of the shelter, and the bus would never come. "Look," Maria asked, focussing on the ground, "I know I'm ignorant, and some men are definitely bastards, but surely there's nothing wrong with men as such?"

Ruth's lips were uneven. "Maybe not, but there's nothing wrong with women as such either, and that's all a women's group is. Christ, with all the hostility we arouse in this campus, you'd think we were terrorists."

Maria watched the gravel shift under her foot.

"I can tell I'm boring you; if it's not your scene, just forget it."

Maria was considering whether, and then how, to say she

was sorry when the bus trundled round the corner. It jogged them home, cold and wordless. In her head, as ever, the words flowed easily: *I have no wish to hurt you,* and *teach me,* and *the room is warmer when you're in it.* Covertly, she watched the reflection of Ruth's dark curls bump against the window beside her. Once their eyes met in the glass, and they almost smiled.

🔒

Was that him, slouching out of the photo booth? No plait. Not a bit like him, really.

"Personally speaking," Yvonne began, "I'm bored out of my tree."

Maria whipped her eyes back to her polystyrene coffee cup. They were squeezed into a corner of the Students' Union, their heels up on a table overflowing with empty popcorn bags. "Ah, but you missed this morning's major excitement," said Maria, yawning. "The dean of arts called us in to the sports hall and gave us a lecture about the importance of mixing. The usual 'best years of your lives' crap, with an extra bit about love, or rather sex, seeing as we're adults now."

Yvonne tapped her ash onto the floor. "What did she advise?"

"She said, 'Please don't fall in love,' with this fatuous simper on her face. As if it was just another of those irresponsible things that students get up to, like doodling on sculptures or roller-skating on the wheelchair ramps."

Maria coughed slightly, and Yvonne moved her cigarette into her left hand and waved away the smoke. "Did she say why?"

"Apparently if we fall in love in first year, we'll miss our chance to make oh so many new friends."

"D'you think she was speaking from experience?"

"No doubt." Maria decided not to chance the dregs of coffee; she balanced the cup delicately on top of the rubbish. "Probably dropped out pregnant in nineteen fifty-nine, had it down the country and put it up for adoption, came back to repeat first year as a model citizen."

"She's right, you know," said Yvonne gloomily. "About the L word."

"What, love? Of course she's right. But it's like saying, don't eat a box of chocolates because it'll spoil your appetite for dinner. I'd always go for the chocolates."

"Me too," said Yvonne lasciviously, folding back a linen cuff.

That simply had to be Damien, his orange sweatshirt just visible behind a pillar. It fascinated Maria, the way his huge hand cupped a thin French cigarette, which he sucked at from time to time in defiance of all the No Smoking signs.

"What's so interesting?"

"Nothing. Just a poster." Her head spun round. "I don't know, Yvonne, maybe we're just not suitable to grace the halls of academe."

"The halls of what?"

"Here."

"Oh." Yvonne took one last drag and stubbed it out on a Coke can. "You're probably right. I'm just here because everyone else is. I've no ambition to be a big success."

"There's more than one kind of success. You've managed to shift, what, three guys in less than three weeks of term."

"Four, actually," she smirked. "Did I not tell you about your man last Friday?"

"Lucky beast."

The coy tone became serious. "It's not luck, Maria, its hard work. Anyone can do it. Well, nearly anyone." She took her feet off the table and sat up. "If you got your hair layered back like I was saying, and wore a tiny bit of lipstick, very pale—"

"I hate the taste of lipstick. No, I think I'll leave you your train of admirers."

Yvonne relapsed into gloom. "I don't actually fancy any of them except Pete, and he doesn't seem too serious about me."

"Give him time." The orange sweatshirt had disappeared. "Come on, it's ten past already."

The lecturer was in full flow, projecting images of monstrous canvases onto the screen. "Get an eyeful of that," hissed Yvonne as they slid into the back row. "Didn't know they had lezzie orgies in the seventeenth century."

"It's the *Rape of the Sabine Women*, twit. They're clinging together for moral support."

"Immoral, more like." Yvonne slapped four different-colored markers down on her refill pad and turned to the main business of the day. "So, you fancy anyone yet?"

Maria rolled her eyes, then wrote out a neat header for her notes: *Baroque War Scenes—Dr. Quentin—October 19*.

Lowering her voice suggestively, Yvonne continued. "Romantically interested in any male humanoids at this point in time?"

"Lay off."

Yvonne sighed. "You're so self-reliant, I really respect that." She began neatening her cuticles with the cap of her pen.

Maria didn't dare look. She knew he was down eleven rows on her right, and if she cast a single glance in his direction, Yvonne would go on red alert. No doubt she would shudder at Maria's taste; one was meant to fall for a long-limbed med student whose daddy had a BMW, or be obsessed with the firm jaw of a Law Soc smoothie. One was meant to aim higher than a bearded knowall in one's own tutorial.

It was only three days ago that she'd noticed Damien at all. As he knotted himself into an argument with the tutor about aesthetic theory, she sat back and stared. When the hour was up he shoved his books into a battered briefcase and stalked off through the crowded corridor, eyes on his feet. She always kept an eye out for his lank braid at lectures after that. He never stooped to taking notes; beside a swarm of girls transcribing all the lecturer's mediocrities, he sat like Julius Caesar.

After a glance at Yvonne, who was still preoccupied with her nails, Maria let her eyes slew down to him. Only the back of his head was visible, and one arm. Hold on, he did seem to be taking notes today—scribbling something on a pad. "Go on without me," she told Yvonne when the lecture limped to a close. "I better finish taking down that structural diagram from the board." Hunched over her notes, she watched Damien through her hair. He was scrunching up his page and flicking it round the desk. She hung around for several minutes after his departure until the theatre had cleared, then ran down the steps and pounced on the document. It was a crudely executed sketch of a suckling sow.

She kept it, neatly labeled with the date and lecture theatre. Maria liked to label the detritus of the past. It scared her that in ten years' time she might be a mother of four in a sub-urban semi, unable to remember anything.

🔄

"It's going to boil over, I swear. Look at those bubbles."

Ruth shot her arm under Maria's to get at the switch. "All you had to do was turn it down."

"But you said I wasn't to stop stirring till the lumps disap-peared," Maria insisted. She dropped the wooden spoon for a second to scratch her forehead, and a drop of scalding milk splashed her wrist.

Hearing her yelp, Ruth took over. "Gimme, I'll finish the white sauce. You could be greasing the dish."

Maria yawned as she rolled down the sleeves of her cardigan. "Sorry to be useless. I don't know how you can stand the stress of juggling pans."

"Practice."

She couldn't see Ruth's expression; steam clouded the features. "Are you pissed off with me?"

"Not at all." The warm eyes turned on Maria. "Now don't do your forlorn puppy act, I haven't time to find you a biscuit."

Maria busied herself with the ceramic dish, buttering its curves. When she had finished, she wandered over to the steamy window and peered down at the pavement. "Mucky day. Can't make up its mind whether it's raining or not. I think I spy our wee Jaelo Submarine hoving round the corner."

Ruth came over, wiping her hands on her jeans. "That'll be her. She looks so harmless from four flights up, doesn't she? Like a carrot top floating in the gutter."

"You can be such a bitch when you try," said Maria appreciatively.

"Mostly I don't try. It's only fair to leave her something to be better at," Ruth explained through a fingerful of white sauce. "You want to start breaking the pasta into pieces?"

A muffled ring from below. "She must have forgotten her key again," said Maria. "Tell you what, I'll run down, if you finish the lasagne."

They tramped up the stairs arguing at full voice. "Would you believe it," Maria announced as she slashed through the bead curtain, "this constipated cow had her key all the time."

Jael blew a sardonic kiss at the cook and started to tug at the dripping zipper of her leather jacket. "Well I thought it was probably at the bottom of my bag, but I was too wet to be bothered rummaging for it. Especially as I knew there'd be a pair of seventeen-year-old legs just longing for some exercise." She sidestepped a kick from one of the legs and got behind the sofa. "Besides, look what I have here." She brandished a sodden copy of the *College Echo* like a matador's red cloth.

"Did they print it?" demanded Ruth, looking up from the cheese grater.

"You bet your bottom they did. Listen to this for quality journalism, youngster. 'Top Profs Feel a Little Fresher.'"

"Ah, god love us, they couldn't have called it that." Ruth ran to grab the newspaper with sticky fingers. After a quick scan of the third page, she aimed a slap at Jael's ear. "I knew you were lying, fiend."

"Let's see." Maria pushed between their shoulders.

"They used the headline I suggested: STAFF IN SEXUAL HARASSMENT SCANDAL."

Jael sank onto the sofa and put her boots up on the fireguard. "If you ask me, it's libelous, even with the proper title. You make accusations of gross indecency against 'a senior lecturer in the Department of Paleography,'" she went on, tugging open the top buttons of her purple silk shirt, "and there are only two of them."

"It's all based on objective research," said Ruth, scrutinizing each paragraph.

Jael sniffed the air. "Is there a burning sauce in the house?" Ruth scuttled to the stove. "I love deflating her when she's on an ego trip," Jael whispered to Maria, clearing her a narrow place on the sofa.

"You mean when she's a brilliant success."

"Same difference," said Jael lazily. "Ah, I suppose she's better off keeping busy, it distracts her from her loveless life. We spinsters have to use up our energies somehow."

Maria was licking the faint buttery taste off her little finger.

The fire was dying into grey ash, but she was too deeply tucked into the sofa to move. "Speaking of our loveless lives," she said, "don't we eat a shocking amount?"

Jael's face was dreamy as she patted the rounded belly of her jeans. "Well personally, I'm eating for two."

"You are *not*." Maria's voice was not quite sure.

"I mean me and my ego."

Toying with the fringe on the tartan blanket, Maria waited till the shake was gone from her voice. "No, but seriously, about food. I know I pay into the kitty, but you two are always buying extras. I amn't offering to cough up any more, because I can't afford to, but I feel a bit mean chomping my way through your sesame rolls and peaches."

Jael erupted into laughter. She rested her heavy elbow on Maria's shoulder and put on her huskiest Hollywood voice. "You can chomp your way through my peaches anytime, sweetheart."

"I wouldn't worry about it, Maria," said Ruth, her voice muffled as she bent down to the oven. "I'm living off savings from my years as a civil serpent, and Lady Muck here gets monthly checks from her loving family."

"Loving, is it?" snorted Jael. "All they love is their stud farm and their station wagon. They pay me to stay away."

"That's shameful," said Maria.

"Isn't it just! Thrust out into the cold at seventeen by my nearest and dearest."

Maria couldn't hide her smirk. "No, what I meant was, it's shameful for a grown woman of twenty-nine to be still collecting pocket money."

There was a short pause—had she managed to hit a nerve? She began plaiting the tartan fringe, three strings at a time.

Jael bounced back. "Every time I feel a pang of guilt, I remember that as a communist it's my duty to squeeze my capitalist parents dry."

"You're a communist in your hole," called Ruth, clanging cutlery in the sink.

"Especially there," said Jael, giving Maria a lecherous wink.

Maria combed the blanket edge loose again and went over to dry the saucepans. "Yes, but what about me?" she asked Ruth as she took a dripping bowl from her hand. "It's not my food."

"You, my dear, are helping us to squander our ill-gotten gains," called Jael, her chin on the sofa back. "We'd be buying the odd chocolate cake whether you were here or not, so don't bother your pretty little head about it."

Maria wiped between the tines of a fork. "But why did you advertise for a flatmate, then, if you could afford the flat yourselves?"

"Wasn't my idea." Jael snapped open the *College Echo*.

Ruth scrubbed at the edge of a plate with steel wire. "It's hard to remember. It seems years ago."

"You were lonely," Jael prompted from behind the paper.

"Didn't realise you'd noticed." Ruth turned back to Maria, and her voice livened. "But it's just as well you're here, or we'd be at each other's throats. One Sunday last summer we came to physical blows over who got to read the newspaper first."

"Mmm," said Jael, "and I remember who won."

Maria looked from one to the other, as she folded up the damp cloth. "So I'm to consider myself some sort of cushion?"

"More like a kept woman," suggested Jael.

🔄

"Now try O'Connell Street."

"Shrawd Ee Cunl."

"It's a *ch*." She pointed at the sign, three stories up. "Try again: Sráid Uí Chonaill."

Galway twisted his mouth with effort. "Shroyige Ee Hunil. Oh, boy, I give up. Why can't they spell it like it sounds?"

"It's like a wartime code," said Maria, watching for a gap in the cars. "The invaders aren't supposed to be able to read the street names," she called over her shoulder as she dashed across the street.

Galway followed her more cautiously. "I guess I won't be fluent in Gaelic by Christmas, then? My grandma will be mad."

"I wouldn't waste your energy on a dying language," Maria advised him. They crossed the bridge, skirting the beggar and her baby wrapped in a striped blanket. "I only know it because it was drilled into me for thirteen years; I'll have purged my mind of it soon enough."

He paused to peer over a scrolled parapet to the dank Liffey rolling forty feet below. "You shouldn't deride your heritage," he told her when she joined him. "Smell that."

She bent obediently for a sniff.

"Full of bones and battle-axes, that smell is. Pure history."

"Dead fish, and Guinness leaking from the export ships, more like." Maria straightened up. "I've had enough bloody history for one morning. I was tired when I woke up, and those cathedral steps nearly finished me off. If I'd known you were going to be such an enthusiast, I'd never have brought you."

He caught her up at the traffic island. "I've just noticed that all the shops are shut. Has there been a bomb alert or something?"

"Sunday, remember? The Lord will smite thee if thou buyest a packet of biscuits." She led him round College Green. "Which reminds me, I've missed mass. Still, my mother used to say it's all right if you visit a cathedral instead, so I suppose they have their uses."

"But wasn't the Viking settlement awesome? And that

trash heap, with bits of eggshell from prehistoric dinners?"

"Please, I've had no breakfast." As they rounded the blackened facade she said, "We should probably go and gaze at the Book of Kells, but I'd rather a coffee and a cherry bun."

"I have to tell you, I'm totally broke."

"Galway, may I buy you a small beverage out of my grant money? Come on, let me feel rich. New Men are meant to be into role reversal."

He looked young in the morning light. "Our tour guide couldn't have been described as a New Man. Did you catch his little jest about the hygiene habits of Viking women?"

"What got to me was the way he kept calling 'Step this way—but mind the step, ladies!'"

Maria found a tiny café, the only door open on the street. "Hey, I didn't tell you," she said over the menu, "I've got a job at last. Office cleaning, at night."

"Go for it," said Galway. "I was a chambermaid in Boston the summer before last. It gives you lots of dream time."

"I'm glad you approve. Everyone else says why don't I do waitressing instead."

"I'd rather sell sweat than smiles," he told her.

"Me too." Maria was always convinced by epigrams. "It's not the sweat I mind, though, it's the stink of window-cleaning fluid."

"Soon get used to it. Who are you working with?"

"A woman called Maggie. She has a lavender overall and flat grey curls and never speaks."

"You'll get some peace and quiet, then."

"Oh, stop it. You could get a Ph.D. in looking on the bright side."

⑤

The grey steps of the administration building were littered with several dozen bodies and three banners. "Rubbers for

Revolution," she read, and one long sagging one that included the letters "HIV" and something that looked like "Cabbage" but couldn't be. Maria dawdled at the edge of the gravel till she spotted Galway's arm waving in a leisurely fashion. She waved back but walked on; it was too bright a day to sit on concrete in the shade. Of course the college should install a condom machine, but somehow she couldn't work up the energy to demonstrate for a product she had never even seen out of its packet. As she strolled toward the main gate, she heard rising from the crowd a slow clap and several chants, including an irreverent "Johnny, I hardly knew you."

Maria got off the bus a stop early, to soak up the yellow sunlight. She considered her new boots with satisfaction: slightly imperfect matte-brown Doc Martens, £15.99 from the stall that shifty-looking guy ran in the arcade she discovered last Saturday. Now she could pass for a real student. Their broad toes scuffled through gutterfuls of sharp leaves.

The door at the top of the stairs was swaying open, so she strolled in and glanced through the bead curtain.

It wasn't her fault; she was in no sense spying. She couldn't help but see the shape they made. Her eyes tried to untangle its elements. Ruth, cross-legged on the table, her back curved like a comma, and Jael, leaning into it, kissing her. There was no wild passion; that might have shaken her less. Just the slow bartering of lips on the rickety table where Ruth chopped garlic every night.

Maria clamped her eyes shut, as if they had not already soaked in the scene as blotting paper swallowed ink. When she raised the lids, the women had not moved. The kiss, their joint body, the table, all seemed to belong to a parallel world. She had the impression that no noise from behind this shifting skin of beads could reach them.

She doubled back to the door, making her brash boots land as softly as slippers. A count of ten, she gave them, as she leaned against the door frame. How long could a kiss last? Five more seconds. It occurred to her that they had no reason to stop. Nineteen hippopotamus, twenty hippopotamus . . . Perhaps they would go on all afternoon. The windows would darken around them, their faces would become silhouettes, the dinner would stay on the chopping board, and all this time Maria would be standing in the front doorway.

"I'm home, folks," she yelled, loud and cheery as Doris Day. They behaved perfectly too, strolling out of the kitchen with armfuls of library books as if they had been rehearsing this little scene all their lives. Which, now she came to think of it, they probably had.

Five hours later was the earliest she could go to bed without having them worry that she was ill. She kept yawning heartily and explaining how her new job really took it out of her, what with the industrial vacuum cleaners and all.

At last she was under the covers, soft candlewick bunched in her fist. She concentrated on blacking out the tableau that was still flickering on the screen of her mind. What bothered her was that there was no distance. The topic had come up before, of course. Girls joked about it all the time in convent school; there'd even been rumours about the gym teacher. At parties they swapped Freudian theories, and Nuala had once claimed to have seen a French film with two women in bed in it. But it was never real. Now suddenly here were two friends of hers kissing on the table she ate at every night. Rapt faces and library books and garlic, how bizarre.

Almost a month, Maria thought. Four entire weeks, and she hadn't copped on, not even after overhearing that first conversation. Nearly thirty days of conversations, blown kisses, suppers, private jokes. The quilt was heavy on her eyelids, blotting out the light. What ludicrous naivete, even for seventeen. How could she not have known? And then, embarrassment swinging to anger, the question reversed: How the hell was she meant to know?

3

DOUBLING

Waking, Maria felt weighed down, as if something was crouching on her rib cage. She lay still for a few seconds until it rushed back into her head: the table, the kiss, the lot. She stretched up to tug the curtain a few inches open, letting an arm of light slide across the bedspread. Daylight made things more manageable.

Certain phrases soothed her, she found, as she lay there trying to formulate a policy. *Consenting adults,* that was a steadying one, along with *nobody's business but their own. Different strokes,* she thought, then rejected it as too vivid an image. What was the phrase the Northerner came up with at the women's group? *Mutual acceptance,* that was it. She would accept them and they would accept her and not flaunt it in her face or push it down her throat.

Maria halted the words flooding through her head. That wasn't what she meant. All she wanted was not to be afraid and embarrassed in her own flat. Flaunting, pushing, that made it sound like a stick. But she didn't know how else to visualise it. An open-winged hawk, a double cherry, a two-way mirror? A kiss on a kitchen table, that was all she had to go on. Somewhere between private and public, terrible and tender. Maria sat up and pulled the curtain fully open. She leaned back, letting the cold wallpaper startle her skin awake.

By the time she emerged, Ruth and Jael had almost finished breakfast. Under her plate she found a saccharine letter from her school about the graduation ball. Automatically she slid it over to Ruth and poured the last drips of milk over her granola. She couldn't be the first to speak; her voice might shake.

Jael was reading over Ruth's shoulder; "If I were you," she commented, "I'd find myself a man pronto. Take one spotty Homo sapiens, insert him in a wing collar, proceed to your grad, and get yourself laid."

Maria's tongue prised a bit of hazelnut out of a back tooth. She was inclined to make a feminist virtue of financial necessity and just not go. As for stage two of the operation, the laying, that struck her as even less attractive, though probably cheaper. "I'm not sure how much I want to spend a night doing 'The Birdy Song' with a hundred schoolmates in pink taffeta," she said. "I know a girl who worked in a bingo hall all summer to pay for her dress, but I couldn't be fashed. Did you go to yours?" she asked Jael.

The eyes crinkled with nostalgia. "Peering back through the mists of time—when was it, late seventies?—I seem to recall that I brought the first friend's brother who was willing to pay his half of the ticket, and the creep got inflamed by vodka and tried to rape me in the lobby of the Shelbourne Hotel." She dropped yet another sugar into her coffee, then added, "I must admit I was tempted. There was damn all else going on. It was really his getup that turned me off; I can say to my credit I've never laid a guy in a bow tie."

Maria's mind lurched. She bent her head and focussed on her tumbler of apple juice. "What about you?" she asked

Ruth after a minute, in case they noticed her silence.

"Didn't go, didn't see the point."

Jael beamed. "Now that is the essential difference between us. Ruth Johnson is a hundred percent Ideologically Sound."

Ruth turned from a sink full of mugs to throw a hazelnut at her. Her—what was the right word—friend, girlfriend, lover? She missed.

⑤

I'M FELICITY, TRY ME was hung alongside SEAN L. FOR CLASS REP, HE'S FULL OF PEP, and below them sagged MARYLOU TENNANT, THE CLASS REP WHO'LL GIVE YOU WHAT YOU WANT. Maria scanned the ten-foot banners of computer paper taped to the steep brick walls of the lecture theatre. She decided against voting for any of the candidates. Only eleven o'clock, and already the day felt old. Keeping the mind on small things, that was the knack. Not to fret, not to make any sudden decisions, not to think too much. She distracted herself by scanning the packed lecture theatre, row by row, for Damien's silhouette. In the far corner her eye found him, under the grimiest patch of wall. He had his head back like a dead bull; perhaps he was asleep. Much the best thing to do. Face on her arms, Maria slumped across the desk.

The professor's drone hovered above the hum of the crowd. "I hope I made it sufficiently clear in my last lecture that the really essential point you must grasp is the significance of the rediscovery of oil paint and the resultant potential in terms of color intensity—"

A nudge jolted her awake. "What?" she spat.

"And a good morning to you, sunshine."

"Sorry." Maria hoisted herself onto her elbows. Yvonne had either been crying or was wearing startlingly pink eye shadow.

"What's up?"

No, Maria assured her, she was not hung over, nor having

her period, nor in love. Her finger traced the generations of graffiti carved on the desk. Famous names of rock, sharp-petaled flowers, the odd swastika drawn the wrong way round. Then the words slipped out past her tongue. "I got a bit of a surprise."

"A nice surprise or a nasty surprise?" asked Yvonne, in what she clearly thought of as her tactful tone.

"Oh, for god's sake, you sound like an Enid Blyton book. Just a surprise, all right?"

"About what?" She was beyond tact now, her eyes bright with curiosity.

Damn it, why had she said a word? Just below her pad was a deeply scored heart, bigger and sharper on the left side; she traced it with her pencil. Taking a heavy breath, she decided to get the whole thing over with. "About my flat-mates going out together."

A brief pause. Then a tentative "Going out where?"

Maria kept her face blank.

"Oh, good jesus." Yvonne's voice went spiralling up to the top of the lecture theatre, and several bored faces turned to stare. "You're telling me they're lesbians? Both of them?"

"Will you shut the fuck up?" snarled Maria under her breath. "No need to tell the whole of first arts."

The professor peered up in their direction, then resumed his monologue. Yvonne leaned over toward Maria's ear. "You poor creature," she whispered, "you must have been so embarrassed when they told you. How did they bring it up—which of them actually said it?"

Engrossed by the carvings on the desk, she stumbled over the syllables. "They didn't have to tell me in so many words, you know, it just sort of became clear."

Yvonne nodded. "Of course, you're pretty perceptive, you'd be quick to pick up the clues. Body language. Had you noticed anything, like, revealing before?"

"They're perfectly normal people otherwise." Maria looked up suspiciously. "And you're not to spread it round campus."

"I wouldn't." Yvonne's voice was hurt. "I can just imagine how I'd feel if a rumor went round college about me—I'd be sure everyone was staring. I won't even tell Pete, I promise."

"Thanks."

Yvonne sat back, dazed. Maria began to hear what the professor was saying. She supposed she should be taking notes. A quick glance across the theatre showed her that Damien had gone, sloped off during Yvonne's little fit, no doubt.

"I just hope no one jumps to the wrong conclusions about you, Maria."

"Sorry?"

Yvonne had got her breath back. "Just because you live with them, I mean. Not that anyone would be likely to, since you've got hair down to your shoulders and you often wear skirts. Well, fairly often."

Maria rested her forehead on the heel of her hand. "Look, they're both very nice. And they wear skirts sometimes too."

"Oh, I know," said Yvonne wisely, "but they'd have to, wouldn't they, as cover?"

🔄

Trailing out of the library with the last studious finalists that evening, Maria found herself unwilling to go home. She wandered round the arts block, looking at dog-eared posters for hot-whisky evenings and medieval farces she had missed. The sculptures in the courtyard were so different by night; they lost all their comic twists and darkened to look like standing stones. She stood with her fingers and nose against the icy glass.

Maybe Yvonne was right; it was hardly what you'd call normal to be sharing a flat with—how would the nuns have put it, if they ever had to?—two active homosexuals. One of them being either bisexual, having implied at breakfast that she liked to lay guys without bow ties, or a convincing liar. The other being the kind of woman Maria would have liked to bring home to her mother. Both being mortal sinners, according to one rule book, and pitiable case histories, according to another. She turned from the window, rubbing the cold pads of her fingers against her jeans.

Could it all have been a hallucination? Or a joke—could they have heard her coming up the stairs and started kissing just to shock her? No, she thought, summoning up the image. And no chance of it being the first time, either; those lips were used to each other. So she could stop codding herself and get on with prising open her mind to fit this knowledge.

Maria scanned a notice on the Hockey Club bulletin board, but the words slid by without meaning. She had nothing against her flatmates, she thought; they lit up the rooms and made them ring with laughter. But the fact remained that she didn't know what to do or be with them. Anger bubbled up in her stomach. It was a bit much that they hadn't warned her before she moved in. Unless—of course, that wretched ad, it must have been some sort of code. Well, how was she supposed to know? It didn't seem too naive to assume that a women's symbol meant women, and no bigots meant generally liberal people.

The phrase turned her mouth cold, as she leaned against a notice board. It meant her. Well, if she was a bigot, she couldn't help it. She didn't understand, she didn't know what to think or why she thought it, she didn't even know the right terminology for it. Oh, damn and blast it, why couldn't they teach this sort of thing at school?

A few limp couples were curled up in corners, deaf to everything but their own whispers. When the ten-thirty siren blared, they straggled out of the building two by two. The night was so mild that Maria decided to risk a stroll around the lake. If she met a rapist, she would gouge his eye out, she reminded herself, and splayed her keys between her fingers as Ruth had taught her. Though of course, now that she came to think of it, Ruth was a bit paranoid about men. The moon looked almost full, just a lick taken out of its side. Avoiding the dark bushes, Maria threaded her way through the trees and reached the rim of the lake.

She found a space relatively clear of white gulls' droppings and crouched down on the paved edge. The nuns never liked you to sit on cold surfaces; they said you'd regret it in later life. Only years afterward did she discover that all they were warning against was piles. Where had all the ducks gone? Probably nesting on the artificial islet. The water looked so silky, though she knew it was full of oil drums and scummy crisp bags. She resisted the impulse to pull off her runners and socks and dip her feet in; no point getting pneumonia for a bit of moonlight. Staring across the stretch of water, she watched the library lights go out one by one.

⑤

A plumber gave them a quizzical glance as he passed down the underground corridor.

"So then she said to me, the cards show that you are having problems in a relationship with a dark-haired man, he is not yet ready for commitment. Wasn't that weird? I had barely mentioned Pete, and certainly not the color of his hair. And then there were quarrels, and after that a love choice, but a definite reconciliation by Christmas. Maria, are you listening?"

"Mmm. Don't move your jaw too much, I'm trying to catch the angle. What else did Madame Zelda predict?"

"No, her name was Doris. Just some stuff about buying a house; I think she overestimated my age. But the emotional stuff was really accurate, wasn't it? She offered to read my palm for another fiver, but I was nearly broke, and anyway

Pete knows this guy from Luxembourg, we met him in a wine bar on Saturday, and he's going to read mine for free."

"Sounds good." She held the pencil out at arm's length, narrowing her eyes.

"You think it's all mumbo jumbo, don't you?"

"Stop putting words into my mouth."

Yvonne arched her back against the rusty blue locker, then stretched one foot out with a slight moan. "You needn't bother drawing me, I'll have turned to a statue if you keep me sitting on this concrete floor much longer."

"Are you cold?" Maria looked up in concern. "I'm sorry, it's the only place I could think of to get any peace. You could sit on my jacket."

"Never mind, I'll survive." She leaned over for a peek at the page, but Maria jerked it out of sight. "So what's up with you today?"

"Nothing's up."

"Well, you've been fiddling over that sketch for twenty minutes now without saying a word, and my beauty isn't all that engrossing, so you must have something on your mind." She flicked a cigarette butt off the side of her shoe. "Is it them?"

"Who?"

"You know right well who I mean. Have you decided whether you'll be moving out?"

Crosshatching a shadow, Maria said nothing. After a few seconds, "I just like to concentrate when I'm doing a picture. You said you wanted it for your wall."

"But you are still upset about them, aren't you?"

"I wish you wouldn't call them Them, like they're Martians or something." She lowered her voice again as a cluster of raucous footballers went past, banging on the end lockers.

"I know their names, that's not the point." Yvonne stretched her arms above her, then readjusted the shoulder pads in her blouse. "The point is, they got a month's rent out of you on false pretences."

"Ah, for god's sake, it wasn't a financial scam or anything." Maria rubbed out a crooked line. "They probably assumed I knew."

"That's outrageous. I mean, it's not the first thing that's going to spring into your head when you go house-hunting, is it? I mean, you don't say to yourself, oh, yes, must check whether my flatmates are lesbian lovers, just in case!"

Maria placed the pencil on the concrete and looked her in the eye. "I appreciate your looking after me, I really do. Now, will you kindly lay off? I've been busy with my job; four evenings this week. I haven't had time to think whether I'll be moving out or not."

"What's to keep you there?"

"For one thing, I like them."

"I know you do, Maria, you're a very friendly person." Yvonne hugged her knees in exasperation. "But they're hardly your sort. I mean, don't you find them a bit, you know?"

"A bit what?"

She squirmed slightly. "Butch and ranty."

"I can't believe I'm listening to such clichés. You've never even met them."

"Well, I know a girl who had one in her school, and apparently she was really aggressive. Like Martina Navratilova."

Maria stared down at the careful sketch; she was sorely tempted to rip it up, but that would be immature. She tried again. "Jael wears mascara sometimes. And Ruth is a dote, I wish you knew her. OK, they're feminists, well, Ruth is anyway, but they don't rant. Like, the other night for example, they had no objection to my watching the Miss World contest."

"Well of course."

"What do you mean, of course?"

Yvonne leaned toward her and cooed, "All those semi-naked women."

"You're sick."

She shrugged her shoulders. "I just can't believe you're being so naive about this, Maria. You're defending them as if they've been your bosom pals for years."

"At least I know them, which is more than you do. And they never wear boiler suits or"—she scanned her memory frantically—"studs in their noses or get their hair shaved off or any other clichés you might care to dredge up." She ground to a halt. "And neither of them has even a shadow of a moustache, so there."

"Aren't you going to finish my picture?"

"Go back the way you were, then. Hands in your lap." Maria sketched in silence. After a few minutes, she had almost lost herself in the faint rasp of the pencil.

When Yvonne, scratching her wrist, whispered, "I never mentioned moustaches," Maria pretended she hadn't heard.

🔳

"Did I not remind you to peel them?"

"There isn't anything to peel, Ruth, carrots don't have a skin."

"Well, they've got a surface, and it's leathery. Here, use the potato knife."

A gull screamed above the open window; Maria glanced up from her knife to catch a flash of white against the smoky sky. In ten minutes it would be dark. From the street below came the rumble and screech of office workers leaving ten minutes early to beat the traffic.

Hard to stave off melancholy these late October after-noons, when the clouds massed so quickly after five o'clock and blocked off the mild light. She had always disliked the moment when her mother would send her to turn on the overhead kitchen lamp and snuff out the day. Especially on lethargic afternoons when somehow she had not got around to doing anything but arranging her paintbrushes in order of size and feeding her brothers' neglected hamster; those times, it choked her to snap the light switch down and admit that the day was over, with no possibilities left but Irish grammar by the fire and cereal with hot milk for supper. Maria used to suspect she would never grow up while she clung to these domestic comforts. To be a teenager you had to brave the twilight and stay out long past teatime, walking along the wall of the graveyard and hanging round the chip shop swapping insults with the rough lads from the travellers' caravan camp. She used to fear she would always be four foot four as long as she stayed under the thrall of the kitchen light bulb, eating the spirals of sharp peel her mother tossed aside as she made apple pie.

"Oh, slice them longways."

"Sorry?"

"Instead of circles, could you slice the carrots into little sticks? Eighths, maybe," suggested Ruth.

"Sure. Sorry, I was dreaming." Maria shifted her weight to the other leg and set to work again on the mouse-shaped chopping board. Her thighs were stiff as girders after scrubbing toilets three evenings in a row. Tonight was hers, she promised herself: a two-hour bath with last Sunday's papers, random television, and a bar of Belgian truffle. The knife skidded through the carrot. "Bloody hell, I fear for my fingers. This is the last time I volunteer to cut up your crudités."

Ruth turned, her face softening. "Ah, pet, I'm really grateful. I'd never have had time to do three dips otherwise. Do you think they'll like the fennel-and-chives one?"

"They're students; they'll probably chomp through the lot without noticing any difference."

"No doubt." Coming back from the sink with a colander of

wet herbs, Ruth paused by the window and peered down. "I wonder what time Jael will be back. Bet she's on a bender with the Spanish crowd."

"She's a big girl, don't worry about her."

Ruth pulled with both hands on the wooden frame, until the window gathered momentum and rattled shut. She snapped the light on, and the table was suddenly bright with orange and green.

"So how come you're the one who gets landed with bringing food to the History Society do?" asked Maria, sliding the carrot sticks into a tub.

"Suppose because I'm the social secretary, and they know I like to cook."

"Sounds a thankless job."

"I'm their token woman. When I lost the auditor election to Graham, I thought I'd take the next most responsible position." Ruth tasted a fingertip of dip abstractedly. "I used to be more like you when I was younger," she remarked.

Maria took a cautious bite of cucumber. "Like me how?"

"Oh, you know." Ruth pressed a lid on a tub with the heel of her hand. "Good at saying no to things."

"Am I?" She was not sure whether to take it as a compliment. "It's mostly just cowardice."

"No, I've been watching." Ruth straightened her back and gave her a thoughtful look. "You say no to most things, to make room for the things you really want."

Maria felt pink.

"I used to be able to do that. When I was in the Civil Service, if anyone had asked me to make crudités for a party, I'd have told them where they could stuff them."

She held a slice of cucumber up to the light bulb; it glowed white, like a cell under a microscope. She fed it to Ruth. "So what happened?"

"Came to college, got happy. Figured I was getting what I

wanted, so it would be mean not to give other people what they wanted. Oh, I don't know," the voice straining to lighten, "I suppose I'm just overworked and overcommitted." She bent to Maria's hand, taking another sliver of cucumber into her mouth. "Sometimes," she said through the crunch, "I'd like to be seventeen again."

"Yuck."

"I could start from scratch. No ties or duties or fixed ideas."

"You poor, world-weary crone."

"Amn't I just. Do you think I should cut the courgette on the diagonal?"

"Don't ask me, ma'am, I'm just the skivvy."

The window was a square of licorice now, and the noise from the street had lulled. This table was floating in a pool of yellow light on top of the city. Maria would never get used to living as high as the gulls. Some nights, as she hauled her knees up the last flight of stairs, she felt like an old usherette, lost in the innards of a Victorian theatre. Coming through the light-dripping curtain of beads into the living room was like wandering onto a stage in the middle of the last act. Even when it was empty, it carried the echo of shouts, whistled tunes, thrown cushions. On her own, Maria sometimes felt so exposed, on this bright platform perched on a block of deserted offices, that she stayed away from the windows. She had to remind herself that there was no one high enough to look in.

Her knife was lolling; she reached for a handful of radishes. "Hey, did I ever tell you about my one and only *cordon bleu* production?"

"What did you cook?" asked Ruth.

"Don't remember; suffice to say it was the hautest of cuisines. The point is, it was meant to be a romantic dinner for my parents' silver wedding anniversary the year before last. I locked the lads into their bedroom with a packet of chocolate biscuits, ushered the happy couple into the candlelit kitchen, opened the half bottle of champagne, and glided out, shutting the door softly behind me."

"Of course."

"You know what the clodhoppers did? They turned the lights back on at nine to watch *Dynasty*." Maria slashed a radish in half.

Ruth laughed, laying her dripping whisk on the bare wood. "With my mother it was the other way round; it was me who was always disappointing her." She reached past Maria for the garlic crusher. "Like, when I was about five, she went into labour with my brother, and I had to call the ambulance for her. I remember running into the kitchen to show her a daisy chain or something, and she was sitting on the floor and making a sort of grunting noise."

"You creature! What did you do?"

"She told me to get the phone, but the cord wouldn't reach. So then she said,'Do three nines, love, and tell them your mummy's having a baby.' She was having a what? Where? That was the first I'd heard of it. So I took about five goes at dialling—with my left thumb, I remember—and told them our address, and they came for her twenty minutes later."

"Hang on. Surely your mother was proud of you then, not disappointed?"

Ruth shook garlic off her fingertips and scratched her eyebrow with one wrist. "All I remember is her look of exasperation while I was struggling with the phone."

"If you had labour pains, you'd look more than exasperated."

"I suppose so." Ruth was staring into space. "It's coming back to me now. She used to tell this story at parties, how she asked me would I like her to bring me a little brother home one day, and I said no, I'd rather a box of chocolates. How honest we are until we reach the age of reason."

🗲

She could never remember which plants needed watering on which nights. That yucca seemed to be keeling over; it was probably too late for a reviving squirt of plant food. Maria considered the matter as she started up the droning vacuum cleaner. Just when her back was beginning to twinge, in the fourth corner of the manager's office, the bag exploded.

Maggie was surprisingly nice about it. She said everyone did it once and few did it twice. After finishing all the rooms on her side of the corridor, she came back to help Maria mop the dust off the manager's keyboard, family photos, and cafetière. Working only inches apart, the women felt their shyness evaporate. Maggie described her grandniece's mysterious rash; Maria gave a brief summary of the difficulties of higher maths. And yes, wasn't the backache an awful curse.

At the end of the evening, wheeling the overladen trolley into the fifth-floor elevator, Maria found herself on the point of blurting out something about the flat. A thoroughly stupid idea. What form would the revelation take: "I think I may be living with a couple of lesbians, Mags, what would you advise?" It wouldn't be fair to embarrass a fifty-five-year-old like that. Besides, she thought, as she watched the light drip down the panel from five to one, she had to make up her own damn mind. How was she ever going to grow up if every time something scared her, she ran, lips quivering, to the nearest mother figure?

"Night, so."

"Night night."

On O'Connell Street Maria paused to change out of her hated pink overall. She sat on a ledge by the left knee of Anna Livia, a reclining giantess in bronze. She put on one thick jumper, then another, but she still shivered in the night air; the wool weighed her down. There were two stains on the front of her overall, but it would do until the laundry on Saturday. She folded it and squeezed it into her denim bag, over the bag of red grapes she hadn't been able to resist on Moore Street that afternoon. She dug in and plucked four of them off the stem; they should give her enough energy to make it to the bus stop.

Behind her, eager fountains were hiding the green nakedness of the statue. A monster, really, all out of proportion, her bony thighs a good seven feet long. But the calm face always comforted Maria as she dragged her sore feet by after work. It was good to see a woman, even a mythical one, sprawling so disdainfully in a giant bath, oblivious to trucks and taxis.

Just get to the bus stop, Maria told herself as she strapped her bag and straightened up. A bus would be sure to come in ten or fifteen minutes, then a ten-minute ride, and no more than four minutes walking, including the stairs. She promised herself a scalding bath within the half hour, lavender oil slippy between her knees, steam lifting all her aches away. These nights she longed for the flat as if it were home. She kept forgetting there was anything to worry about.

⑤

With a forkful of apple crumble halfway to her mouth, Ruth was staring at her watch. "It's stuck at half five."

"Ten to seven now," said Maria.

"Why didn't somebody tell me?" she wailed.

Her mouth bulging with crumble, Jael pointed at her bare wrist.

"I was meant to be working out a strategy with the team, and now we'll all be contradicting each other."

Jael cackled, sliding the wine bottle toward Maria. "Who's going to notice the difference? After a sherry reception all arguments about European unity sound the same."

Ruth was rummaging in the pockets of her suede jacket. "Speech, lozenges, tissues, lip balm."

"Ignore her, you'll be grand," said Maria. "Your black cap's on the telly. Listen, are you sure you don't want us to come?"

Jael rapped her fork on the table. "Oy, speak for yourself. No offence, but I'd be bored rigid."

Ruth gave Maria a twist of the mouth. "I'm better on my own. See yez later." The door slammed behind her, and a faint call came up the stairwell.

"What did she say?"

"Keep me some apple crumble, I think," said Jael, and topped up Maria's glass. "Or it could have been, Teach me how to rhumba, but that's less likely."

Maria licked the last trace of sweetness off her fork. "How come you don't have a watch, anyway? Surely the stud farm could finance one."

"Just don't like them, they're like handcuffs. Besides, if I want to know the time, there's usually somebody to ask. No better way to chat up a stranger on a train."

"You're so bloody suggestive about all those years of travelling," commented Maria from the window. She scanned the pavement but couldn't see Ruth yet. "I bet you were a dishwasher in a series of little German teashops."

Jael swirled the dregs in her balloon glass. "Wouldn't you like to know?"

"Couldn't care less, to be honest," said Maria. She stared over the rooftops. "But if I'd spent ten years on the move, I'd never shut up about it. All those trilingual puns and stories you must have."

Jael was pressing the last crumbs of pastry onto the back of her fork. "I do use them at parties, or sometimes I make them up, because the best stories are lies. Like that time I was climbing in the Tyrol and slipped down a glacier—"

Maria turned, belligerent. "I believed that one."

A whoop of laughter. "It must have been a good one, so. But mostly I find the present more interesting."

"Seriously?"

"Seriously." Then, casting her a concerned glance, Jael asked, "Why, is your present life so dull?"

"No, no." She fumbled for the words. "It's different for me, because things are so, well, different nowadays. I mean Dublin and all. Whereas you've got a past worth talking about."

Jael tipped the wine bottle up to get the last mouthful. "Live long enough, pariah, and you too will be a Woman with a Past."

"Maybe." Maria turned her gaze back to the window. There was Ruth at last, a dark figure bobbing in and out of the crowd of shoppers. Maria waved her fingers.

"Anyway, why isn't your own past worth talking about?"

She turned. "Ah, because. It's only home, and it's still there, I haven't got right away from it yet."

"I don't think we ever get right away," said Jael softly. "Tell me something about it."

"Like what?"

"Something small."

Maria turned into the room, frowning in concentration. "Can't think. Well, the TV screen always has a sort of figure-of-eight smear on it from Mam, from my mother, she wipes it with a wet rag every Saturday morning. And we once had a budgie, but it flew out the window in a storm and didn't come back. There's a little statue of Our Lady with the hands chipped off, and a field out the back full of cowshit."

"Look, don't satirise it for my benefit," Jael broke in. "I'm not a journalist."

"What do you mean?"

"Just, if you liked it, don't try and be sophisticated by slagging it."

"I am not trying to sound sophisticated," said Maria in fury.

Jael leaned her forehead on her fist. "That came out wrong. All I mean is, I come from the country too, I remember the smallness of it all."

"Thought you were a filthy rich Prod from a stud farm." Maria's voice came out even more hostile than she intended.

"Horseshit, cowshit, what's the difference? You can't wipe it off your feet all at once." Jael held her stare. "Do you ever get homesick?"

"What is this, a joke?" said Maria warily. "That's not a Jael-type question."

"Whatever you say." Jael began piling up dirty plates. Crashes interleaved with silence. The stack was a hand's breadth high when she burst out, "Only whenever I try to get to know the real Maria, you act like you're about to be raped."

Maria put down the tea towel and rested her hand above Jael's elbow for a moment. "Hey. Hey. Take it easy."

With a self-deprecating grimace, Jael walked out of the room. Maria sank onto the sofa and wiped her hands with the tea towel; a headache was beginning to lace its web behind her eyes. With her right hand she squeezed at her shoulders, trying to loosen the taut muscles; tugging open the top button of her shirt, she slid her fingers round to the nape of her neck.

"Need a rub?" Jael swished through the beads behind a newspaper.

Maria stood up, folding the tea towel. "I'm fine."

Jael snapped the paper open, leaning against the back of the sofa. "You should get Ruth to give you a proper massage someday; she's a lifesaver when my back starts acting up. Her kind is called 'healing bodywaves'; she learned it at a week-long workshop on goddess spirituality."

They exchanged queasy grins. "Whatever you're into," murmured Maria, checking that she had shut the fridge door properly.

"Here we are," exclaimed Jael, peering at the small print on the back page. "'Taut and riveting, reminiscent of . . .' blah blah . . . 'dreamy fetishism . . .'"

"Sorry?"

"Oh, didn't I ask you already?" asked Jael. "It's the last night of that French thriller at the Lighthouse, and I thought, well, that you mightn't have anything better to do."

Maria's shoulders stiffened. "I'm sort of tired."

"Yeah, but not actually doing anything, are you? Not hitting the wine bars with your bimbo friend, for instance."

"If you mean Yvonne, she's not a bimbo." She settled herself in the rocking chair and put her feet up on the hearth.

"Don't tell me," hissed Jael. "She's actually an undercover Kremlin spy, *masquerading* as a bimbo."

Maria started unlacing her shoe. "If you'd ever met her, you'd know she's a really decent person."

"Nice, even?"

"No, decent. There's a good nature behind that fluffy facade. She laughs at all my jokes. Besides, I need some friends who aren't on pension." She avoided a swipe from the rolled-up newspaper.

"Anyway, what about the movie?" continued Jael.

Yawning, Maria wriggled deeper in the chair. "I really should be doing that essay on frescoes. And what about the washing up?"

"Only social rejects stay in on Friday nights."

"Why didn't you go with Ruth last week?"

Jael shook her head impatiently. "She dispproves of French

films; apparently they're all voyeuristic. Complains loudly every time there's a close-up of a pair of legs, even if they're Charlotte Rampling's."

"I really don't—"

On her knees, Jael dug her fingers into the straggly rug. "Please. I'm begging for company. Am I going to have to kiss your foot?"

Maria's socked toes wormed away. "All right. Stop *getting* at me."

"Yippee."

"I'm a bit broke though," she complained as she put her shoe back on.

"No problem, I'll pay," Jael said, her voice muffled by the coat cupboard.

"You will not."

She found herself being tugged out the door. "Shift a leg. We've only ten minutes to get there, and I hate missing the trailers."

"OK, but I'm paying for myself," shouted Maria, clattering down the stairs. "And kindly stop treating me like an aunt."

She could tell it was an arty cinema, because the seats were black instead of red plush, and among the couple of dozen watchers there wasn't a popcorn carton in sight. After a long credits sequence, with reverent close-ups of tomatoes being sliced, the film started to flow, and Maria slid down in her seat and relaxed. But there was one scene about halfway through that left her rigid. As the heroine and hero squabbled in the foreground of a smoky café, the camera shifted to focus on the table behind them: two slim men with moustaches locked in a kiss. A sound of revulsion began to rise from the cinema audience. Maria sat stiff and blushing— whether for the men or for the audience, she wasn't sure. Jael, tossing Smarties into her mouth by the handful, didn't seem to notice.

When they emerged, blinking, the sky was navy blue. A furious dispute was going on by the ticket office; Maria recognised that woman from the women's group—Pat, wasn't that the name?—insisting that her wheelchair was not going to block the aisle. Maria gave a little wave, but Pat didn't seem to recognise her. Jael had hurried on; Maria had to dash along the side street to catch up.

"Will we walk the long way home?" Without waiting for an answer, Jael turned down a cobbled alley.

Maria was lost already. She peered around her. "Is it safe?"

"You'll be all right if you stick with me, kid. I keep a hat-pin in my lapel."

The beggars had packed up for the night, leaving only a few cardboard boxes and, on the slab where the alley ended, a smeary chalking of the Last Supper. Jael slowed to a stroll. "I love films like that, with fishnet tights and snarling violins and not a social issue in sight." She watched Maria as they paused on a curb. "You didn't enjoy it much, did you?"

"Oh, it was beautifully filmed," said Maria quickly. "Only I'm not sure I'll be able to get to sleep tonight. That bit where the cat leaped out of the kettle . . . "

Jael ducked in front of a truck; Maria held her breath till the coppery head emerged on the other sidewalk. By the time she caught up, Jael was peering at a menu framed in a heavily curtained window. "Are we hungry or are we *hungry*?"

"Peckish," said Maria. "But what—"

"You are about to traverse," intoned Jael in the voice of a car ad, "a frontier in culinary excitement. Those innocent taste buds are about to experience the fiercest chicken vindaloo—to be strictly accurate, the only chicken vindaloo—in Dublin's fair city."

Maria's protests lowered to a whisper as they entered the dim hush of the Indian restaurant. "Chinese is cheaper, and anyway, shouldn't we be getting back to find out how Ruth's debate went?"

"Chinese is for wimps," Jael hissed back. Then, resignedly, "All right, we'll get a takeaway here and take it home. But don't tell me you prefer Chinese when you're a vindaloo virgin."

Maria crossed her arms and leaned on the counter.

"Trust me, sulky," murmured Jael in her ear.

She stuck out her tongue, but had only just time to whip it back into her cheek when the waiter trotted up.

They were rounding the corner of Beldam Square by half ten. "Let's take a shortcut through the square," Jael proposed, heading for a gate half hidden in the hedge.

"It'll be locked."

"Maria," said Jael with a sigh as she wedged her foot into the wrought iron and clambered over, "you musn't let these little circumstances get in your way. Swing the dinner bag over."

Poised on the top bar, Maria clung to Jael's bobbing head for support. "Stop laughing," she ordered; "if you let me fall on one of these spikes, you'll put an end to my marital prospects."

"Ah, sure what harm," murmured Jael, heading through the trees.

Maria picked her way over the grass after her; it was too dark to see anything but leafy mounds and tree trunks. "Wait for me," she called. "I'll bet this place is crawling with rats." Stumbling onto the gravel walk, she found Jael balancing on the arm of a park bench, craning over the treetops.

"You can see the flat from here."

"Are you sure?" Maria climbed up behind her. "How can you tell it's ours?"

Jael shaded her eyes from the streetlight. "That has to be

Ruth, walking past the kitchen window. She keeps reminding me to buy a blind for it, but it always slips my mind."

"Look, she's taking off her cap," said Maria. The small figure four floors up was black against the warm light. Then, with a shiver, she jumped down. "Let's not. I'd hate it if I didn't know I was being looked at."

Jael grinned down at her. "You like to know you're being looked at all the time?"

"Don't correct my grammar, beast," answered Maria, catching her leather cuff and hauling her onto the gravel. "I meant, if I was being spied on from a squalid park bench, I'd rather know about it."

"It can't do Ruth any harm," said Jael; "she's guarded by the goddess's personal troupe of angels." She picked up the leaking paper bag and led the way toward the gate.

🔄

It was Hallowe'en morning, and Maria was dividing her attention between her scrambled egg and a page of diagrams.

"We Scorps," announced Jael without warning, glancing up from *Motorcycle Monthly*, "are not the green-eyed monsters society has labelled us, but rather sweet, unassuming creatures."

Maria gave her a blank look, then turned back to the geometry.

Swallowing her toast, Ruth explained. "It's the lady's birthday and she wants a tin of chocolate Brazil nuts."

"How do you make sense of all that verbal diarrhoea?" asked Maria.

"Practice. It takes at least a year to get to know all her little quirks."

Jael made a troll face over her granola. "Would the pair of you kindly stop bitching and nip down to see are there any cards for me. I heard the postman ages ago."

"I'm busy," said Maria, eyes following a parallelogram.

"Nip?" repeated Ruth. "Nip down four flights?" But she went.

Maria abandoned her maths book. She began the washing up rather halfheartedly and was soon distracted by a page of wet newspaper under the kettle.

"Mmm?" inquired Jael through an unpeeled kiwi fruit.

"Listen to this, Scorpion," said Maria. "If it's your birthday this week: 'You have a headstrong personality and would make a good actress, sewage worker, detective or undertaker.'"

"You're lying through your teeth, Murphy. Bring that paper over here."

"Look, down in the corner."

Jael snatched at the page. "God, they actually say sewage worker. I wouldn't mind the others—even undertaker—they've got a certain grandeur. But a sewage worker!" She sighed, reaching for a banana. "Let's see whether Aquarians get any kicks this week."

Maria wiped the page with a towel. "It's a bit blurred, but I think it says I'm to watch out for marital conflict and risky investments."

Ruth reappeared, coughing. "Three brown bills for me, one parcel and one postcard for the birthday girl, and . . . ha ha, look at this, a card from Maria's tutor wondering why she's missed three statistics classes in a row."

"There's twenty-three of us squashed into her tiny room, reciting figures," complained Maria. "I don't see the point."

Ruth's answer was cut off when Jael handed over her postcard. She looked down at the blue-and-white village scene, glowing under the sun. "What's this?"

"Read it," said Jael brightly. "She's on Mykonos."

Ruth handed it back. "No thanks, it's yours." She turned away to finish the washing up.

Jael brushed past Maria at the door of the bathroom and

muttered sharply, "What do you bet she read the whole post-card coming up the stairs?"

The safest answer was a shrug.

⑤

At dinner that night they drank toasts to the pope and the plight of the aged—Jael having difficulty in blowing out her thirty candles. To the strains of flamenco music on Ruth's dragging tape recorder, they ducked for apples in a wok full of water, which Maria managed to overturn on the carpet. Tonight she would not watch them, would not worry and analyse and hold back. Tonight was for having a good time, all girls together. Jael and Ruth overdosed on chocolate nuts and whisky while Maria nursed a glass of wine. At two in the morning she left them tangoing on the sofa, roses (impro-vised from red paper napkins) stuck between their teeth. Her bed wrapped her in a cool embrace, and she slept almost at once.

It began as her usual bird dream, with her rising above the bed, melting through the window, gliding over the roof and away. But this time she found herself hurtling through a canyon, her wings flaring out behind her. Gradually she realised that the cliffs at the end—or were they skyscrap-ers?—were too close together. She hunched her feathered shoulders and tried to slow down, but as the gap came nearer and nearer, the wind forced her eyes shut. She knew that the gap had narrowed to nothing.

There was no crash, just a quietness; like in a cartoon when the cat skids out over a precipice and sits for a few long sec-onds, rigid and bemused, on thin air. Gradually a set of pale lines formed themselves into striped curtains, barred with street light. Maria knew where she was, but she was still waiting for the fall. She wanted to crane back over her shoul-der to see where solid land ran out; her stomach was clenched against the drop.

A glass of ice water, that would bring her back to reality. Pulling her dressing gown on over her thin pyjamas, Maria crept down the corridor. Before her hand touched the beads, a faint sound stopped her. Shadows were twisting on the rug in front of the dull embers.

She held her breath until her pulse thumped in her throat. As her eyes got used to the dark, she could see firelight edging over a tangle of limbs. It wavered on Jael's long brown back arched over Ruth, their arms like the dark interlacing bars of a hedge. Ruth lay askew, her lean body stirring under the weight of her lover. Maria had to strain to hear the rough breathing, the indistinguishable words. She had no idea how long she had been standing there, all her senses riveted to the scene, when a frantic whisper began to spiral from the bodies. She couldn't tell which of them was making the sound. It was like nothing she had ever heard. As it clawed its way upward she wrenched herself away and ran back to her room.

Furled up in the foetal position, the quilt over her head, Maria waited for calm. She thought perhaps she was going to throw up, but it was too far to the bathroom, so she swallowed it down. I'm a voyeur, she told herself, mouthing the words into the pillow to make them real. I'm worse than them. To do it is one thing, that's their business, but to watch it, to spy on friends at their most exposed . . . how can I look them in the eye tomorrow morning?

Outside, the rain had begun, rumbling and spitting at her window. She found her cheeks latticed with tears for the first time since she came to Dublin. So that's what it's like, she thought, bewildered.

4

CUTTING

Looking at a flattened curl on the back of Ruth's head, Maria wondered whether she had been hallucinating. This frail, cuddly woman could have nothing to do with the shapes by the fire last night. Leaning against the sink, Ruth washed two aspirins down with orange juice. She was colourless as paper; tiny wrinkles showed round her eyes.

Jael lay diagonally across her futon with a sockful of ice on her forehead, rejecting Maria's offers of hangover remedies and breakfast. "I'm thirty fucking years old," she commented, eyes shut, "so what good will a poached egg do me?"

When Maria came back into the kitchen, Ruth was picking up sticky wine glasses and tattered napkins. They washed up wordlessly, their hands dipping in tandem. Half an hour later they were curled into the sofa, swapping family photos.

"Is that your little brother in the suit?"

"It was far too big for him, but Mum insisted," answered Ruth. "He's doing law; she'd love him to become a diplomat."

Maria contemplated three photos of the same triangle: a

woman sitting in an armchair with a boy at one shoulder and a young, slightly sullen Ruth at the other. "Is that what she wanted you to be?"

"Oh, no, the Civil Service was much more suitable for a girl, no need to live in foreign parts. It broke her heart when I ditched it. Maybe if I go on and get a master's, it'll make it up to her."

The next sheaf of photos showed Ruth and her mother walking on hard shingle. "What would you research?"

"Medieval nuns. My professor tells me it's a soft subject, but I think they led such fascinating lives." Ruth looked up and smoothed the lines out of her forehead. "What about you, Maria, what are your plans?"

"Plans, woman?" She shrank back into the folds of the tartan blanket. "I'm not old enough to vote yet."

"I keep forgetting."

Maria tapped the photos into a neat pile. "You know how, when you're small, adults can never think of anything to ask you but what are you going to be when you grow up? Well, I used to say a bus driver just to shock them. And because I liked buses."

Ruth grinned reminiscently. "I always said air hostess, just like every other little girl in my class. Jael said terrorist once and got slapped for it. At least that's her story."

"Should we try the malingerer again?"

"Why not."

Finding the bedroom door open, Maria picked her way through strewn jumpers and coffee bowls to the window and pushed it a few inches open.

Eyes shut, Jael ordered, "Shut that damn window."

"We were going to go for a walk as far as the river," said Maria, nudging it farther open.

The reply was prompt: "You can go for a fuck in the park for all I care, ducky."

"Oh, come on," Ruth called from the corridor, "let her fester."

The sunlight was turning to violet in the oil-streaked puddles. How familiar the streets were to Maria now, as if she had spent years in Dublin rather than weeks. The grimy corners, bus stops askew, green street-name plaques so high on the red brick walls that tourists had to crane up as if looking for Superman. The city was always quiet after a holiday, especially the debauch of Hallowe'en. Orange streamers were coiled in gutters, and some joker had left her witch's hat on the skull of a bronze patriot.

Once they had left the square behind, Ruth slowed down, polishing a plucked leaf between her fingers. "Nice day."

"Mmm." Maria was watching the chimney tops for birds.

"Sorry Jael was so foul."

"Not your problem."

Ruth spiked the glossy leaf on a railing and folded her arms. "Actually I'm glad we're on our own because there's—" She stopped and let out a little snort of amusement.

Maria looked at her warily.

"Sorry, it's just—of all the clichéd phrases—but I can't think of any other." Singsong, almost parodic: "There's something I've been meaning to tell you."

Not now, thought Maria. Not now that I know the curve of your hip, the sounds you make. I've no right to be told anything anymore.

"You may have guessed this already, I mean we really should have got around to saying something before, but I mean, you do know we're lovers, don't you? Me and Jael."

It was a relief to have it spoken. But how unnerving to watch those words being exhumed into the chilly daylight.

"Well, yes. More or less." Three long seconds. "Fine by me," she added hurriedly.

"Great." Ruth's voice leapt up an octave.

They strolled for a minute or two, both studying the trees through the black rods of the fence. Say something nice, Maria ordered herself, but the silence nibbled away her words.

"Wasn't sure how you'd take it," Ruth commented at last. "Most people have been fine, but you never know. A couple of good friends from school—they didn't exactly spit in my face, but I saw their eyes glaze, and I could never be comfortable with them afterward."

Maria ran a twig along the railings. "I suppose most students would be fairly liberal, though."

"Do you think so?" Ruth's eyebrows were sardonic.

"Well, I don't know. After they get over the initial shock, maybe. If it is a shock." Shut up, stop flailing.

The rotting leaves were sticking to Ruth's low heels; she paused to scrape them off on a kerb. "I find it's the opposite, actually," she commented. "Students have this tolerant surface—they cheer Martina's serves and hum along to k.d. lang—but inside they're panicking and twisting like hamsters in a cage."

"You can't know that," said Maria desperately, dropping her twig. "And even if some do seem hostile, it's just ignorance. Like, you're the first one I've met. As far as I know. I mean the first two."

A quick smile flashed like a dragonfly. "Yes, but some of the warmest reactions I've got have been from people who didn't know the first thing about it but had tolerant instincts. Like that old woman I was telling you about, the one I pickled gherkins with in Germany."

Maria counted the cracks on the pavement. "Why do you tell people if they're going to be horrible?" she asked at last. "If I'm scared of something, I just don't do it."

"I doubt that," said Ruth gently. "You must know what it's like when you're so scared of something your guts are churning, but you do it anyway, and the adrenaline rushes through you, like a flag going up."

"Suppose. Not very often, though."

"Well, I don't come out to people every day of the week; it would be exhausting. I lie low for a while, then go on a crusade, hit them with it, make all the jaws drop." Her hand was light on Maria's elbow, ushering her across the road as the lights changed. "Most of the time I do it just to feel free. I can't stand those old euphemisms about good friends and flatmates."

"That's the way you talked to me." Maria moved away slightly, unable to keep the hurt out of her voice.

Ruth paused to peer into a cobbled alley and murmured, "The river's down thisaway." Then, "I'm a terrible procrastinator, Maria. I was—we were both—afraid you might go."

"Why would I go?" asked Maria. Her lips were taut with the effort of not saying *I nearly did*.

"Jael told me that instead of barging in there as usual, I should give you a chance to find out on your own. And once a couple of weeks had gone by, we were too embarrassed to make an official announcement." Her tone lightening, she went on. "She suggested we stick a little sign on the fridge, saying 'To whom it may concern: Jael and Ruth indulged in unnatural relations last night.'"

Maria laughed, a little shortly, and commented that unnatural relations sounded like hard-hearted aunts.

Brown office blocks stared at grey ones across the streets that still surprised Maria by their gracious proportions. Out of basements stuck the unlit neon titles of nightclubs and neat plaques offering acupuncture or laser printing. Farther into the old city, buildings sagged, one seeming to lean on a single thirty-foot wooden support. Dandelions tufted from the rubble.

By the time they reached the quays, the conversation had

wandered to the ethics of meat. "I remember the first time I ever wanted to be a vegetarian," Ruth said as they crossed the Ha'penny Bridge. "My mother called me in before mass to show me how to joint a chicken. 'Listen for the crunch,' she kept saying."

Maria nodded vehemently, running her finger along the railings. "What got to me were the names—the breast meat was 'his chests,' and that sort of triangle at the bottom, Mam called it 'the pope's nose.'"

"My mother would never have been so blasphemous. She probably referred to it as 'the bird's posterior.'"

"Does she know about you?" Then Maria wished she hadn't asked.

"Not yet." Ruth put her head through the pale blue slats of the footbridge and stared down. "Water's going at a fair lick, isn't it?" She grinned up at Maria, her face striped by the bars. "The worst thing about the chicken was its little bag of organs, do you remember? For years I was convinced that all my innards were carried in a slimy pouch too, and if I sneezed, they might shoot out."

"I worry about you, woman. Come on, let's go back the long way. I want to show you that peculiar duck I found in the green. And maybe if we give Jael a full hour, she'll have repented and heated up a frozen pizza."

"Bet it'll be a ham one," said Ruth, leading the way back across the bridge. "I'd have become a vegetarian long ago if it wasn't for her, you know. Maybe even a vegan."

⑤

Maria had taken to avoiding mirrors. Every time she saw herself she looked younger, as if her handful of years was flaking away. The nose a little flatter, the cheeks paler, the hair more helpless each time she caught her reflection in a polished shopfront. Since she came to Dublin her clothes had been hanging wrong on her shoulders. As for the overall she wore two evenings a week, it made her look like a fifties-era unwed mother, scrubbing floors in a convent. She would have asked Yvonne's advice, if Maria had not been avoiding her since their last argument about the flatmates. Galway was hardly an expert on clothes, since he wore nothing but skinny jeans. And Damien—glimpsed in lecture theatres, hallucinated on street corners—never noticed her, whatever she wore or however she tied back her drooping hair. So the list of friends ended after two, she noted. Friends her own age, that was, not including Ruth and Jael. It was all too easy to spend a merry evening in the flat and forget that she was playing gooseberry to a couple of lovers.

One evening Maria came in for dinner metamorphosed.

Ruth's forehead creased. "But it was nice the old way."

Jael took one look at Maria's skull-hugging hair and whooped. "What does it think it is, a punk sheep?"

She felt her throat scald. "I just felt like a haircut. I was bored with sweet seventeen."

Jael produced her vampire smile. "The problem is, my dear, you're now so cute you put me off my dinner." She gave the furry scalp a tentative stroke, as if it were a squirrel, and dropped her hand as Ruth walked over to the table with a wok full of steaming vegetables.

"I think it'll grow on me," said Ruth. "It's just the shock of seeing your eyebrows, and—oh, what tiny ears. Lookit, Jael, did you ever see such defenceless earlobes? They're going to get so cold!"

Maria squirmed out of their grasp and sat down to eat, claiming the chair with the armrests.

"Oh, by the way," commented Jael, passing the soy sauce, "I hear you guessed our murky secret, and you're not intending to call in the vice squad."

She blinked and picked up her fork. "Not unless you make me do the washing up."

Ruth, sliding onto her seat, had dark bags under her eyes. "We had assumed our last flatmate knew, you see—"

"A portly bitch in first law called Annabel," Jael interrupted.

"But when she found out by accident, she made a ridiculous scene, threatened to tell the landlord, and stomped off bag and baggage without paying that month's rent."

"Not that heterosexuality ever did much for poor Annabel," Jael murmured, stealing a mushroom from Ruth's plate.

After dinner Maria left them bickering pleasantly over coffee and went for a walk in the cool deserted streets. She had brought her sketch pad, but it was too smoggy to make out more than the wooly forms of cars and brick walls. The clammy air stroked her cheeks. A black cat slunk by across the path. She crouched down and whispered to it; it cast her a curious glance before slipping into a tiny basement garden. She would like a cat someday, curled up in a sagbag in a flat of their own. Perhaps her mother was right, and she would never get around to getting married; she could just paint her flat sky-blue, lock the door, and walk round on her deep-pile carpet with nothing on.

As she passed the petrol station her eye was caught by some golden freesia, and she bought a pound's worth. Ruth and Jael brightened up the flat with their Women's Music Festival posters and pot plants and television; the least she could do was bring home a few flowers once in a while. They were lovely to her, really; Maria could hardly remember why she had considered leaving. They didn't quarrel any more than ordinary couples. Most of the time she could just think of them as friends.

But as she headed up the second-last flight of stairs, she was overcome by a wave of exhaustion. Her back was twingeing after having had to scrub that filthy bathroom floor last night, and her shorn head was cold. From the flat above she heard the theme music from "Glenroe" and then a brief scream. For a long moment there was no air to breathe in the dark stairwell. She sank onto a step and listened. On the count of six, she was relieved by a muffled roar: "Jael, get off me this instant, I mean it."

Maria immersed her nose in the rich stain of the flowers. Taking a sweet breath, she started up the stairs.

⬚

She stood at a casual angle to the door, pretending to be absorbed in *The Dublin Event Guide* but glancing into The Pit every now and then. She had never been near such a place before; her mother always implied your bag would be snatched as you walked in the door. It was almost empty; a couple of punks leaned on the Space Invader games in the far corner, and the bottom table was occupied by three rather intimidating women in suede waistcoats. Two tables up, playing against himself, was Damien.

She hadn't caught more than a glimpse of his plait for weeks. Today, after a lecture on the salient points of Romanesque versus Gothic cathedrals, she found herself pursuing him from the lecture theatre, past the men's toilet (she had to loiter outside, reading a poster headed "What Has Jesus Got to Say to You???," and then down to the university's subterranean pool hall. Rollie butts sprinkled the floor of The Pit like leaves at the launch of autumn. On the longer wall, titans and demons clashed in a seventies-style mural, all purple and silver. Some graffitist had penned in a lacy garter on one giant's muscled calf.

Beneath it Damien leaned purposefully over his cue and potted a ball. Maria reminded herself, as she watched his plait loll over one shoulder, that he was utterly unaware of her existence. Odd; here she stood half hidden behind a yellow metal door, watching him chalk his cue, and he didn't even know her name. She would never have the nerve to accost him in the corridors, and anyway, what had she to say that was any less banal than the usual fresher's chitchat? Turning aside to watch the game more discreetly over the rim of her magazine, she caught sight of her blurred reflection in a panel of steel. A peaky little face still, even with the trendy haircut. A face to launch a paper boat.

Which was about all this fixation on a stranger amounted to—something to watch, to push, to fill in the spare minutes. Maria waited till Damien had potted two more balls, then walked away.

She blew her nose as she waited for the lift. Were they ever going to turn on the central heating in this damn state-subsidised university? Dawdling past the maths department notice board to see if the results of that painful midterm test were up yet, she came across Galway, leaning out precariously over the bannisters. So much more likeable he was, so manageable a friendship—even if that silly bimbo in the stats tutorial did keep referring to Maria's "American boyfriend."

"Yo, stranger, what are you up to?"

Galway straightened up. "Spying on a couple of love-birds," he explained in a low voice. He pointed down through the wooden slats to the bench just beside the foot of the stairs. "It's a cyclical ritual. They exchange tongues for maybe twenty seconds, then spend three minutes scanning the crowd to see who's noticed them."

"Pathetic." Maria peered over the bannisters.

"But fascinating. I never understood the angst of Yeats's love poems before. Courtship is so tentative and giggly over here; don't you guys ever just go fornicate with each other?"

"Sex in Ireland is a scary business," she told him. "We can get pregnant if sperm so much as splashes on our knees. It swims its way up."

"You trying to fool a gullible Yank?"

Her voice wavered between anger and amusement. "Look, in my school, we were given one hour's class per year, called Preparation for Life. At fifteen it was on thrush, the next year the nurse talked about praying with your husband, and last year the nuns finally allowed her to mention the rhythm method of contraception. By which time most of my class-mates were on the Pill anyway, having told the doctor they needed it as a period regulator."

"I want to go home to Brooklyn," he said. "Hot dogs, mug-gers, sanity."

"Come for a bracing walk to the cafeteria."

"So, life is good?" he asked as they tramped down the stairs. "I notice you've lost some hair."

"Apart from cold ears, life is all right. Well," she added, spurring herself on, "apart from the occasional blip. It turns out that my flatmates, they're both gay."

He turned, his eyes narrow. "So why does that cause blips?"

"It's complicated," Maria assured him, in what she hoped was a tolerant tone. "Basically they couldn't agree about whether or not to tell me."

Galway nodded thoughtfully. "It's great they did decide to come out to you. They must trust you."

"I hadn't thought of it that way." She hurried to keep up with him as they crossed the concourse.

"Two of the chambermaids I worked with in Boston were dykes; they were such a laugh," he said nostalgically.

"Ah, yeah, the flat's great crack." It's true, Maria thought, so why does saying it make it sound like a lie?

🔄

The next Sunday she woke late again. She was sleeping a ridiculous amount these days, as if hibernating for the win-ter. She fumbled with the loose handle of the top drawer, reaching in for her watch. Ten past eleven, too late to have to decide whether to go to mass. Besides, she could hear the rain against the glass. Maria scratched the fuzz at the nape of her neck.

She padded down to the other room; when she knocked she heard nothing but the sound of a hair dryer. Putting her head cautiously round the door, she saw Jael cross-legged on the futon; she had to shout to make herself heard. Jael jumped in shock, then snapped off the hair dryer and swept the red curtain of curls off her face. Static strands clung to her cheeks, and she shoved them away.

"Sneaking up on me, were you?"

"I was just wondering if you were finished with the paper. Where's your lady friend?"

"Ruth's gone to Mumsie's for lunch, so I'll have to do. Here you go, though there's nothing worth reading except a nice bitchy review of the Lorca play," Jael said, handing over the paper. She began yanking a brush through her hair.

Absorbed in the headlines, Maria knelt on the edge of the futon. Something was nagging at her; she glanced up. "Why is it Ruth never mentions her dad? And he wasn't in any of the photos either."

"Didn't you know?" Jael arched her eyebrows. "She's a secretive little witch. The Johnsons got a legal separation when Ruth was six; the father hasn't been seen since."

Maria's face twisted in sympathy. "That must have upset her."

"Well, she still has vivid memories of the fights and the financial hassle, so I'd imagine she loathes the absentee."

Maria sat, lost in thought, on the edge of the rumpled duvet. She was trying to remember whether she had ever heard her father raise his voice to a shout. "Do you think that's maybe partly why?" she asked, then added hurriedly, "No, forget that."

"Why what?" Jael kept up her sardonic stare till Maria's

eyes fell. "Oh, I get it—why Ruth was so easily seduced into Sapphic lurve."

"No, I mean—"

"You mean the trauma of her parents' breakup turned her off men, so she waited, what, eighteen years, then ran into my arms for consolation."

Maria rested her chin on her knees. Out of the entangled pattern of the wall hanging, a tiny monkey's face smirked at her. "I'm sorry, it was a deeply stupid question."

"That hoary old theory's no stupider than all the others, tufty." Dropping her brush, Jael put out one palm and lightly stroked Maria's hair from the neck up, against the grain. "It tickles," she observed. Maria wriggled out of reach.

"Listen, most of the queers I know love speculating about causes and influences. My own favourite is the Mummy-didn't-love-me."

"What's Ruth's mother like?"

Wrenching the brush through her fringe, Jael rolled her eyes. "Total martyr; I bet she wouldn't get a divorce even if it was legal in Ireland. Her handbag is always leaking pearl rosaries, and she says things like 'no cross, no crown.' Ruth has this kind of masochistic devotion to her."

"What's masochistic about loving your mother?" It came out too sharp; Maria considered the floorboards.

"Hey, it's not an insult. I've a weakness for handcuffs myself."

Maria ignored that. She tugged on the duvet. "Go on about Ruth."

"Well, she's Mumsie's hope and joy. It took me months to persuade her to move out and share this flat."

"She was telling me her mother has no idea about you two."

"Did she say that?" Jael's brush paused at the end of a stroke. "The double-thinking old bitch must know something's up by now. She's always dropping caustic comments about Ruth's short hair and unsuitable friends. But she won't admit it to herself, of course; she can just about cope with a spinster daughter so long as no one mentions the L word."

Maria had found a pillow to wrap herself around. She stared into the shadows of the wall hanging, distinguishing leaves from faces and wings. Jael yawned, stretching her arms above her head, and with a jolt Maria was aware of her again. "What about your family, don't you ever visit them?" Awkwardly, she added, "If you don't mind being interrogated like this."

"Not at all, I love telling stories, especially my own. My folks, yeah, I turn up at the stud farm on occasion." Jael gave her hair a last brisk slap and tossed the brush onto the windowsill with a clatter. "My mother found me in bed with a girl when I was seventeen. She let me stay till I got my leaving cert, then I headed off to Spain."

Maria realised she was gaping and shut her mouth. "What happened to the girl?" she asked lamely.

"It wasn't a long-term thing," Jael reassured her.

"I suppose it must be different if you're both women."

Jael let out a low snigger as she leaned back against the pillows. "Well, yes, in several significant ways—there's anatomy, pace, frequency—"

Maria could feel her face burn, but she knew her blushes never showed. "All I meant was, if it's another girl, I suppose you could go, like, all the way—I mean as far as you like—without it having to be a long-term thing, whereas if it was a guy, you might have to worry . . . Look, I really don't know what I'm talking about, forget it."

Jael took pity on her confusion. "You mean, if it's a guy, you have to hope it's a long-term thing in case the rubber bursts."

Maria winced and nodded.

"Or, as Ruth would put it," Jael went on satirically, "sexual behaviour between two adults of the female gender, being nonreproductive, need not be circumscribed by Western bourgeois morality's condemnation of female 'promiscuity.'"

"She would not put it like that," Maria protested. "You make her sound like a lefty politician."

"She's that way inclined. But to get back to our original example, me and Sonya up to mischief at seventeen. I have to admit that I'd have done the same thing if it had been a guy. Occasionally did, in fact. Only my mother wouldn't have let a guy spend the night in my room. The thing about being a dyke is, you get away with a lot!"

Maria said she supposed so, and if Jael wanted a cuppa, it would be in the pot.

She leaned her hips against the cool ceramic of the sink. While the tap water spluttered and gulped into the kettle, she tried to clear her whirring mind. She held one finger under the cold flow of water. Soon she could feel nothing as far as the knuckle. There used to be a stream halfway home from school, its water faintly brown from the turf. After the occasional bad day, Maria used to throw down her bike when she got there, crouch on the stones, and dip her hands in to the wrists; when she had held them to her face, she was herself again.

5

HEATING

November had decided to do nothing but rain. Slouched against a window in the arts block, glaring at the drizzle, Maria saw Yvonne trotting by under a huge golf umbrella. She knocked loudly on the glass and waved. Yvonne stopped, stuck out one finger, and rolled her eyes. Evidently some reciprocal gesture was called for: a tragedy mask, a thumbs up. Maria peered through the glass till it steamed up, then gestured to Yvonne to meet her at the door. "What's wrong with your finger?"

"Nothing's wrong with it, nerd."

Maria studied it. "I've seen your Claddagh ring before."

She clicked her tongue, shaking the drain off her umbrella. "But today it's turned inward again. Which means that Pete and I are officially back together."

"That's wonderful," said Maria. "If you're happy about it."

Yvonne slumped down on the nearest bench. "You've never liked him."

"Don't start that again. I've nothing against the guy."

"You said he had big ears."

"So what if he has?" Maria straddled the bench, leaning

toward Yvonne. "Hang on, wasn't it you who said that about his ears?"

"Well, but you agreed." Yvonne rolled the dripping umbrella off her foot. "You've depressed me now."

"I didn't do—"

"Came out of that sculpture lecture on a high, and now everything's grey." She stared down at her wet suede court shoe.

"Ah, would you stop working yourself into a gloom." Maria inched closer, trying to get Yvonne's eyes to turn. "I only reacted oddly because I can't keep up with the pair of you. This is, what, the third time you've got back together?"

"Fourth."

Maria sat in silence, then asked, "What does it mean, being officially together?" Answering Yvonne's defensive look, she added, "No, I'm not getting at you. I'm ignorant and curious."

"What's your question?" Yvonne's bottom lip was shaking almost imperceptibly.

"All I was wondering was, what does it mean to be together if you're fighting and breaking up every other weekend?"

Yvonne nibbled the edge of a fingernail, considering the question. Then she brightened. "We're not together, the in-between times." She paused, fumbling for logic. "Officially together stops after we've had a slanging match and I go home on the bus and turn the Claddagh ring outward. So the together bits are fine."

Maria watched her twist a limp curl between her fingers. "What do you do in between?"

"Watch more television."

"Talk more to pariahs with antisocial haircuts," Maria suggested.

That won a smile. "I only said it was a bit short."

"I could tell you were restraining yourself; your eyes were out on sticks."

"Well, at least you got rid of that floppy fringe," said Yvonne philosophically. "I'm getting sick of the Goldie Hawn look myself. But Pete likes it, and this time me and him are going to last," she went on, with a resolute slap of the knees. "I've a feeling in my bones."

"You'll have a feeling in some other parts before the weekend's over. Ouch, gerroff." Maria beat her away. "People are watching, they'll be starting rumours about us. Listen, are you coming for lunch?" She got off the bench and stretched her arms above her head.

"Ah, I'm sorry, I promised to meet the heartthrob in the bar." Yvonne waved from the door, struggling to erect her umbrella.

Maria sat down on the bench again, cross-legged this time—for variety. She could not quite bring herself to stroll to the canteen on her own and carry her meagre tray past the crowds of indifferent watchers. She was not that hungry anyway, having placated her chocolate craving a hour ago. Where she should be was in the library, mulling over group theory. What she should be doing was anything except watching the rain, the least original form of melancholy. She had misspent too many pubertal afternoons hanging round the shop in the holidays, listening to rain puddling in the striped canopy Dad put up every May. He used to think up favours for her to do him, like sweeping the storeroom or counting the unsold oranges. At the first sight of the bleary sun, he'd send her out with the broom to poke up the canopy and spill the rain all over the path. That always left her feeling as competent as any boy. Not that there was any real need to empty the canopy straightaway; it could have waited till Mam unhooked it, last thing before tea at six. That occurred to Maria now for the first time, as she watched a knot of medics scurry toward the canteen, holding their lab coats up like sheltering kites.

That had to be Ruth, the face half hidden behind a pile of multicoloured folders. Maria ran after her and tapped one shoulder lightly. "Hey, fairy godmother, want to bring a poor girl to lunch?"

The preoccupied face lit up for a moment. "I'd love to, but duty calls, or rather, Gaysoc." She folded her arms and rested her chin on the folders.

"I saw the stand in Freshers' Week, with pink balloons all over it."

"They were condoms, actually." Ruth had a way of gently mentioning things that, coming from anybody else, would have made Maria feel so stupid. "But they all got burst by right-wing vandals."

"You weren't on the stall, were you?"

"I did a couple of hours, but I can't say I enjoyed it; people tend to glimpse the banner and walk this wide circle round it."

"I meant to sign that petition, but I never got around to it," Maria said guiltily. She nodded at a passing seminarian from her trigonometry tutorial, then turned back. "Sorry, am I keeping you?"

"No bother."

"I have to admit I assumed the Gaysoc was just for men."

"Apart from a couple of stalwart females." Ruth's tone was cheerful as she rested her burden on one hip. "College is crawling with dykes, of course, but when you take away the closeted hockey players, the nonpolitical semiclosets like Jael, and the radicals who won't socialise with men, that leaves just about three of us."

"Has Jael not come out, then? And her always presenting herself as the daring one," added Maria with satisfaction.

"She hops in and out as the fancy takes her," said Ruth

wryly. "Her official policy is that she doesn't give a fuck what anybody imagines she does in bed, and her self-respect is perfectly healthy without queers' coffee mornings, thank you very much." Her eyes focussed beyond Maria; she waved one hand. "Wait for me?" she called to the woman with dozens of hair braids, but Pat gave a brief wave and rolled on.

Maria's eyes followed hers. "You good friends with her?"

"Pat and I used to be like this," murmured Ruth, holding up her first two fingers pressed together.

"Used to be?"

Chin jutting over the folders, Ruth looked at her from miles away. "She's a strong woman."

"She looks it," said Maria, to fill the gap.

"We had the same kind of choice to make, once," Ruth went on, picking out her words as if for a child, "and we chose differently, and she despised me for it."

Seeing Maria's stricken face, she broke into a smile. "Ancient history now, all long gone and forgiven. Listen, it's twenty past, I must head. You on for learning stuffed peppers tonight?"

She watched Ruth until she was out of sight, then set off for the canteen before apathy could lay its limp fingers on her again.

Details swarmed through her head. On days like these Maria wondered whether she had any life of her own at all or was just an eavesdropper on other people's. When would she have a story, a theme, something people stopped her in the corridor to ask about? The kitchen staff were stacking dirty plates on trolleys, shouting pleasantries to one another. Nothing under the red light but two deformed croissants. She bought a carton of milk and found a nook in the nonsmoking section.

A grunted greeting, a man with a beard sliding his tray against hers. Jesus Christ. Or rather, Damien.

"Oh, hi." Well, that was a start. Breathe deeply now, Maria, gather your thoughts, make conversation.

Luckily he spoke first. Unpeeling a banana very slowly, he inquired, "What happened to your hair?"

"I had an accident with a microwave oven."

Damien nodded, not smiling. "So what do you think of Watson?"

Glory be, he recognized her from the tutorial, even with the haircut. Better be noncommittal. "Well, he does his best," she began, "but the man's not the most dynamic of teachers, is he?"

"I think he's a fine mind."

"Well, yes, of course." How could she get out of this one? "I just mean he could be a little more receptive of our ideas." Receptive of? Receptive to? And what ideas had her mouth ever produced in that tutorial?

She watched Damien eat halfway down his banana. Finally, "You have a point there, Maria."

He knew her name and how to pronounce it.

"So how are you finding the *verfremdungs-effekt*?"

"Not too bad." What the hell was a *fremdunksect*?

Damien spread honey on his ham sandwich; she watched, hypnotised. "So the anonymity doesn't bother you—the lecture halls full of sweaty teenagers, the spaghetti corridors?"

"Not really." Come on, rally your forces. "I rather like it. In my part of the country there are no strangers, only neighbours."

He nodded over his sandwich, then, swinging his heavy plait off his shoulder, he launched into an analysis of the repressive politics of college architecture, how the theatres encouraged intellectual dictatorship, how the only central point for student demonstrations was the bottom of the lake.

She felt perhaps she should be taking notes.

Suddenly: "Do you play pool?"

"No, not really. Not at all, in fact."

"You should, it's very relaxing."

He couldn't have spotted her the other day outside The Pit, he really couldn't. Maybe pool was his single hobby, maybe he always talked about it to total strangers.

"Are you free now?"

Maria blinked. "What, you mean right this minute? I do have a lecture."

"Come on downstairs, I'll teach you to play."

Superior macho shithead. She gathered her possessions and stumbled after him.

🔄

The dark was fuzzy on her eyes; she strained to make out the details of the medieval Virgin. Blast these slide viewings anyway; she had meant to go home every few weekends, or at least do something better with her Saturdays than sit in a lecture hall that smelt of cheese sandwiches.

I'll write home tomorrow, she promised her mother telepathically. Turning over the pad, she jotted down a reminder.

Noticing the date, she realised she had missed yet another Holy Day of Obligation. It wasn't that she was deliberately lapsing, more that she found it hard to motivate herself to get up in time for mass without company. At home it was automatic; the whole village plodded through the carpark in unison at two minutes to ten on a Sunday. But here she knew nobody to go with. The other day she had mentioned it to Ruth, who explained that for her it was not exactly loss of faith either, more the fact that the latest pastoral letter from the bishops had advised Catholics to abhor homosexual activity but have compassion for the congenital homosexual, and if that was all the church had to offer, they could stuff it up their cassocks. Ruth still went to mass whenever she spent Sunday with her mother, of course; she couldn't not.

Maria decided to worry about religion some other time.

She peered down at her red ink scratchings. The lecturer had advised them to make brief sketches of the famous pictures on screen, but how could you reduce a portrait to a squiggly torso? It was too dark anyway. She flicked back over the three pages of notes; how similar they all looked, women slumping over bloated baby boys.

She began to build up a profile in feathery biro strokes; it looked rather like Ruth, the soft mouth turned down at the corner. She added the velvet cap and began to draw Jael's profile emerging out the other side. Not so good—the nose was too hawklike. Maria studied the sketch at arm's length. Rather like a two-headed monster in a fairy tale, the kind of thing the hero had to fight every morning. Or a gargoyle, with two tongues for waterspouts.

The door at the back of the hall lurched open, and a shaft of light shot down the steps. Damien slid in beside her and plucked the sketch out of her hand. "Who's that?"

"It's a bad drawing of my flatmates. Give it back."

She reached for it, but he held it over her head. "I like it. Maybe you should get into horror comics. Are they the two you were telling me about the other day? The redhead who can't play the guitar, and the raving loony feminist?"

"I said no such thing," she whispered. "Gimme."

He tossed the sketch onto the desk. "You did say one of them was down the S.U. all lunchtime handing out leaflets on triple oppression for women in the Third World; sounds a bit extreme to me. So are they always ranting about us phallocrats or what?"

At last, an opportunity to crush him. "No, I can't say we often talk about men at all. It's not a fascinating subject."

He just smirked, watching the screen, no doubt formulating one of his theories. There was no use trying to be witty, Damien was never impressed. What an arrogant profile. The Greek nose sloping down the face, the black beard strengthening the jaw. She stared at it gloomily out of the corner of her eye. That tug in the pit of her belly again—longing or lust or one of those words. He twisted round suddenly, flicking his plait off his shoulder. "Fancy a game?"

"Now?"

"Unless you really need to see fifty-seven more icons to pass your exams."

"Where's that lanky French tutor you usually play with?" Her tone was sulkier than she expected.

"Philippe? Gone to Derry for the weekend."

Maria put the cap on her fountain pen. "You just like playing pool with me because you always win."

"No, it's for variety," he explained, getting to his feet and letting his seat bang upright. 'Remember your first game, last week, when you knocked the black right off the table?"

🔁

Late on a grey-skied Thursday afternoon Ruth found her in the corner of the deserted library, drawing intricate spiders' webs on the back of her pad. Maria glanced up guiltily, then made room on her desk for Ruth. "You've got to help me with this essay. *Discuss how Turner's works are expressive of the spirit of Romanticism.*"

Ruth gagged obediently.

"I mean, I could always rehash what the books say about the lonely artist prancing round on tempests and mountaintops, but I'd rather say something original."

"I know exactly." Ruth took the pen out of Maria's hand and added a fat fly to a web. "I used to try and find a fresh angle for every essay till my tutor lost his temper and told me there just weren't any women's issues in the Franco-Prussian War."

"So there weren't." Jael's face stuck up over the top of the partition.

Ruth raised her eyebrows at Maria. "Do you think she'd

know the Franco-Prussian War if it bit her on her woman's issue?"

"Ladies, please, we are in a place of lofty learning." She slid in between them and sneaked a few nibbles at Ruth's neck.

Maria looked down tactfully and tried to concentrate on her essay plan. So far it went Introduction, Historical Context, Numbers Two to Five, then Conclusion and Bibliography. She heard Ruth hiss, "Get your tongue out of my ear," then a painful thud.

"Are we disturbing you?" Jael was rubbing her elbow.

"Not at all," Maria told her. "I'm stuck. Can't think of anything to write that's not totally banal."

"So give the bastards what they want," Jael said in exasperation. "Let them eat clichés. I just copy mine out of old library books."

"Yeah, well, you've got about as much intellectual integrity as a toilet roll," said Ruth, straightening her shirt collar.

"But I'm so much more romantic," she drawled, striking a Marlene Dietrich pose against the partition.

"Well, that's a fact."

"Romantic?" Maria looked up from the blank page, yawning. "Our wee Jaely?"

"Ach, you should have known us in the early days," Ruth told her. "We had quite a courtship. Well, two weeks actually, but she brought me roses and gave me rides on her motorbike till she crashed it."

Maria leaned back, balancing her chair on two legs. "Red roses?"

"No, sort of dirty-coloured ones."

"Enough!" Jael slapped the desk with the refill pad. "I paid fifty pence each for those wretched flowers; they were meant to be black, a new species. I was trying to be original."

"You must admit they were horrible," said Ruth indulgently.

Jael put the pad over her face and made sounds of despair.

"Go on," Maria told Ruth, letting her chair drop into place with a bump. "Tell me more romance."

Ruth's forehead furrowed with the effort of memory. "She took me on a ski holiday last New Year—did I ever show you the photos?—and she dragged me out of several drifts."

"Don't show her the nudie ones," said Jael in horror, dropping the pad.

"Of course I won't. Do you think Maria would have any interest in perusing your parts?"

Jael stage-whispered, "I'm keeping them for blackmail when she's a Labour politician."

"Anyway, what else was romantic?" Maria tapped her pen against the partition impatiently.

Ruth seemed to be running out of memories. "Well, she sat up late so many nights helping me to revise for last summer's exams that she failed her own. How's that?"

"Ten out of ten." Maria's eyes went from one to the other.

Jael grinned as she got up and stretched. "If my memory serves me right, it wasn't revision we were at at all."

"She doesn't need the details. Leave the poor girl to her essay."

They blew handfuls of kisses from the escalator. When they had sunk out of view, Maria put down her pen and let her head slump onto her arms. Ten minutes' dreamtime before really tackling Turner.

She could see Damien if she craned her neck to the left, but she wasn't going to. He was nothing worth pining over; he should wash his hair more often, for starters. But as soon as she shut her eyes, she could conjure up a broad-shouldered genii in a cloud of blue smoke, a Damien who smiled like Paul Newman and, lazily tossing back his heavy plait, murmured, "Let's not talk about linear perspective, Maria, let's talk about you and me." Not that the real Damien ever said anything like it, but you never knew.

🖪

Near the end of November she decided to skip a few lectures and get the train home for the weekend. "That'll be nice," commented Yvonne wistfully. "It must be good crack, and the fresh air and all." Maria peeked at Yvonne's ring finger; yes, the silver heart was pointing outward again. She could only deduce that her friend was a single woman and had no parties to go to that weekend; she invited her home.

Things began to go wrong at the station. Their train was delayed an hour and a half, and Yvonne claimed to have caught a cold sitting on her carpet bag on the draughty platform. Maria pointed out that any virus took several days to incubate. Yvonne resented the remark and spent the four-hour journey huddled in a corner of the carriage, sniffing loudly behind an old copy of *Image*.

They were met by Maria's Uncle Jim and driven home in his rather doggy Fiat. "Is there a funny smell, or is it just my flu?" was Yvonne's sole remark until they got home.

Opening the back door as the car chugged across the gravel, Maria's mother was wordless at the sight of the new haircut. Yvonne, with a regretful giggle, said, "I know just how you feel, Mrs. Murphy. When I saw it first I thought, what has the girl done to herself?"

She perked up a little over dinner, setting Maria's teeth on edge by apologizing every time she reached for the salt. They watched a James Bond film; Maria was annoyed with herself for wincing whenever one of her brothers shouted "There's a gun in the umbrella!" or picked his nose.

The only place where she could be on her own was the bathroom. Maria slid the bolt over and sat on the sheepskin bath mat, a present from a butcher uncle five Christmases ago. Its creamy tendrils were soft between her fingers. She leaned back against the edge of the tub and let her eyes shut. Five minutes or so she could afford in here, before Yvonne would start worrying and knocking on the door to ask if Maria had cramps. Five minutes of silence, and the milky wool under her palm. Not that this felt like home anymore, now that she had brought a stranger to it. She always knew it was provincial, but this was the first time the house had made her cringe. Framed prints of anthropomorphic mongrels and little Dutch skaters over the beds, a footless Royal Doulton shepherdess on the mantelpiece, and (how could she not have remembered to hide it?) an old yellow-duck nailbrush lying on its back in the bath. Maybe she, not Yvonne, was the stranger here. Less than two months away, and already she had lost that sense of being home.

Time to hostess again; she slid back the bolt. Yvonne did not warm to the idea of sharing a double bed. Her beige silk pyjamas looked out of place against the blue cotton sheets. Maria lay stiffly in the dark listening to Yvonne's "little tickly cough" and checking that all her limbs were on her side of the bed. God knows what conclusions would be jumped to if she shifted over even slightly in her sleep.

The next morning Yvonne didn't think it advisable to go out in that downpour; they played a few mediocre games of chess, watched a Doris Day comedy, and irritated each other. Maria was just overcoming her urge to ask "Instead of constantly sniffing why don't you just blow your nose?" when Yvonne asked languidly, "So what does one do on Saturday nights down here?"

Maria called up a precise mental image of Hogans's fuggy interior; her dad's farmer friends, the accordion player, the few male school friends of hers home for the weekend whom Yvonne might note under the heading of "talent." No, she couldn't face it. "Well, usually I'd head out with a gang of friends, but I thought we'd take it easy this weekend, seeing as you're not well."

"Just so long as I'm not spoiling your fun." Sniff. She followed Maria upstairs and wandered round her bedroom looking at ornaments and tapes. A charcoal drawing of a horse chestnut tree caught her eye. "Did you do this? It's excellent. Though I must say I didn't think that one you did of me was very like."

"Nobody can see their own likeness; anybody else would have recognized you from it." Maria yawned, covering her mouth. "A likeness is a sort of mask that everyone but yourself can see."

"So my mask has hair on the bridge of its nose?"

Maria opened her throat to laugh for the first time that weekend. "I told you, it was shadow, not hair. The pencil was too hard."

"Well, if you drew that Damien guy you're so besotted with, you'd need a special oily charcoal."

Maria couldn't decide whether or not to ignore the remark. She wrapped her cold hands in the bulge of her Aran jumper. "Are you being subtle or something?"

Sliding down on the bed, Yvonne remarked, "I just can't work out what you see in him. He's a greasy, pretentious git."

"I suppose so."

Having expected more resistance, Yvonne halted and changed tracks. "And I wouldn't be surprised if he turned out to be, you know."

"What?"

"That way inclined."

"No way." She lightened her tone and untangled her fingers from the harsh Aran wool. "You're really getting paranoid about the sexual orientation of my friends, aren't you? Don't worry, there are a few straight men left in the world."

Reclining on her elbows, Yvonne balanced her white pumps on the footboard. "Well, that plait is a bit suspect. And he never socialises with the girls in our class."

"Most days he's too busy having lunch with me." Instantly, Maria regretted her tone.

"Well, excuse me!" Yvonne's mouth twisted in amusement. "Just tell me, what's the attraction?"

"Don't know. There isn't any. He's just worth talking to." Maria slumped against the wall, her finger dusting the rim of the bookcase. "Yvonne, don't you ever get sick of girls? The way they—we —talk about the weather, and smile to soften any harsh remark, and nod devoutly whenever they're listening to some prat pontificate?"

"Isn't that exactly what you do with Damien?"

She paused, wiping her dusty finger on her jeans. "No, that's quite different. He treats me like an intellectual equal."

"Gosh."

At this rate they would have murdered each other before the end of the weekend. She could hear Mam chasing the lads up to bed; she lowered her voice in case they listened through the wall. "What are you getting at?"

"Just, I don't see where you get your less-girlie-than-thou attitude," Yvonne answered. "I mean the kind of generalisation you've been making about girls, you'd never let a guy away with that."

"Yeah, but this is off the record," said Maria with a strained grin.

"What about your famous flatmates? I'll bet there's nothing coy and girlie about them."

"That's different, they're not really girls, they're women."

"I thought we were all called women nowadays."

Maria played for time, readjusting the lid of a china ring box, a present from Thelma she had never used. "Well, then, they're dykes."

"That's a really offensive word, Maria."

"No, it's not," she protested, turning. "They use it themselves, it's been reclaimed. Ruth says it comes from the Greek rain goddess Dike."

"You're the expert." A minuscule curl of the lip. "But you still haven't explained why it's any different for, for women like them."

"I'm only guessing," Maria answered uncomfortably. "They don't seem to have to play the same games as we do, with men. They play their own games."

"Like what?" Yvonne leaned her elbows on her knees, eyes bright with curiosity.

Maria was tempted to whisper "Racquetball," but thought better of it. "Ah, I don't mean anything specific. How should I know, anyway? Just, their 'going out together' seems like our 'best friends' with a bit of 'enemies' thrown in."

Yvonne nodded wisely. "You mean it's more emotional than actually . . . sexual."

"I didn't say that."

"But they're not promiscuous?"

Maria shifted, her back against the wall. "You're worse than a priest in confession. No, Jael and Ruth aren't, but I don't know if it's a general rule."

Yvonne meditated for a minute, then said, "It's really rather sweet, isn't it, that they have each other." Then, catching Maria's stare, she said, "Sorry, did that sound patronising?"

Lining up the battered spines of her George Eliot novels, Maria hunted for words. "See, I know it might be a bit sad later on when they've missed their chance of having kids, but for the moment it seems a perfectly valid way of life. Doesn't it?"

Yvonne gave a tiny shiver, shifting to the rim of the bed. "I just find the physicality of it so hard to imagine."

"Well, don't try to, then."

She ignored that. "And how can you put up with being a gooseberry? I shared a flat one summer with a pair of newly-weds, and it was so awkward."

"They really don't make me feel left out," said Maria. She heard herself bleating and cleared her throat. "Remember those diagrams in electricity for the leaving cert? Well, I'm not blocking the circuit, I'm a loop in it."

"What circuit?"

"Ruth and Jael. I think they need me to absorb some of the static. They say they'd be fighting like cats if I wasn't around to distract them."

Rubbing her forearms, Yvonne gave her a doubtful look. She suggested they go back down to the fire, as the cold was starting a tickle in her throat again.

That night the temperature dropped hour by hour. Maria lay flat on her back and willed blood into her feet; she curled up and hugged her icy knees to her breasts. She could not get warm. Two feet away, Yvonne's satin back hunched. The crack in the curtains let in only a chill strip of moonlight. Maria inched onto her side. She pulled a tiny feather from the old pillow and tickled her upper lip with it. A childhood fantasy came back to her: She wished she had six sisters, three to each side of her, folded together like spoons, their warm brushed-cotton ribs rising and falling in unison.

She buried her nose in the smooth pillow and tucked the edge of the blanket round her ear. Mam's aunt, she remembered, used to carry a hot potato in her coat pocket to school every day, so that she would be able to hold the chalk to write a sum on the board. It occurred to Maria now that the potato was a talisman. No doubt the great-aunt's fingers still went numb but were comforted by the feel of the brown skin.

And where was her own hot potato tonight, this term, this lifetime? Maria edged down the bed until her head was submerged in rough blankets and the air grew musty. She had had enough of loitering on the outside, playing the chilly virgin, everybody's helpful agony aunt. She wanted to feel something, anything, so overpowering that it would fill the space between her ribs with radiance. Not that she required happiness, at least not straightaway—just something hot enough to burn her hand.

⑤

"No, honestly."

"Schmonestly."

"Can't handle another, I'll pass out." Maria's belly hurt from laughter. She nudged the pint away.

Damien shoved it back across the table; the creamy head bobbed and almost slopped over. "You have to drink it now I've carried it through the madding crowd of elbows."

She rested her lips on the rim of the glass and let the cream seep between them.

"Here, let me draw a face on the head, and if it stays all the way down, it's a good pint."

"Get those mucky fingers out of my head," she roared. The law students at the next table raised their eyebrows. "I can do it myself." She finished the cartoon face, then added a cross underneath.

He peered over her elbow. "What's that, the Campaign for Nuclear Disarmament symbol?"

"No, it's the wimminy thing."

"Spare me!" Damien grabbed the pint and drank, widemouthed, till the imprint had disappeared. "No feminism allowed after eleven o'clock or you'll turn into a pumpkin. Come on with you now, let's be having a wee dance." He pulled her into the circle of bodies.

"Would you be imitating anyone's accent there?" she shouted in his ear.

"Divil a bit!"

Maria gave a wrench to his beard. "Beast. Listen, I'm not sure if I can stand."

"Here comes a slow set now, all you have to do is sway. How come I'm still in control of my limbs if I've had three more than you?"

"Boys have bigger bladders. Or maybe it all goes into the plait."

She leaned against his bulk and let her eyelids slide shut. The music pivoted them, limp as hibernating bears. It was one of those songs that envelops you in its saxophone intro, and you think you remember and love it, and by halfway through it has become one of those sloppy ballads they play every Christmas. What was the name of the damn thing, something about a year or a heart. Weren't they all? She put her head back to ask Damien and found his mouth on hers. It seemed impolite to twitch away. He tasted of smoke, oddly savoury. She opened her eyes but found his overhanging nose alarming, so she shut them again.

People are looking, thought Maria. The right people or the wrong people or the don't-give-a-shit people?

His tongue in her mouth was harmless, thick; that came of talking too much, she decided. The dark curls of his beard were warm against her chin. She turned her mind off and dug deeper into the kiss.

Her name. Damien had disengaged and was shaking her shoulder.

"What did I do?"

"It's past closing time; they're kicking us all out."

She shook herself awake. They were alone on the neon-outlined dance floor. The crowd was trickling out the swing doors; she saw a hand wave and recognized Galway's wry smile. She waved back, shamefaced, but he had disappeared. The lethargic bar staff were upturning orange chairs on wet tables. "Oh, good lord, my bus."

"I've got rooms," he commented as they opened the swing doors and the cold air slapped them.

"I'd better not," Maria told him, softening the words.

"You mean you'd rather not."

"I mean . . . I don't know what I mean," she said, coughing in amusement. "Night, so." She patted him on the shoulder, an awkwardly intimate gesture.

Damien pulled his plait inside his collar, turned up against the wind. He nodded and headed off toward the buildings.

"See you tomorrow," she called, but he was out of earshot.

All the way home in the bus she kept her eyes shut, and her disbelief switched off, holding on to the warmth.

5

Tuesday, Wednesday, seven and a half hours of Thursday and still no sign of him. Not even the usual hallucinations. Maria killed some twenty minutes at the modern languages notice boards, wandered down a corridor dusty with light, and her eye caught sight of that French tutor she'd seen in The Pit. She spoke before her nerve could decide not to answer the summons.

"*Excusez-moi,* sorry."

His face was long and tapered like a Brazil nut.

"I'm a friend of Damien's. Just wondering had you seen him round at all today?"

Philippe's shoulders would have liked to shrug. "I presume he's still in London," he told her with the faintest of accents. "He did say it was only for the weekend, but I wouldn't be surprised if he stayed all week."

"Of course," Maria answered brightly.

It would be rude to truncate the conversation with that, as if she had no interest in the man except as a source of information. As was the case, she reminded herself, and felt doubly guilty. Her smile bared a few teeth. "You must be missing your games!"

He stared.

"Your games. Pool. I've seen you play, you're brill." Maria told him her name and how nice it was talk to him and that she would no doubt bump into him again sometime. Then she put her fingers over her mouth and cleared her throat, to halt the flow of words, and walked away—the wrong way down the corridor, so she had to lurk in the staff toilet until she could be sure Philippe was gone. Brill, she repeated into the mirror with an extra-wide grimace, to mortify herself. How seventeen.

🝰

She was paddling up gradually from sleep when her alarm piped. An irritating little sound, like a squirrel being strangled. Ten o'clock; once again she had forgotten to set it to half eight for weekdays. The lecturer would be straightening his grey tie outside the lecture theatre by now, ready to deliver his commentary on the salient points of rococo ceilings. Maria was aching in all her own salient points, after a crippling evening washing every window in an insurance company office.

There was no one who would notice if Maria went in today or not. Yvonne and she had exchanged only a few hellos since that disastrous weekend at home. As for Damien, he had been back for over a week, she calculated, and it was as if that blurred incident in the bar had never happened. He was reliably friendly; every time she stage-managed an encounter with him on the corridors, he stopped for a chat, impervious to the crowd swirling past them. They even had a short game of pool together, and one threesome with Philippe. But none of it added up to anything.

Maria wrenched back the duvet and reached for her long johns. She would not come home early again today; warm evenings in the flat were a luxury to be rationed. She mustn't keep leaning on Ruth and Jael, tagging along. Surely they would get bored of her if she had no life of her own to joke about. Besides, they could do with some privacy. Though it was not her fault, last night; it didn't count as eavesdropping if the voices carried right through the wall. Words like *self-respect* and *typical* and *self-indulgence* and *cliché* came ripping through the cloud of murmurs. Every few lines, one voice reproved the other with a piercing "Shh!" Maria had lain there, troubled for them, sometimes trying not to listen, sometimes straining for the words.

Now she sat on the edge of the bed again and took off one runner, shaking it to loosen a tiny pebble, which hit the carpet and leapt under the bed. Maria rested the shoe on her lap and shut her eyes. If she was lonely, it was her own damn fault. If she was bored, why didn't she do something about it?

By the time the bus got her onto the campus, lectures were over for the day. Maria made a draughty pilgrimage round the notice boards and, steeling herself to it, signed herself up for backstage work on the Dramattic's Christmas Panto.

That evening she wandered down to the basement before the fourth rehearsal of *Snow White and the Seven Bishops*. A minimal welcome was offered, over plastic cups of coffee. The rehearsal was protracted and irritating, with the lead bishop fluffing his lines at nine crucial points. Afterward the crew all sat around listing the production's faults. Maria liked the look of one girl, a scene painter with coal-black hair who claimed to be named Suzette. Hearing Maria's name, Suzette turned to her, her huge ponytail swinging. "You live with Jael, don't you?"

Maria couldn't think of anything to say that wouldn't hurl her through a trapdoor of implication. She nodded uncertainly.

"I know her from way back," the girl explained. "Has she learned to play that guitar yet?"

"She thinks she has."

Suzette turned away to get some instructions from the tetchy director. Maria was just pulling on her gloves to go when Suzette glanced back. "Aren't you coming to the bar for a nightcap?"

"Sorry, got to dash," mumbled Maria, and made for the stairs.

Another adolescent panic attack; out at the foggy bus stop she cursed herself systematically under her breath. One, she had turned down a rare and valuable social overture. Two, being an old acquaintance of Jael's did not automatically make Suzette a lesbian. Three, even if she was, she was only being friendly, and was hardly intending to molest Maria in the college bar.

She got home at midnight, bone tired and sick of herself. Letting herself in quietly in case Ruth and Jael were asleep, she was surprised to hear only one voice in the living room. Maria glanced wearily through the beads; it was Jael, huddled up in her flame-coloured kimono, the phone cord spiralling round her knees.

"Mmm. Whiling the hours away all on my lonesome. No, the youngster must be at college still. So what have you and Mumsie been up to?"

A long pause; Jael shifted on the sofa, tucking her feet under her. Go to bed, Maria told herself, yawning silently. She couldn't decide whether she wanted a cup of tea.

"Me too." A low, throaty laugh. "Wouldn't say no. Why do you have to stay with her tonight? Possessive cow." Jael listened, then broke in. "I'm not insulting her, I'm just lusting after her daughter. I won't be able to sleep, you know. I'm just going to have to parade starkers on the roof till someone takes pity on me."

Maria decided against the tea. A hot bath before bed, maybe? Her shoulders slumped in indecision.

"It is not ovulation, you're a week out. I'm always horny on

Friday nights. And no wonder, after your shameless conduct in the shower this morning. You didn't learn that in the Department of Pensions. I bet you're still wet." The voice slid down. "Come on, tell me. No, your mother won't hear through the wall. Aren't you even the slightest bit wet for me?"

Maria leaned against the smooth wallpaper; she could feel her face heat up in the dark.

The words were almost inaudible. "Where are you, the hall? All right. Imagine I'm sitting on the stair just below you. Concentrate now, stop sniggering. Imagine my hand sliding up between your knees. Are you wearing those stockings with the—" A roar. "I am not kinky. OK, piss off, go get your beauty sleep. See you in the morning. How about breakfast in bed?"

Maria slouched in. "Evening, all."

Jael was staring at the receiver in her lap. She looked up, pulling the kimono around her neck. "Kettle's still warm if you want a cuppa. I was just talking to Ruth, she's on filial duty tonight."

"I'm sure she's glad to get a break from us, have her dinner made for her once in a while."

"You haven't met Mrs. Johnson," warned Jael, dropping the phone on the matted hearth rug. Then, watching Maria's limp arm lift the kettle, she asked, "How's the poppet?"

All her walls of independence crumbled; she felt like burying her tired face in Jael's lap. Instead, she took a gulp of steaming tea. "Hunky-dory."

"That bad?" Jael raised one eyebrow.

"I've signed up for the Dramattic's Panto, and I think I'm going to hate it."

"Drop out."

"No, I can't do that now."

Jael let out a huge sigh that turned into a yawn. "I'll never understand you honourable types. Ruth's just as bad. Tell

you what, we were planning a picnic in the hills this weekend; why don't you forget about those thespy shites and
come with us?"

"Shouldn't you check with your other half? I don't want to
be in the way."

"Rubbish," said Jael, positioning another brocade cushion
behind her head. "What do you think we'd be getting up to
on a mountaintop?"

"The mind boggles," said Maria, and carried her scalding
mug down the corridor.

"Besides," came a shout, "some things are even more fun
with three."

🔄

The bus wheezed slowly into the mountains; Ruth's chocolate supply ("for blood sugar") had dwindled to nothing by
the time they reached the terminus. They set off up a random
muddy path, held up at intervals by Jael stopping to photograph interesting patches of tree bark. "God, I'd love a cig-
gie," she remarked wistfully.

"I didn't know you smoked," said Maria.

"Oh, I don't anymore, not since I shacked up with your
woman."

"'Shacked up with' sounds like cattle," Ruth complained;
"couldn't you use 'met' or even something nice like 'fell
for'?" She turned to Maria. "After the first fortnight, I dared
her to give up smoking." Lowering her voice to a whisper,
she added, "She stank."

"I heard that," called Jael from the hedge where she was
poking around for late blackberries, "but I'm mature enough
to ignore it. Speaking of stink, hadn't that infant on the bus a
bit of an aroma?"

"It couldn't help itself," commented Ruth. "Just imagine
having no control over your anal sphincter. I thought it was
fairly likeable, as babies go."

"Would you ever mind not having kids?" asked Maria.

"No way," said Jael comfortably. "Call me selfish, but they'd cramp my style."

Ruth paused in deliberation, scanning the panorama of purple heather and black turf. "Well, having children can be part of heterosexist oppression ... Ah, no, to be honest, I'm just more into women than men and babies put together. The theory came later."

"There's always squirting," suggested Jael.

Maria's eyes bulged.

"She means self-insemination," Ruth explained with animation. "This couple we know in England, Wendy and Deirdre, they've been together for twelve years, and they've just had a baby boy that way."

"But how exactly—"

"You get a friendly milkman to leave you a bottle of fresh HIV-negative semen," Jael told her, "then you get a turkey baster, lie on your back, and ... " She performed a graphic mime, almost falling over a boulder.

They exchanged a grin at Maria's expression. "Sounds a lot more fun than the usual method, if you ask me," murmured Ruth.

The women climbed through a gap in a barbed wire fence, holding it up for each other, then headed up a boggy field. Maria and Ruth picked their way delicately through the bushes. "The best way," announced Jael, "is to run so fast that you don't put any weight on your feet." They watched her scamper up the field and burst into simultaneous applause when her foot sank into a moist cowpat. Staggering to the fence for support, she wiped her runners along a cushion of moss. "Well, at least I've made your day," she told Maria. "That's the first smile I've seen on your face all week."

"Is it?" And then she was sick of evasions and blank expressions. "There's this guy at college."

Jael snorted.

"It's no big deal," Maria rushed on, "I just thought he liked me, and now I doubt it."

"And there was I thinking you had definite D.P. Oh, well, another one bites the dust." Jael kicked a stone theatrically, then used it to scrape some mud off her heel.

"What's—"'

"Dyke Potential," Ruth filled in. "Jael was planning to convert you by the force of her personal charms, weren't you, pet?"

"I'd have done it by Christmas," Jael agreed mournfully. "And now some handsome brute has ruined all my good work—"

"He's not particularly handsome at all," said Maria awkwardly.

"Do we get his name?" asked Ruth gently, leaning on a five-barred gate.

"It's really not important. I just like talking to him."

"I'll bet." Jael started climbing over the gate at the wrong end.

"What?" asked Maria, stung.

Jael turned with a manic grin, her feet clinging to the highest bar. "Come off it, Marianissimo. If you just liked talking to him, you wouldn't be upset. Why not just say you want to go to bed with him?"

"Because I'm not upset, and I don't want to go to bed with anyone."

Cantering down the field, Jael bawled back, "Famous last words!"

Maria's throat seized up in fury.

"Ignore her, it's hormonal," murmured Ruth. "She needs a few sozzled nights on the scene, and then she'll calm down."

"What scene?" Maria was relieved that the talk had shifted from herself; she led the way down the field.

"Oh, you know, pubs and stuff. Which for us means Saturday nights in one tiny inner-city lounge walled with women in paisley shirts and Docs. I can't say I'm enthralled by it."

"But Jael goes?"

"Sometimes. She used to go a lot on her own or with friends, but over the summer there were problems." Ruth stared down the field after the tiny jogging figure.

"Like what?" asked Maria, then wished she hadn't.

"Ah, I won't bore you with the details, but basically we do our drinking at home nowadays."

Maria sucked her lips. Only after picking a handful of coppery leaves did she think of something that would be safe to ask. "But if you don't like pubs, how did you two find each other in the first place?"

"I owe it all to feminism," said Ruth, taking one of the leaves from Maria and examining its veins. "We met at a Women and Literature symposium; Jael always claims she was there for the free sherry afterward."

"But were you already—"

Ruth interrupted her as she fumbled for the right phrase. "Hard to tell. Who knows what we all are before anything happens?"

"I suppose," said Maria soberly. After a minute, she returned to the question. "But were you surprised? Did you expect to fall for a woman?"

"Will I be perfectly honest with you?"

"You will."

"I was twenty-two, and I'd never had more than the occasional unfulfilling snog behind the bike sheds. I thought I was probably asexual, like a plant."

"Oh, you're very like a plant," Maria commented in amusement.

"Whereas her ladyship had gone out with lots of women and a few guys as well. So I still don't quite know how we got together. But I can't imagine it any other way."

Maria considered the details in silence.

"I'm not usually like this, you know," Ruth went on. "I'm the quiet, reticent one, known in the women's group for extracting intimate details of everybody else's lives without giving any of my own!"

"So what's changed?"

"I think you're good at questions; you just seem to start the words spilling out of me." The look she gave Maria over one shoulder, as she pushed through a gap in a hedge, was half grateful, half worried. "It's because you seem so interested, and I know you're not likely to use the information against me."

"You've said nothing incriminating so far, but by Christmas my dossier may be complete."

"Speaking of which," resumed Ruth more lightly, "have you given any thought to the holidays yet? How long are you likely to stay up?"

"I'll probably catch the afternoon train on Christmas Eve, then come back up after New Year's. There's never much going on at home apart from the annual aunt invasion."

"You'll be here till the Eve? Great stuff," said Jael, who had trotted silently from behind the hedge to fall in step with them. "So, lads, will we go the whole hog and put up a tree?"

"Yes, dear," said Ruth, patting her on her windswept fringe, "and you get to sit on top in a pair of wings and a silver G-string."

⑤

Walking back from the supermarket with a bottle of milk and a batch loaf, Maria felt her leaden mood begin to lift. The sun was setting over the park railings; tall willows were blocked out against the ginger light. She hummed the first two bars of a tune that eluded her as she headed up the stairs, swinging the grocery bag.

Opening her bedroom door, she was disconcerted to find Jael slouched on the duvet, her head back on the windowsill. "What are you doing in here?" she asked, too curtly.

"Sunbathing," said Jael with a yawn, lifting her head. The ebbing sun made a fuzzy halo of her hair. "This room is magic in the evenings, isn't it? I used to play my guitar in here."

Resting her elbows on the windowsill, Maria looked over the glinting roofs.

"We never got around to repainting it. Does the orangeness not get on your nerves?"

"I thought it would, but it's sort of grown on me; I like the way the curtains catch the sun. I think I get fond of anything after a few months."

"Dangerous habit," murmured Jael. "I see you've left up the calendar of monsters. It was a present from Ruth one Christmas; I couldn't bear the way they looked at me."

"Ah, but the December starfish is rather loveable, look."

She shuddered. "Turn back to the harmless seaweed. Now, what I like are your posters, especially the Bogarts."

"Do you?" Maria's face turned in enthusiasm. "He's nothing special on his own, but with Bacall he's fabulous. I've always had a soft spot for screen couples."

"One of my earliest sexual fantasies," Jael confided, leaning up on one elbow, "involved Greta Garbo, John Gilbert, and a gauzy four-poster bed."

"Perv!"

"It was hot stuff. Unlike the real thing, which I didn't try till I was in Berlin."

"Which real thing?"

"Three in a bed," explained Jael. "Take it from me, it's overrated. Someone always gets left out."

Maria was failing to look blasé. "Better put the milk in the fridge," she said, picking up the grocery bag.

Jael followed her up the corridor. "Who's your favourite of them all?"

"Film stars? Dunno. There was a time I'd have died to look like Audrey Hepburn."

"There is a slight resemblance." Cross-legged on the hearth rug, Jael contemplated Maria's profile as she bent over the grate.

"There is not." Maria struggled with the last match. "She had lovely dark hair, for one thing."

"Yeah, but otherwise the urchin look is similar. Same little pointy ears. Are they pierced?"

"They were, at fourteen, but I've let the holes close over."

Jael put out one finger to touch Maria's neat lobe. "Ah, look at the size of them."

"Gerroff, that tickles." She smacked the hand away harder than necessary.

The firelighter finally sparked into life. Maria dusted her hands and sat back with a cough, watching the flame grow. "I'm worn out now, and all I've done is a bit of shopping. Must be PMS."

"Lie down on the mammoth's hide, and I'll make you a cuppa."

Flat on her back, Maria waited for the dizziness to pass. The rug smelt of firelighters. She let go of her muscles one by one and allowed her mind to slide into deep water.

A thump, a cackle, and she found herself being rolled up in the rug, arms crushed to her sides. She came to rest face-down, her nose tickled by a curl of brown fake fur. As she began to writhe, a thigh came down on the small of her back, and hot breath touched her ear. "Got you now, little girl. That'll teach you to snooze in the spider's parlour. Now, what shall I do to your ears?"

Maria let out a bellow. "You wouldn't dare."

"Now, that wasn't very clever. Do you not know by now I

never refuse a dare?" Teeth snapped just behind her ear, and the heavy body shuddered with laughter.

Maria gave a furious wrench and said murderously, "Get off me this minute." Then, seeing the absurdity of her position: "I surrender, you dirty wee fucker."

The bang of the front door relieved her; she squinted up as Ruth staggered through the curtain with a bale of turf briquettes. "Hello there," Maria panted. "Could you possibly get your evil girlfriend off my back?"

"Oh, for god's sake." Ruth's voice was cold. "You've let the fire out, and we've no more matches. Would you ever stop acting like a pair of hyperactive infants and get out of my way." She stepped over them to poke at the cinders.

Abashed, Maria rolled out of the rug and stood up. "Is there anything I can be doing?"

Ruth didn't answer, and Jael tugged Maria away by the sleeve. Halfway down the corridor, she whispered, "Let's stay out of her way, she'll be all right by dinnertime. Why don't you show me the rest of your posters?"

"Nah, I've got theorems to revise." Maria shut her door. Her head was spinning. She sat on the bed, her feet sticking over the edge. The gaps between her jeans and socks were goosepimpled. If ab is equal in length to cd—What the hell just happened? Let there be a circle of radius gh. Why was Ruth so cross? Maria put down her pen, dry-mouthed.

She wandered into the kitchen and filled a glass of water from the tap. Go on, she told herself, you're meant to be good at questions. "You OK?"

"Fine," said Ruth, breaking spaghetti into a steaming pot. "Sorry I snapped at you."

"What's wrong?" It came out less like a question than a statement.

Ruth sat down on the kitchen stool; her back made the shape of a comma. "I'm not sure."

Apologies for the fire and the general mess rose to Maria's tongue, but she stifled them. She took the spaghetti packet from Ruth's hands and broke the rest into the pot, then turned up the flame.

"Maria." The voice was thoughtful. "Have you ever had a suspicion that something was going to happen, but not been able to tell anyone because the effects of the warning might be just as bad?"

Her forehead furrowed. After half a minute, "No."

"Oh, well, leave it, then."

Maria found the lid of the pot at the very back of the cupboard. "Hang on," she said, straightening up. "I once saw a film about an earthquake in Los Angeles, where the mayor was terrified to announce it on the radio, in case there might be a mass panic, which would make everything worse."

"But also," Ruth went on, "the mayor might be afraid that people would think her motives for the warning were selfish." Noticing Maria's doubtful expression, she added, "Oh, I don't know, to influence the share price index or something. Besides, what if some people thought the earthquake was a good thing, and didn't want to be warned against it?"

"A good thing?"

Ruth snapped a strand of spaghetti into one-inch sections. "They might want the earthquake."

"How could anyone want an earthquake?"

"That's where our metaphor falls down, doesn't it?" asked Ruth; her eyes were scalding.

Maria took hold of Ruth's shoulder, which felt surprisingly fragile under the angora wool. "Then why not drop the metaphors, and tell me what's the matter?"

She stood up; rather than letting Maria's hand fall, she lifted it off her shoulder and gave it a squeeze before letting go. As the pot began to leak white foam, she turned down the flame. "Lots of good reasons why not."

"Like?" Maria's tone was irritated.

"I'm sorry. I didn't mean to flirt with your curiosity like this. I'm just thinking out loud, I'm tired, I'm sorry."

"Just—"

"No. Because you'd think I was greedy and suspicious and paranoid, and I probably am. And it might not do any good, and really it's none of my business."

Maria growled like a maddened dog and gave up.

"I'm sorry I brought it up. Ignore me, I haven't been getting enough sleep."

"I just want to help you, woman."

The eyes were soft, like peat-browned water. "I know that."

"At least let me finish dinner," said Maria, resigned.

"If you could—"

"It shouldn't be beyond even my abilities to move pesto sauce from the fridge to the spaghetti. Go on, have a wee lie down, rest those baggy eyes." She watched Ruth move out of the kitchen like a zombie.

🖳

"Have you decided to stick with the job, so?"

Maria prised the paper clip out of the vacuum cleaner's nozzle and straightened up. "Might as well, as I haven't any other. The doctor says I'm doing my back no harm, it's just tired."

"Ah, sure my back's been hurting for thirty years," Maggie told her. "You get used to it."

"Is that how long you've been cleaning offices?" she asked respectfully.

"God forbid. That's only the last five years. Before that I ran a B&B, but with the fall of the dollar there just wasn't the trade anymore." The woman paused at the door. "I'll be in the toilet having a fag if you need help shifting that big sofa."

"Thanks, Mags."

She blew her nose, the sound trumpeting through the empty office. The carpet was streaked with mud; it had been raining for five days. Maria pulled the moaning vacuum cleaner backward and forward over the smears until they faded to beige. She remembered a story her mother had told her on the phone last week, about how the town council had tried to house Nelly the Nutter in a cottage beside the chicken factory. One businessman fitted it up with basic furniture; another provided a secondhand vacuum cleaner for her to keep the place nice. A visiting social worker found Nelly sitting on the floor beside the vacuum cleaner, which had been on at full suction for five days. Nelly said she liked the sound. She wheeled her vacuum behind her when she went back to her rug under the bridge. Maria thought it was a lovely story and hoped the council would have to pay the electricity bill. She was always nervous when she came face-to-face with Nelly on the steps of the library, in case the woman would say something unanswerable, but from this distance, Maria remembered her with respectful affection.

What would Nelly make of a room like this, four flights up, its wet windows sprinkled with the city's lights? Maria blew her nose and bent to the switch; silence caressed her ears. At least this work was real. The carpet was definitely cleaner when she had finished with it; the windows let in more street light when her cloth had passed over them. Office workers she would never meet had slightly pleasanter mornings because she had remembered to wash their coffee-stained mugs. Not forgetting the money, of course—little but undeniably real, notes in her palm every Friday, coins for vinegary chips on the way home. Whereas that last essay on Celtic spiral motifs—what good did that do anyone? It might get her a job in the long run, she supposed. Only she was having difficulty imagining a long run. Even Christmas seemed out of sight, at the end of a queue of cold December evenings. Damnation, she was out of tissues now. Maria felt tears welling up as her nose began to run.

This was ridiculous, she told herself, with a loud sniff. She sat in the director's chair and spun herself around. What she wanted was someone to walk through the swing doors and hand her a silk handkerchief, a white rose, and two tickets to Jamaica. Or even to the pictures on Saturday afternoon. Maria dragged her feet, halted the chair, and spun it the other way. Her back subsided against the firm leather of the seat. Someone, anyone, to ring her up and ask her out and take these maddening questions out of her head. She pulled up her overall and felt in the back pocket of her jeans until she found a last fold of toilet paper. Her nose hurt from blowing. She dragged the vacuum cleaner into the next office and turned it on.

Her mother would laugh if she could hear these thoughts. She had been supportive enough about Maria coming up to the uni, but at the suggestion of an M.A. she had raised her eyebrows. In her experience, girls started out as ambitious as the lads, but by the age of twenty they were usually itching to settle down with someone nice and put up curtains. Maria had poured scorn on this argument, she remembered now. She told her mother that this was just one more stereotype of female behaviour that, given enough career guidance, newspaper articles, and flat-heeled shoes, would evaporate. Mam said she would believe it when she saw it, and wasn't it a good thing girls were the way they were or it would be a cold and nasty world full of careerists crashing into one another's fancy cars. Maria argued that there would always be some girls who wanted engagement rings and curtains, but personally she would rather a degree and a fancy car.

And here was the loudmouthed feminist, moping over a vacuum cleaner, wishing she had a date instead of a work-sheet on differential calculus. Come on now, ten minutes more hard work and she could go home. Hot buttered toast by the fire with Ruth, gossip and snatches of poems out of broken-backed anthologies—wasn't that something to look forward to?

They plodded up the shiny street under Maggie's broken-winged black umbrella, avoiding the splash of a lorry's wheels. "Enjoy your walk, so," said Maggie at the corner.

"Do you think I'd be walking on a night like this?"

"Sure weren't the buses off after nine tonight?"

"You're codding me." Maria's cheeks were numbed by rain already.

"It's a work-to-rule, they're protesting after that double-decker was toppled by yobbos in Finglas the other night."

"That's right, I heard about it." Maria pulled up her collar. "I think it'd choke me to spend an hour and a half's wages on a taxi."

"I haven't so far to go. Have a lend of my brolly."

"I won't, Mags, but thanks for offering." Maria waved and trudged off into the darkness.

6
WAITING

When the stage crew had nothing to do, they arm-wrestled.

"What the hell is that?" asked Maria, hearing screeches from backstage.

Suzette tightened her grip. "Don't even try to distract me. It's just the cast having a scream session to loosen up their voices."

Maria pressed the flat of her other hand to the grimy boards. Her back was writhing. "Another of Jennifer's innovations?"

"Indeed."

"Stop moving your elbow in. Ow." Maria's wrist was crushed to the floor.

Suzette sprang to her feet, shaking the dust off her fringed shawl. "If Jennifer could see us now, she'd say our attitude was—what's that phrase of hers?—'less than professional.'"

"Just because she did a theatre course last summer, she thinks she knows it all." Maria rolled down the mingled sleeves of her three jumpers. "She found me peacefully reading *Anna Karenina* the other day and told me off for not being busy painting publicity flats."

"That's nothing," said Suzette, straddling a broken-backed chair. "Last night after rehearsals, right, me and Yves were roller-skating peacefully round the stage singing *'Non, Je Ne Regrette Rien,'* and she walked in and threatened to kick us out of the crew."

"I hope you told her where she could stuff herself."

"More or less," said Suzette evasively.

Maria blew her nose, trying not to hurt it. "If I'd known backstage work meant sitting round in arctic conditions waiting for Jennifer's orders, I'd never have signed up."

"You know what, you should volunteer to help that malnourished American with lights. I'm sure he could do with some company."

She peered across the theatre at the dimly lit sound box. "Hey, I know him." Clambering up the ladder, she had only time to call "Hi, gorgeous" before giving her head a blinding crack off a speaker.

A bony hand reached down from the darkness. "Everyone does that once," observed Galway.

"Since when have you been a technical wizard?" She climbed through the trapdoor and slumped on a chair.

"Picked a bit up here and there; it's easy enough if you keep your eyes open. Like, for example, that's a light filter you're sitting on."

"I give up." Maria wriggled out of the way. "I came to volunteer my services, but all I seem to do is smash things."

Galway patted a backless swivel chair beside him. "Nice to see you, Maria. Sit. Now there's just one thing you've got to keep in mind: If you bring a switch up too fast, you'll blow the bulb."

Her hands flinched from the lighting board.

He reached past her for his plastic cup of coffee and a photocopied sheet of cryptic diagrams. "There's the lighting plan; watch me once and you'll have no problems."

"Could we have a little hush, people?" inquired Jennifer from below.

🔄

". . . goin' to Scarborough Fair . . . sage, rosemary and . . . "

Maria could hear the faint pattern of the guitar chords as she sprang up the stairs; that must be Jael singing, much too low, so her bottom notes were barely audible. Opening the front door softly, she laid her rucksack of books by the coat cupboard. The music halted for a moment when her face divided the beads. "Hippie nostalgics!"

Ruth gave a vague smile and continued massaging the guitarist's neck in time with the chords. Sighing with pleasure, Jael let her head slump so far forward that her sheaf of hair obscured the strings, and the song trailed off. "Don't mind us," she said through her curls, "we're ever so slightly stoned."

Maria put the kettle on.

"So, what has you looking so perky?" called Ruth, taking hold of Jael's hair by the curls and swinging it from side to side.

"We got the bathrooms done by ten this evening," said Maria cheerfully.

Jael shook the hair out of her eyes. "Come off it. I bet it's that mystery man we heard about a few weeks back."

"Well, yes, as it happens, he did go without his pool game today to buy me lunch. And he told me I should always wear purple."

Jael giggled into her collarbone. "Do you know what that means, the colour purple?"

"No, and I doubt I want to."

"Suit yourself." Jael let her neck roll back into Ruth's lap.

"Don't mind her," said Ruth sleepily. "It's just the traditional queer colour. You know—purple, lavender, nowadays pink."

"I should have guessed." Maria rushed to turn off the kettle. After a minute, she called over, "And he said we must go to the pictures sometime."

"So you said, 'Yes please, when?'"

"Ah, give the girl credit for some subtlety," protested Ruth, plaiting Jael's long fringe.

"I just said, 'That'd be lovely,' like my mammy taught me." Maria carried over the tea tray laden with mugs.

"Sounds like you've got it made," said Jael, pulling herself upright. "Who is this boy-germ, anyway? Is he worthy of you?"

"If I tell you his name, will you promise not to laugh?"

Jael brightened. "Is it something really poncy like Edgar?"

"Worse."

Ruth reached across Jael for the milk jug. "If she laughs, I promise to twist her vertebrae out of joint."

"Well, it's Damien."

After a pause, Jael asked, "He wouldn't happen to be a big guy with a beard? And a plait? And a boyfriend?"

Maria could feel herself heating up. "Will you stop playing games with me? You don't even know him."

"I do," Jael insisted. "Or at least I know a friend of a friend of his. Swear to god, Maria," she went on. "I wouldn't joke about it, not if you're really into him. But the guy's had a scene going all term with some Frenchman."

Philippe, of course. How could she not have noticed? How could she have known?

Ruth broke in anxiously. "Maybe it's not the same guy; I've never seen anyone with a beard at Gaysoc."

"Yeah, well a lot of us don't feel the need to join a club to announce who we sleep with," said Jael witheringly, and Ruth flinched.

Maria bit her lips. She just wished she had never mentioned his name, or better still, never met him. Her exasperation welled up; "But he kissed me."

Ruth and Jael exchanged a glance.

She stared into her steaming tea and answered herself: "Not that a kiss proves anything. I've been reading every damn signal wrong; it never occurred to me about Philippe."

"This Damien guy is probably bi," said Ruth encouragingly. "Don't give up too soon."

"He can be a necrophiliac for all I care," snarled Maria. She sipped her tea; she had forgotten the sugar.

Jael's mouth twisted. "Bad luck, pardner. Hemmed in by pervs on every side."

🔄

It wasn't hard to avoid Damien, since she was missing most of her lectures anyway. Rehearsals for *Snow White and the Seven Bishops* were stepping up, and even when Maria wasn't needed, she liked to hover round the theatre, absorbing the warmth of overheard conversations.

Yvonne dropped by once or twice to examine the half-painted scenery and compliment Maria on her increasingly fluffy hair. One day she announced that Pete kept insisting on going the whole way in the back of his mother's Volvo.

"Why?"

"What do you mean, why? I'm not that much of an eyesore."

Concentrating on her paintbrush, Maria fumbled for words. "I don't mean why does he fancy you, just why does it have to be that? I mean, lots of people nowadays are sticking to nonpenetrative sex, it said so in *The Guardian*."

Yvonne rolled her eyes and sat cautiously on the edge of a wooden piano. "I can't answer for your trendy feminist types, Maria, but in the real world petting doesn't count as sex, and everybody prefers the real thing."

"Do you?"

"It's nice, yeah," she said defensively.

"Only nice?"

"Pretty nice. How do you measure these things?" Her stare turned harder. "You tell me, Maria. How many orgasms a night do you call nice?"

Catching a stray drip of red paint with her little finger, Maria wavered between anger and mollification and made her usual choice. "Ah, Yvonne, don't be like that. I'm talking from a position of complete ignorance here. I was just asking what it's like."

Yvonne's voice went lower, as she busied herself brushing dust off the piano. "It's not that it's not nice, it's that I'm scared. I don't trust those damn condoms, I've had one burst in me. When I had to take the Morning After in August, I threw up for a week, and I'm not going through that again."

"You could get a prescription for the Pill—"

"Cop on. I'm only seventeen; the doctor would tell my mother."

Maria put the brush down on an old newspaper and turned to Yvonne. "Then tell Petesy babe to go fuck himself."

"There's no need to be hostile when you barely know the guy."

"I think we need a cup of coffee."

Maria had never drunk so much coffee in her life; it was the fuel the Dramattic ran on. Each day hours slid by as she tinkered with tapes and silhouette filters up in the sound box. Galway and she enjoyed dissecting the character of every cast member in turn, using a mixture of Freudian terminology and gross generalisation about national characteristics. He was a good listener. The one thing he never seemed to do was look at her. Once she was wearing Jael's exotic purple eye shadow, and he never noticed; it was probably too dim in the sound box. She began to feel like a disembodied voice in the dark.

Of course every friendship had a certain element of what you had to call attraction. She didn't exactly fancy Galway, he wasn't her type. Not that she had a type, strictly speaking, but he was far too haggard and several inches too short to be it. There was just one time, near midnight after a rehearsal, when she came back for her gloves and found him up on the lighting tower, swinging from bar to bar like a demented Tarzan, and thought she might like to hold him.

"Maria," he called in a low voice when he noticed her standing in the shadows, and she ran up to the precarious structure he was straddling. "Could you possibly get that apple butt out of the way of my wheels?"

🖻

They sat round the fire swaddled in duvets, comparing flu symptoms. "My eyes are nearly too sore to read, even," complained Maria.

"Did you finish that book I lent you?" asked Ruth.

"Halfway through," said Maria, showing where the book-mark was. "I find it hard to get into short stories, even if they're well written."

Jael looked up from peering under the sofa. "Who's trying to convert her now?"

"It's good literature that happens to be by lesbian femi-nists."

"Brainwasher!"

"I asked to borrow it," Maria intervened. "I'd got *The Well of Loneliness* out of the library, but Ruth said it'd put anyone off."

"You're being recruited for the cause," said Jael ominously. "Next thing you know, she'll have you strapped to the kitchen table, showing you pictures of James Dean alternating with electric shocks." She took the poker from Ruth and started raking under the sofa with it.

"What are you at now?"

"I'm positive my tarot cards are under here somewhere. I want to tell Maria's fortune."

"Don't let her do it," Ruth warned Maria. "She hasn't a clue."

"Are you impeaching my psychic powers?" Jael sat up, red-faced.

"Psychic knickers," said Ruth, wrapping the duvet round her shoulders. "The tarot has to be studied for years to be properly understood."

"I use intuition, not some scholarly shit—"

"If you can't find the cards," Maria interrupted, "why do we have to fight about them now?"

Jael reached for the bottle on the rug. "Ruth's just ratty because she has to come out to five hundred strangers in an hour and a half."

"No, I'm not," snapped Ruth. "I've been looking forward to this debate all term."

"Another hot whisky?" Jael asked Maria. "I'm on my third, and you two are still hugging your first."

"I'm grand," she said, helping herself to another slice of lemon. "I prefer to stay with the pleasant buzz; if I have any more, I'll make a fool of myself."

Jael's eyes lit up. "Come on, let your hair down for once, it might be interesting."

"I've no hair to let down."

"What are you afraid of, Maria?"

She cradled the glass to her belly. "A hangover. And I want to be sober enough to understand the speeches tonight."

"You've got to take some risks in life." Jael reached over with the whisky bottle.

"I said no."

"Leave her alone." Ruth's tone was harsh, startling them both.

"She can look after herself, Mumsie," said Jael; "she's not the teenager you treat her as."

"Maria's got double your ration of maturity anyway," muttered Ruth, shutting her eyes and leaning back into the cushions.

"What about another little tot for you then, dotie?" Jael went on, poising the bottle over Ruth's head. "You're well past twenty-one and have never been known to mind making a fool of yourself." Getting no response, she stood up and stretched, knocking into the light bulb and making shadows waltz from wall to wall. She slung on her leather jacket. "I'm off in search of better drinking company. Ta-ra," she said as the door slammed.

Ruth's eyes stayed shut.

The fire was sinking into orange embers. As Maria watched, a turf briquette fell apart in perfect layers, like a wafer biscuit. The occasional bright flame grew from a bed of blue, licked itself, and slunk away. Her sore eyes watered, but she stayed there, looking until she could see every hairline crack along the glowing briquettes. Very little mattered, she thought, when she really looked at a fire; the day's collage of images was singed off her retina, and all her petty worries and indecisions baked away. Sharp voices were swallowed up in these lazy flames. There was nothing left but the pleasure of heat on the backs of hands, melting the eyes, the pleasure of orange flames going straight to the brain.

Ruth took a long, slightly ragged breath. Maria was alert again and reached for the radio dial, hoping that music would calm Ruth's nerves, but all she could find was strident rap. "You'll be grand," she told her.

"What? Oh, the debate, yes."

"I'll be in the front row, and I'll start clapping every time you dry up."

Ruth pulled herself upright and started a deep breathing exercise. "I never dry up."

"Touch wood."

"Don't be daft." But her hand reached out to pat the arm of the rocking chair. "You should stay in the bar till eight, you know; the reading of the minutes is so tedious." She stared into the fire. "All I'm afraid of is that the heckling might be so loud I'll forget the order of my points."

"Your points won't matter," said Maria, tidying up the lemon slices and glasses from the hearth. "People will be so impressed that you've got the guts to stand up there and say it."

Ruth smiled faintly. "What if I develop a sudden lisp? 'Ladieth and genthemen, I'm a lethbean.'"

"You can pretend lethbeans are a new oppressed minority who do it with kidney beans," said Maria, kneeling on the arm of the sofa. "What's the wording again?"

"That homosexuality is a blot on Irish society."

Maria got up again and twiddled the knob of the radio, looking for soothing jazz. "It'll be a doddle. That suede jacket of yours will stun them into silence."

"Maybe it's too dykey; I don't want to confirm their clichés. Maybe if I put the silk scarf back on?"

"Stop fretting, you look lovely." She clicked the radio off.

Ruth held her breath for a count of ten, then let it out slowly and noisily. "You never said what you thought of my picture."

"Which? Oh, is that the one you framed yesterday?" It was an old sepia photograph of three suffragettes with defiant expressions, their arms round one another's corsetted waists. "Where did you come across a treasure like that?"

"Mum's basement. Apparently the middle one's my great-aunt Lily."

Maria turned to consider the picture. "Does it have to be

stuck square in the middle of that dark wall, like pictures of ships always are in a B&B?"

A hiss from Ruth, pretending to be wounded. "I can only apologize for having no visual sense whatsoever."

"May I?"

Ruth gestured her toward the photograph.

"This other wall is best because it gets some natural light from the kitchen window. What if we put it here, so people can see it as they walk in? Two thirds of the way from the sideboard to the ceiling, I think; there, is that about eye level?"

Watching in admiration, Ruth asked, "How can you be so sure?"

"It just looks right. Doesn't it?"

"Yes, even I can see that. You're a genius. Though Jael would probably say that after a joint all the pictures look right."

"I think"—should she chance it?—"maybe you worry too much about what Jael would think."

"Oh, I'm not worried . . . " Her voice trailed off. "You're right, actually."

When Ruth had finished running through her speech notes one more time, Maria brought her a fresh cup of tea. On the saucer were poised two lemon puffs, for blood sugar. Maria thought Ruth could probably do with some distracting conversation too. "Had lunch with Galway today. I begin to think he's a little bit interested in me."

"Sounds lovely," said Ruth abstractedly.

"I mean the majority of guys in college are sexist louts, but Galway's all right."

The corners of Ruth's mouth twisted as she bit into a lemon puff. "Stop apologizing," she mumbled, "the race needs a few breeders to perpetuate itself. Anyway, to coin a cliché, some of my best friends are men."

"No, they're not," objected Maria.

"Well, colleagues; guys in my study group. We can have great arguments without anyone getting their feelings hurt. I just wouldn't want to go to bed with one."

Maria rocked precariously on the arm of the sofa.

"I'm a potential masochist anyway," Ruth went on lightly; "it's bad enough that I mammy the pair of you, but if I were with a man for a few weeks, I'd start washing his socks!"

"I've been meaning to ask you about that," said Maria penitently. "We seem to have got into a sort of rut, with you doing practically all of the cooking and housework. I keep meaning to make a rota, but I forget."

"Can you see Jael doing her share of a rota?"

"How could she not?" asked Maria, uncertain.

Leaning her head back onto a brocade cushion, Ruth explained. "In the first place, she'd claim the flat only needs a minimum amount of cleaning and that things like dusting are extras that I choose to waste my time on. And then she'd drag in her bad back—"

"Yeah, but it's one thing your lover exploiting you, and another thing your flatmate doing it," said Maria.

"Why is it all right to be exploited by a lover?" asked Ruth, her eyes shut.

"I didn't mean it was all right."

The flustered tone made Ruth look over. "I don't feel exploited, exactly; I was just pushing the point. That's what debaters do."

"But it's true, you put up with too much."

"The fact is, I only do about the same cooking and tidying as before you moved in, and you've taken over some of my jobs, like vacuuming and washing up."

Maria was a little comforted. "But I still don't see why we can't make Jael shift her lazy arse and do a bit of housework. I mean, you wear that 'No Means No' T-shirt to college all the time, but you're not much good at saying no once you come home."

"I know." Ruth rested her forehead on her hands. "But it's not that kind of relationship, with negotiations and promises and rotas. We're together as long as we both happen to want to be, and if I make life irksome to her, you know what'll happen?"

"No," Maria lied.

"She'll walk out the door. Just like she did this evening, only more permanently."

Maria's voice was almost a whisper. "Why do you assume she'd be the one to go?"

"Ah, open your eyes, woman. Because I love her more than she loves me." The hands gripped the head till the fingertips were lost in dark curls.

Failing to think of anything helpful to say, Maria asked, "Does that make you sad?"

"Not as sad as waking up on my own would." Her face emerged. "Don't worry about it. I do like cooking. Tell you what, you can clean out the oven from now on."

"It's a deal." The heartiness jarred on their ears.

Ruth studied her watch and rose, straightening her jacket. "Must be on my way, pet. See you there."

Maria reached up to push a wandering curl under Ruth's black cap.

5

The bar was filling up with stragglers from late dinner at the canteen. Fresh smoke hung like a rumpled curtain along the row of barstools.

"She didn't!"

"She did, I swear to god." Jael finished her whisky with a gulp and waved at the bartender for another. "It was one in the morning on a rather seedy street near King's Cross, and I heard something whack off the wall beside us. We hadn't been snogging or anything, just walking along arm in arm. Well the next thing I knew, Ruth spins around and hisses, 'Those bastards threw a stone at us!' Then she takes off down the street after them."

"Are you making this up?" asked Maria. "It sounds most unlike her."

"I'm telling you, Ruth can be a tiger, especially on behalf of someone else. Though the stone hadn't come within a yard of me. But off she goes hareing down the street like Christine Cagney. I was scared shitless."

"Did you go after her?"

Sheepish, Jael spun a beer mat. "There didn't seem much point, I was in really witchy new shoes, and my lungs can never keep up with hers. But I did yell after her to come back."

"So what did the men do?"

"Luckily they just hurled a few unoriginal dyke baits and disappeared into a pub. She screamed at them for a minute, then came striding back to me."

Maria was halfway down her new drink without realizing it. "So . . . were you proud of her?"

"Proud? The cretin could have got us knifed." Then, sipping her whisky, Jael added, "She's a tough cookie, is Ruth. Here's to her."

They clinked their glasses. Maria felt a slight unease; "How long have we been here, would you say? Do you think the speeches will have started?"

"No idea. Let's have another quick—"

"I'd better ask the bartender just in case."

It was twenty past eight. She rolled her eyes at Jael and made a dive for the door, wriggling through the smoky crowd.

By the time she made it to the lecture theatre, Ruth was back in her seat, with her note cards in a torn pile in her lap.

Maria stepped on several toes as she squeezed in beside her. "Did I miss it?" she whispered frantically. "I'm so sorry, I really am. I met Jael in the bar, and we forgot the time."

Ruth blew her nose. "It doesn't matter. Jael never comes to my debates."

"Yes, but I'm not her, and I meant to be here."

Ruth looked at her and let the corners of her mouth turn up.

"Were you brilliant?"

"It went all right. A Corkman called out, 'On a point of order: you are an abomination to God,' but that's routine."

"You brave creature. I wish I'd heard you. I had no idea we'd been gabbing that long in the bar." She added, "We were talking about you, if it's any consolation."

"Forget about it, it's no big deal." Ruth's hot hand covered Maria's for a moment. "Shh, listen to this one, she's a journalist."

After the debate, they looked for Jael in the bar, but she had disappeared. Shivering at the bus stop, they waited for the motionless number seven to open its doors. The sky had that tight-packed look that hinted at snow. Breath billowed momentarily into white speech bubbles from pale lips.

"Tell me, Maria," Ruth asked softly, "am I boring?"

"No," said Maria, startled. She tucked her gloved hands in her armpits for warmth. "Why do you ask?"

"I feel boring."

"Well, you never bore me." She hoped it sounded even half as true as it was.

Ruth leaned her head against the icy bus shelter. "I suppose I should rephrase my question then: Am I boring Jael?"

"I haven't noticed. Do you think you are?" Jogging on the stop to loosen her numb feet, Maria remembered. "At the flat this evening, she was just having a wee tantrum. Is that what you meant?"

"Oh, stop deflecting my questions, you sound like a god-damn cocounsellor." Then Ruth bumped her head against the glass. "Sorry."

"That's all right."

"I'm losing my grip on people. Like that audience tonight—I was saying the right things, even making them laugh, but I could tell I wasn't really touching them."

"Audiences are shits," said Maria. "If there was a barrier tonight, it was homophobia, that's all."

"It's not just audiences; I feel I'm losing my grip on every-body. Even you, if I keep droning on about how boring I am," she added wryly.

"How could you ever lose your grip on me? Remember, you're my mentor, cookery instructor, and mother figure, as well as lender-of-fivers-on-demand."

Ruth breathed heavily on the glass of the bus shelter, which fogged up against her mouth. "No need to pile it on, I feel old enough already."

"Ah, pet—" Maria wrestled with exasperation. "That mother figure stuff's just an old joke. The punch line is that you're all of twenty-four, remember?"

Drawing a stick figure on the clouded glass, Ruth nodded.

"Tell you what, I'll drop the jokes." Maria felt oddly shy, but pushed on. "The room feels warmer when you're in it, you know?"

Ruth turned; one eye was in shadow, the other glittered in the orange light. "That's about the nicest thing anyone's ever said to me."

Maria considered her shoes, then leaned out to scan the bus for signs of life.

"Just hope the room stays standing."

"What room?" Maria asked, rubbing her cheeks with the backs of her gloves.

"Never mind."

Maria yawned. "You're at your metaphors again, I can tell."

"It's a bad habit. You know who you remind me of, Maria? I've just worked it out."

"Greta Garbo?" she suggested, cupping her hands over her nose and blowing hot air into them.

"Myself, five years ago, when I was a minion in the Service. Wish I could get back to her. She was a tough girl, that Ruth was; excellent at saying no. Why didn't I have you for a friend back then?"

"Five years ago I was a twelve-year-old with a facial tic, so I wouldn't have been much use to you."

"Suppose not."

The cold started a shiver in the small of Maria's back, which spiralled to the top of her ears. She stared over at the motley collection of campus buildings. A huge crane was garlanded with red lights; it dipped over the muddy foundations of a new block like an emaciated mother bird. Acres of trees, broken only at the entrance to the dual carriageway, blotted the dark line of the horizon. No sign of another bus. Ten yards from the bus shelter the number seven sat motionless, its only light the pinprick of the driver's cigarette. Maria turned to share some flippant remark about the driver, but stopped when she saw Ruth's face. "Ah, pet, what's wrong?"

"Isn't it obvious?"

"It's hard to tell what's going on with you and Jael. Sometimes I hear you fighting, but then the next day you're all glowy."

"Oh, yes," said Ruth softly, "nothing like a good fuck for the complexion." Then, turning her face to the freezing glass, "Ignore me, Maria. Please, don't listen when I get like this. I'm not like this."

"But it—"

"This isn't me. I'm somewhere else."

Maria shut her mouth and turned back to look at the bus.

🔳

She knew Galway had something on his mind tonight, it was just a question of waiting for it to rise to the surface like a trout. He'd been abstracted all through the rehearsal, missing three lighting cues, even leaving the lead bishop standing in the orange glare of a swastika left over from last week's political comedy. A couple of times he glanced over to where she sat, moving the switches silkily up and down.

"Maria," in a voice that was meant to be flippant, "would you say I was attractive?"

She bent over the speakers to push in a plug, thinking rapidly. It seemed a rather vain opening to the conversation, but then again, all the books talked about the fragile male ego.

"Fairly attractive," she said, not wanting to betray too much enthusiasm. He finished his coffee in one gulp. "You're not going to believe this, but underneath this suave, confident exterior lurks a spineless amoeba."

"Amoebae are usually spineless, Galway. What are you on about?"

"Irishwomen, Maria."

She scratched an eyebrow. "What about them? I mean us?"

"Well, I can chat away to them as friends, but when it comes to the murky business of wooing, I seize up as if I had a ferret in my Levis. It all seemed so much easier in the States."

Maria swallowed hard. She mustn't laugh, it might put him off. Just then Jennifer called: "Hey, people, I know it's a drag, but could we go through the lights in Act Two one more time?" Maria cursed under her breath.

Half an hour later they were free to whisper again. "Go on with what you were saying," she encouraged Galway.

"Nah, it was nothing really."

"Go on," she said sternly.

"It's about Suzette."

"What is?"

"Do you think you could find out is she dating anyone or has she anyone in mind? I'd really love to ask her out, but I don't want to barge in if I'm not welcome."

Maria shut her eyes for a second. "Sure, I'll get talking to her at the next rehearsal." After a minute, she forced herself to add a jocular "Best of luck!"

"Take five," drawled the director from the shadows at the back of the stage.

Take a fucking hike, thought Maria.

🔄

Trailing out of her lecture on vectors the next day, Maria walked into Jael's hip.

"Aha, little girl, I was just looking for you. Come into the woods with the Wicked Witch of the West."

"What are you on about?" asked Maria blankly.

Jael grabbed her by the hand, despite her protests—girls didn't hold hands in broad daylight unless they were three vodkas over the limit—and tugged her over to the swing door. She brandished a black plastic bin liner: "Today I feel like picking holly for Yuletide, so what do I do, I look up a snotty little fresher's lecture timetable and turn up outside the door and kindly invite her to join me and she had better not say no."

"You're practically a fresher too."

"I am not," said Jael in outrage. "Repeating first year is quite a different thing."

"Well, I want some lunch first," Maria insisted, leading the way toward the canteen.

By the time they were settled with their trays—on the very

edge of the nonsmoking section, so Jael could catch just a whiff—Maria had stopped sulking. "If you don't want to be an eternal fresher," she asked, "do you intend passing your exams this time around?"

"What, you mean in June?" Jael considered the matter as if for the first time. "I might well. You never know."

"But you never do any work."

Jael smiled enigmatically, tucking the bin liner into her leather cummerbund. "It may look that way, but actually every time you see me playing my guitar, I am soaking up the atmosphere of Spanish literature."

"Right. And what about Hebrew?"

"Well, I might go live on a kibbutz between second and third year, so this year it's just a question of cramming some grammar, isn't it?"

"You're a terrible chancer." Maria's eyes strayed to the canteen windows, daubed with giant leering Santas and bow-legged reindeer, the work of the Art Society she had never gotten around to joining.

Jael began on her second banana. "Actually, Maria, I'm thinking of packing it in."

She stared. "But you could easily—"

"It's not that I'm afraid of the exams. I just can't see myself as a bobby-soxed coed anymore, you know? Maybe I better grow up and get a job."

"If that's what you want."

Jael finished her banana with a satisfied swallow. "Dublin is beginning to bore me out of my tiny mind again. Just between you and me, I was thinking I might try the States."

"When?"

"Sometime."

Maria's eyes were steely. "With Ruth or without her?"

Jael laid the banana skin carefully along her plate. "That'll depend more on her than on me. Lighten up, will you? This is just a vague contingency plan, in case things don't work out here in the long run."

Maria looked down at her plate of vegetarian spaghetti and attempted a forkful. She drew breath to speak, then let it out slowly.

Jael picked up a pear and asked, "What about you, are you happy here?"

"Fairly."

"What's up now—the transatlantic heartthrob?" Jael blocked her furious glance. "I know Ruth wasn't meant to tell me, but I can prise anything out of her during pillow talk."

"He's not a heartthrob, and he has no romantic interest in me," said Maria. "I just can't believe I nearly made a fool of myself for the second time this year."

"Did you want him a lot?"

Maria's exasperation mounted. "No, I keep telling you, what annoys me is that I fabricated the whole thing in my head. I was just looking for someone to fancy because that's what you're supposed to do."

"Don't force yourself," advised Jael, amused. "It's disruptive enough when it happens for real."

She looked down at her cooling dinner. "Galway's just my friend. He's a nice guy."

"There's a few of them around."

"Do you like men, yourself?"

Jael wrinkled her nose. "I don't like many people, and certainly not half the human race. Let's say I'm open-minded."

"Yes, but what I was wondering was, do you still actually—"

"Fuck 'em?"

Maria could feel the heat rising from her throat. "I didn't mean to be nosy."

Jael was triumphant. "Yes, you did. And yes, I have, and will no doubt again. Fuckum, fuckest, fuckarama."

"Could you keep your voice down just a little bit?" asked Maria despairingly. The seminarian from her tutorial was only two tables away.

"But in the meantime," Jael went on through a mouthful of pear, "it's good crack being a demon dyke. Just like half the other dykes I know, who are bisexual too but haven't the guts to admit it."

"So on a scale, are you like, fifty-fifty?"

She smiled ruefully as she licked pear juice off her thumb. "I don't know anyone who's fifty-fifty. Nah, my libido is more like a compass needle, swinging all over the place. For the past while it's been jammed at women, but I can't predict what it'll point at next."

"Phallic or what!"

"Point taken." They groaned simultaneously.

Out in the woody part of the campus, Jael ran round looking for mistletoe, her orange silk skirt snagging in brambles. Maria methodically snapped off bits of holly.

"Where's Ruth right now?" Maria asked suddenly.

"Dunno."

"Why didn't you invite her to pick holly?"

Jael shrugged. "She's probably in the middle of a feminist interpretation of the Black Death or something."

Maria busied herself with the holly, but the words bubbled up in spite of her. "She's not happy, you know."

The branch tore off in Jael's hand. "Since when did you qualify as a marriage guidance counsellor? I'm perfectly aware that Ruth isn't happy."

"And?"

"And people are responsible for their own emotions." The skin under the red fringe was paler than ever. "I'm not ecstatically happy either, but I still feel like picking holly."

"But maybe if you were nicer to her—"

"Niceness was never what Ruth chose me for." Jael shoved

leaves into the plastic bag. "Besides," she went on thought-fully, "she rather likes being unhappy. It gives her something to fill her diary with."

"Anyone would think you didn't give a shit about her."

Jael flung down her plastic bag and faced Maria. "How long have you been living with us now?"

"Two months. And a bit."

"And you still don't seem to have noticed that I love the woman."

"Well, then," said Maria sullenly.

"Well, what? In seventeen years, have you not copped on to the fact that love isn't enough, that it doesn't make every-thing hunky-dory?"

Maria looked away from the blazing eyes. They resumed their search. After five minutes, Maria was sufficiently uncomfortable to make the first overture. "Can't find any blasted holly berries."

"Me neither." Jael straightened up, supporting her back with her long hands.

"We could always cheat and use the reddish berries off that bush."

"You're my type of woman," said Jael. She plucked off sev-eral branches heavy with berries and carried them over to the bag. "Rather experimental gloves, aren't they?" she com-mented, taking Maria's hand between hers.

"The holes aren't part of the design, they're what hap-pened when I snipped off the yellow bobbles."

"Yellow bobbles?" Jael's eyebrows lifted.

"Christmas present from baby brothers," said Maria, tak-ing back her hand. "I didn't want to hurt their feelings by not wearing the gloves, but I couldn't bear the bobbles."

"The art of compromise. Not one I've ever learned."

"You're young yet," said Maria, dropping a holly leaf into Jael's collar.

🖪

"Yo, babes, I'm home." Maria clumped down the corridor to her room.

The voices in the living room trailed off. Ruth's head shot out through the beads. "You have a visitor," she said brightly. *Your aunt,* she mouthed.

"My what?" Maria hurried past her. "Thelma! What are you doing here? This is wonderful," she added unconvincingly.

"Oh, I was just zipping home after Christmas shopping in Grafton Street and I thought I'd pop in and deliver some season's greetings to my scholarly niece." Thelma nodded significantly at a beribboned box at her feet, then snuggled back into the rocking chair. "This is a nice place you girls have, I must say. Very bijou."

"I always think an open fire adds a touch of class." Jael's voice was so genteel it verged on parody. She was even sitting with her legs crossed at the ankle.

Maria's mind was rigid. "You'll stay for dinner, Thelma?"

Ruth caught her apologetic glance and murmured, "No problem, it's nearly ready."

Jael soothed all the visitor's protestations and engaged her in a conversation about the merits of solid-fuel central heating. Maria beckoned furtively from the door, and Ruth followed her down the corridor. "Mother of god, what'll we do?"

"Relax, Maria, she won't be taking fingerprints."

"No, but she mustn't find out. I mean she wouldn't—"

"I know exactly. The Womyn's Folk Festival poster is gone from the toilet, and as soon as she arrived I took the 'Dykes on Bikes' badge off the kitchen notice board."

"Bless you. What about the labrys painted on the window?"

"She's unlikely to know what it means, unless she's one

herself. You didn't, when you moved in," Ruth reminded her jokily.

"All you told me was that it was a goddamn Cretan axe."

The dark head dipped. "I know. I chickened out."

Maria could feel the sweat breaking out under her arms. "I'm sorry, I didn't mean to snap. Thelma's put me in a panic. She could have given me some warning, and I'd have worn a skirt."

Ruth nodded comfortingly and headed for the bead curtain. Halfway down the corridor, Maria grabbed her by the sleeve of her Aran jumper. "What's that they're talking about now?" she whispered.

"Travel in Eastern Europe, as far as I can tell."

"Please let Jael not say anything too outrageous."

"Relax, she can be a proper lady when she tries. Now get on in there and make conversation."

"Ruth?" Maria's voice was suddenly forlorn.

"I've got to check the lasagne, Maria."

"Yes, but I want to say I'm sorry. I mean, you having to take down your posters and stuff. It's not that I'm ashamed—"

"It's no big deal, honestly. I'm used to dedyking the flat whenever my mother comes to dinner."

"Ruth? If that's a box of chocolates she's brought me, you can have it."

Their hands touched, warm on cold.

🔢

"So the way I see it is, feminism has had its day. You girls have got the Pill and equal pay, so why do you have to keep rabbiting on about 'Ms.' and 'chairperson'?"

Maria murmured "Excuse me, be right back" to the stranger expounding at her elbow and went off to queue up outside the toilet. It would be a long wait; the guy inside occasionally responded to bangs on the door with "Give us three minutes" while his companion erupted into muffled giggles. Maria slumped against the wallpaper and examined a beer stain on the black satin waistcoat she had borrowed from Ruth. This would be the very last Dramatic piss-up she was ever getting dragged along to, she promised herself.

Snow White and the Seven Bishops had drawn to a triumphant close that night, despite the rumour that the bald guy snoring in the third row was the critic. Everybody who could claim to have been in any way involved had hitched a back-carrier ride to Jennifer's flat for the party. Maria enjoyed the first few hours of energetic dancing, but by one o'clock some loner had taken over the stereo to play his personal Leonard Cohen/Morrissey/Dylan mix; as the melancholy ballads droned on, a succession of incoherent boys waved their beer cans at Maria. In the corner Galway and Suzette were having what looked like a meaningful conversation. By half two they were holding hands; he caught Maria's eye and gave a victory sign.

At three she shared a taxi home with the couple who had finally emerged from the toilet; every time the guy touched his girlfriend's leg, she gave him a playful shove that impaled Maria's hip on the door handle. She comforted herself: With any luck Jael and Ruth would still be up and she could ask them what they wanted on their Christmas glasses.

But there was a barely legible scrawl on the back of a phone bill; she found it resting on the black velvet cap, which was draped over the teapot. "Gate-crashing slight acquaintance's party," it read. "Hope yours was fun. Excuse paper. XOXOX. R. (& J.)"

Maria felt unreasonably depressed. When ten minutes of ice-skating on a satellite channel had failed to snap her out of it, she got out the glass goblets and box of enamels and set to work. Jael and Ruth both being water signs, she contemplated a zodiac theme; since scorpions and crabs were beyond her technical grasp, it would have to be mermaids for them both. Jael's would be red, with big sensuous swirls of hair and serpentine tails. Maria was usually a perfectionist, but tonight she painted quickly, trying to make the ruby figures come alive. She stopped when the whole glass was swarming with mermaids, three elongated ones forming a spiral chain around the stem. The other glass, for Ruth, was more difficult. It was shiny black enamel, and the effect was sombre. The mermaids got smaller as her hand began to ache, until they looked more like octopi than women. Maria added a few strands of green seaweed around the base, then gave up and left them both on the windowsill to dry. She was damned if she was going to sit up all night slaving over a Christmas present they mightn't even like anyway.

After half an hour between the sheets Maria was still wide awake. The floor was cold underfoot as she padded into the kitchen. While the kettle boiled, she tried on Ruth's black cap, pulled smoothly over her tufting hair. Her reflection in the window startled her; the tight velvet halo made her face recede above the round collar of her nightshirt. She looked like a chaste pageboy, trotting through some seventeenth-century painting of a banquet. A wan smile failed to break the illusion, and she turned away.

Waiting for her cocoa to cool, blowing on its steamy surface, Maria paced up and down the corridor. If she looked through the bead curtain, she could see the glasses glinting on the dark sill of the kitchen window. The beads swayed and clicked in the night draught. She had no idea what to do next.

Finding herself at the door of the other bedroom, she took a strengthening sip of cocoa and turned the handle. There was nothing to see, of course—just the usual bare square of carpet around the futon, the same pale walls. The only rich colour in the room was the huge, battered wardrobe, which caught the light from the corridor and turned it mahogany red. Maria stepped delicately between an empty bowl and what seemed to be a fingerless glove. The carpet was restful on her bare soles. She set her cocoa mug on the window ledge and looked out on a clear view of empty offices, a jet descending toward the airport, and a giant crane silhouetted in fairy lights. Below, the street seemed deserted, except for the single red dot of a motorbike disappearing round the corner.

On her way out, the back of Maria's hand skimmed across the polished wood of the wardrobe, which was interrupted with scratches. She tried the intricate metal handle, half of which came off in her hand; as she was fitting it back into its hole, the door swung open. The first thing that billowed to meet her was a taffeta ball gown; she could not imagine which of them had ever worn it. Left must be Jael's side. Maria recognized her second-favourite leather jacket, and three pairs of jeans bunched up on a hanger with a cerise silk shirt draped angularly over them. Ruth's clothes took up roughly a third of the space; an occasional flash of cream or white broke the sweep of black shoulders. Shutting her eyes, Maria let her fingertips follow the clothes, hanger by hanger, trying to identify them by texture and the shape of a collar or elbow. After a run of heavy cottons and denims, her thumb fell on velvet and sank into it.

Crouched on the floor of the sturdy wardrobe, her head wrapped in hanging folds, she breathed in. That must be lavender—a sachet from Ruth's mother. A tang of stale smoke, definitely, and a whiff of boot polish from the Doc beside her bare knee. Something under her left foot—a strap or lace—was hurting. Maria reached out for the bottom edge of the heavy door and pulled it as far shut as she could without trapping her fingers. Now she was cloaked in darkness on four sides.

Something infinitely soft touched her cheek. She twitched away in fright, then turned back to find it with her lips, but it was gone. Whatever was cutting into her foot mellowed to a gentle ache. Perhaps ten minutes passed in this way, with her breath getting deeper and the slow boom of her heart the only sound. Then Maria reached under her nightshirt and touched herself for the first time since she could remember.

Eventually there was a small, familiar sound, like a bird pecking at a tree. The sound of a key in the front door. Maria lifted her head off her knees so fast that a heavy winter coat was pushed backward, and several hangers jangled in protest. She held her breath. The front door was shut, very gently. Footsteps at the top of the corridor. *Remember O Most Gracious Virgin Mary that never was it known that anyone who fled to thy protection, implored thy help or sought thy intercession . . .*

Footsteps in the kitchen. The gurgle of the tap, filling the kettle. Maria stopped praying, with a brief "ta" in the direction of the hangers. Bending low, she slid out of the wardrobe without too much disturbance and shut it softly behind her. She crept to the door. A moment later she was opening her own bedroom door loudly behind her and walking into the living room.

Ruth, alone, leaning against the fridge.

"Top o' the mornin' to ya," Maria said, too heartily.

"Want some tea?"

"I just came in for a glass of water."

They sat in companionable, exhausted silence.

"The cap looks wonderful on you."

Maria jumped, having forgotten she was wearing it. "Hope you don't mind, I just thought I'd try you on. I mean, it."

"Anytime."

She reached up for it, then, with a jolt, remembered; keeping her fragrant hand by her side, she used the other to pluck off the cap and hand it to Ruth. "Where's your bit of skirt then?"

Ruth grimaced obediently at the phrase. "Learning to lambada. She was enjoying the party more than I was, so I came on in a taxi."

"Are you all right, pet?"

"Mostly," said Ruth. Meeting Maria's eyes, she reassured her: "I'm waking up, that's all."

"Waking up, how?"

"You're the one who told me that it didn't matter how you got woken so long as you were awake," she reminded her slyly.

"Did I?"

"About coming to college."

"I don't remember. What a profound young thing I am, ey?"

Ruth threatened her with the dregs of her tea.

"It's no time to be waking up, woman; even the sea gulls have gone to sleep." Maria yawned.

"I'll go in a minute."

The tired words hung on the air like feathers, then zigzagged down to the ground. Maria emptied her glass of water into the sink and held her fingers under the tap. As she left she rested her cold hand on Ruth's bent head: "Sweet dreams."

Only when she was halfway down the corridor did she remember that neither Ruth nor Jael drank cocoa and that her mug was still on their windowsill.

🔄

"I asked Santa for a white Christmas, not a frigging freezing one," grumbled Jael as they bumped the tree up four flights of stairs to the flat. She stopped at the bottom of the last flight to suck her numb fingers, letting the tree sag against Maria, who was doubled over, coughing.

"Well, whose bright idea was it to wait till teatime on the twenty-third?" Ruth called from the door above them.

"That's when we'd pick up the last-minute bargains, you said. You're not telling me that misshapen monstrosity is all they had left?"

"This elegant nine-foot spruce fir," Maria panted as they heaved the tree through the doorway, "enhances the grandiose proportions of the Georgian tenement in which it is presently—what's the word?—erected."

"Ouah!" added Jael.

They disentangled the tree from the bead curtain and wedged it into a deep casserole dish with dictionaries and Spanish novels. "Its somewhat assymetric stance," continued Maria, brushing needles off her jumper, "symbolises the, shall we say, unusual bent of its owners."

By nine o'clock they had spotted the flat with wisps of holly and red crepe-paper bows. Jael had wounded her thumb on a spiky leaf; at intervals during dinner she sucked it and told stories about famous guitarists reputed to have lost digits to gangrene. They had intended to leave the presents lying decoratively under the tree, but when Jael produced a decent bottle of wine, Maria decided to give them their glasses. Ruth couldn't stop laughing as she compared them: "Jael's mermaids look like they're having an aquatic orgy, while mine are lining up for the Dance of Death."

"Yours are subtle," Maria protested. "You have to look hard at them."

"Whereas mine are crudely obvious, I suppose," added Jael, with a wink. She went to on propose a toast to "Maria Murphy, the only known flatmate who pays her rent in advance and never leaves visible hairs in the bath."

They had clubbed together to buy her a radio, as a more sociable alternative to her Walkman. She swallowed hard as she unwrapped it; Christmas always made her irritatingly sentimental.

Jael was already wearing her present from Ruth, a pair of

vicious-looking earrings in the shape of broomsticks. "I picked them myself," she confided to Maria. "They bring out the witch in me." She sent Ruth off to their room for her present; "It's under the futon in a classy green plastic bag," she explained, "but don't worry, it was dead cheap, probably off the back of a lorry."

Ruth reappeared a few minutes later in a little black wool dress; her smile was dubious.

"Gi's a twirl, madam!" shrieked Maria.

But Ruth sat straight down to her chocolate mousse. "You're trying to make either a femme fatale or a total fool of me," she said to Jael, "and I'm not sure which. But I like it. I think."

They played poker, badly and enjoyably, most of the night. "Winner gets to take Maria to her grad," announced Jael, and raised the bidding by twenty pence.

"No, she'd better take us both," called Ruth, going over to the fridge for more ice. "Two for the price of one, special offer while stocks last."

"I'm not going," said Maria, suddenly decisive.

"Yes, you are, and you're taking me," murmured Jael in her ear. "I look very nice in a tuxedo." Her breath smelled of whisky and chocolate. Maria elbowed her away; she looked up to find Ruth watching them.

Ruth sat down; she was moving so strangely tonight, coiled up in that dress. "Won't your mother be disappointed?"

"When?"

"About your grad."

"Oh, that." Maria felt serene. "My mother can stuff herself."

At half past five she remembered the roof. The landlord had admitted that the skylight had a pull-down ladder, and they had been waiting to try it out. Jael grabbed a handful of holly and a sweeping brush; Maria ran after her. "I'll be up in a minute," called Ruth from her room; "Just got to get out of these blasted heels."

The skylight resisted a few thumps from the brush, then creaked open, sprinkling rust down on them. A wave of cold air hit their flushed faces. Maria gasped as she climbed through the narrow hatch.

"It's the frost that's making me slip, not the whisky," explained Jael as she staggered along the dip between the roofs. She worked her way over the slates to the wall and started waving to the tiny figures getting into cars on the streets below.

Maria stood still. She craned her neck back to see the full bowl of luminous clouds, satellites and stars. Dizzy, she had the impression she might topple right off the building. Gradually she became aware of Jael standing just behind her, holding a strand of holly high in the air. "What's that for?" she asked.

"No mistletoe," said Jael briefly, and bent round to kiss her.

Later, trying to remember whether it was a short or a long kiss, an acceptable peck or a dangerous fusion, Maria had no idea. It was somehow balanced on the knife edge between these definitions when Ruth's head came through the skylight. In the second her eyes took to get used to the dark, they had lurched apart.

"Oh, sorry," said Ruth. The blank oval of her face disappeared down the hole.

They were mute, staring at the skylight; then Jael made a dash for the ladder. Maria could hear heavy footsteps in the corridor, Jael's muffled voice protesting, petering out, then silence.

It was getting colder, she thought, as she inched, one foot at a time, along the dip between the roofs and squatted down in a nook beside a chimney. Too cold for snow. She wondered whether there was snow on the mountains. She wondered what the hell had just happened.

Maria tried to fix her attention on the stars, then on the icy slates under her, but her head was whirling. Such a confused dread. Like when she was a child at mass, putting her tongue out for Holy Communion, and heard her own unspoken whisper of resistance: This is too much for me.

By six she was cold to the bone, her knees locked stiff. She would go for the half seven train home; Mam would be glad of the help at lunchtime. She waited for the first lick of dawn on the mountains, taupe and snowless.

Maria climbed down the ladder; her numb fingers lowered the skylight clumsily. The flat was hushed. Once in her room, she fumbled a few jumpers and jeans into her rucksack and tiptoed down the corridor. Better leave a note on the kitchen table so they wouldn't worry.

But when Maria reached the bead curtain, she realized that they were still there. She stood rigid, convinced that they would see her or hear her breathing, but the couple by the fire were oblivious to everything. All she could make out clearly in the red light was Ruth's face. Her head sagged back on the top of the sofa, and her face was a blank page. The folds of her new black dress were crumpled over her stomach; her legs were limp as a rag doll's. Jael was sprawled between them; all that could be seen of her was her long back and some copper waves of hair spilling over the lap of her lover. Maria watched, as if this dance, this coupling, was the key to the whole story. The bodies shifted together like a knot of seaweed.

It was not until Ruth's eyes opened, glittering straight at her across the room, that Maria backed away and slipped out the front door.

7

STIRRING

The train coughed its way to a halt at every tiny station between Dublin and home, but Maria barely noticed. She sat curled up in the corner of a smoky carriage, thawing out. After half an hour her fingers had uncurled, and she picked up a *Farmers Gazette* somebody had left behind on the seat. She found it impossible to concentrate on the print; her eyes skewed toward the pale orange fields framed in the rushing window. On page three a headline leapt into focus: "Homosexuality an Affliction Says Archbishop." She folded the paper in fours and tossed it onto the opposite seat.

At Limerick Junction she thought she spotted Ruth in a crowd on the next platform, but it turned out to be some skinny stranger. Ridiculous, anyway, because what would Ruth be doing in Limerick Junction? By now Jael would be bringing her breakfast in bed, no doubt. How would she explain last night, Maria wondered—a sociable peck on the cheek, perhaps, or a joke, a mock kiss staged between the two of them for a laugh. She would not put it past Jael to claim that Maria had started it. Not that it was long enough to start or finish; it could only have lasted half a second. All this fuss over a momentary contact of dry lips.

She leaned her elbow on the edge of the jolting window. God knew, she had never been more than friendly with that wretched woman. Painstakingly Maria ran the past three months like a film in her head, but it began rolling too fast for her to pick out more than the occasional detail. She had felt so at home in the flat. So absurdly safe. It had not crossed her mind that a woman might want to, well, kiss her. Her mind jerked through the weeks. It was undeniable that Jael's behaviour had been odd, sometimes intense and flirty, but that was just her way. Similar to the way friends had talked to Maria all her life; just schoolgirl humour.

There was Nuala, now that she came to think of it. On sunny days they used to bunk religion class and slip out the back field to lie in the long grass and eat Kola Kubes. The odd time Nuala's eyes might catch hers in a lingering stare, and Maria would wait, but then the pale eyes would drop, and the next remark was always banal. That was all—no scandal. Nuala had left in fifth year anyway. It was hardly fair on the girl to start interrogating her in retrospect.

Maria wove her way down five carriages to buy a plastic cup of coffee. As she was carrying it back to her own carriage, the train hiccuped and slammed her hip against the door. She felt nothing. In her mind she was taking off from the roof of the train. Her taloned heels thrust up from flat metal, kicking away rags of cloud, firing up into the icescape.

⑤

Her mother noticed her yawning over lunch and gave a disapproving glance. "It's the heat," said Maria to forestall any remarks about dissolute student life-styles. "The house is stifling, I don't know how you can bear it."

"Isn't it the only thing for your mother's arthritis," put in her father. The boys had legged it out straight after dessert to watch the circus on TV. What a boring little house.

Maria withdrew to her room, slid under the quilt, and put the most soporific pop music she could find on her Walkman. It did no good. She could neither drift into sleep nor wake out of this cotton-wool numbness. The savour of something cooking drifted in from the kitchen: mince tarts? Cursing under her breath, she sat up and changed the tape to Handel's *Messiah*. Hallayloo, hallay, hallaylooya ... After ten minutes Maria staggered up, stretched, and went into the kitchen for a mince tart. She passed her mother in the hall; even after shutting the kitchen door, she could hear the high-pitched phone voice.

"And what in Heaven's name is she going to do with it?" A hush. "Would she not think of adoption, for the good of ... no, of course, Thelma, it's her own decision. It was just a suggestion. And what about ... " A stifled sigh. "Not much help from that quarter, I imagine. Well, Alexandra has always gone her own way. I suppose we should be grateful. Thousands of Irish girls going over on the night boat every year, they say. Terrible."

Her tone brightened. "My own lassie? Came down early, this morning. Oh, the hair, yes indeed." And a cackle of laughter as she listened. "No word yet, but maybe she's shy of mentioning names. Oh, I'm sure. The studies seem to be going all right, though she's not killing herself with work. Is that the truth? Aren't they all. Still, so long as she keeps well and passes her exams. The laddibucks can wait!" Her voice spiralled up into laughter again.

The tart was dry in Maria's throat. For a moment she wanted to walk into the hall, take the receiver from her mother's hand, and batter her across the forehead with it. Instead, she went out the back door into the garden. The crooked bird table was still standing, half hidden by rhododendrons. Laddibucks, what a word; they were the least of her problems. Maria kicked a mildewed tennis ball down the side of the lawn.

⑤

Between mass and dinner on Christmas morning, while the uncles were discussing tax, Maria was handed a baby cousin to keep entertained. She quite enjoyed making obscene faces to disconcert it. She wondered idly, as she handed it back to its mother, what it would be like to be in Alexandra's situation, her body swelling with a creature of her own that she couldn't hand back to anyone. A quick shiver; she dropped the baby's rattle on the carpet and reached for the choked magazine rack.

Two quizzes for her in *Femme*: "Are You a Witch or a Wimp?" and "Know Your Passion I.Q." Turning to an article on fantasies, Maria read that, according to the latest survey, 10 percent of women imagined ("occasionally or frequently") having sex with animals, and 70 percent imagined it with other women. She slapped the magazine shut; why did she always happen across this kind of statistic? Sliding her eyelids down, she leaned her head back on the sofa, trying to conjure up the memory of that one wretched little kiss. It had happened so fast, she didn't have time to enjoy it or not. Well, yes, there had been a certain electric shock, like when a friend's hand might brush against hers by mistake. But it could by no stretch of the imagination be called a big deal. So why was she worrying herself sick about it?

She nodded abstractedly at an uncle who had turned to the women for confirmation of one of his more biting statements on V.A.T. The smell of dinner, heavy with sage, was seeping from the kitchen.

And if she did turn out to be that way inclined, Maria asked herself, for the sake of argument, what would she do then? She looked round at her family and relations, their plump indifferent faces, and imagined clearing her throat and beginning (in a rather Southside Dublin accent), "There's something I've been meaning to tell you ... " How their ruddy cheeks would cave in. It might be a perverse kind of fun, so long as she could spirit herself away on a magic carpet afterward.

Or was she underestimating them? Auntie Bronagh would probably be sharp enough to guess. Perhaps, Maria thought, with a chill settling into her stomach, even a kiss showed, no matter what your motivation had been. The kiss of a woman might leave some kind of mark, a twist in the curve of the mouth.

"Are you dreaming on us?"

Maria looked up guiltily. Her mother had come in from the kitchen with floury hands for a brief sit-down. "Read us out the horoscope there, pet."

She flicked through the pages and found it. "This one's yours, Mam: 'A financial bonanza in the near future, if you act cautiously.'" She turned to her own. "Aquarius, here's me. 'Your usually calm heart is invaded by a whirlwind romance this week. Let it happen.'" Her brothers sniggered, but Maria looked uneasily at the tiny sketch of the water-bearer, straining under the precarious load of two buckets. Then she turned to check the date: It was the July issue.

🔁

The steam rose in blue clouds, gleaming on the window. Maria let her shoulders sink into the scalding water, eased herself down until cold enamel touched the nape of her neck and made her jerk forward. The water stung her thighs. Maria liked her baths sinfully hot and with the light off.

Well, she had behaved like a normal, healthy young woman for four days now, and the strain was beginning to tell. Asking for second helpings of plum pudding, watching a repeat of *The Two Ronnies Christmas Special*, even going for a six-mile tramp in the coldest bloody fields in Ireland just to please her father. He liked birds. Maria herself could never tell the difference between a swallow and a sea gull, but mumbled "Look over there" and "Could be" convincingly enough. They had got back stiff and numb when tea was nearly over, and her mother had announced that Maria had a grand colour on her. Now she was thawing out in the bath, trying to plan her life.

One, find a new flatshare, staying with Thelma in the meantime. No doubt about it. The questions, the embarrassments of returning would be too much. She paused to imagine a flat without Ruth and Jael and shrank from the thought. Maybe she could loiter in the library sometimes to say hello. On with the list. Two, get seriously involved in theatre or something next term so she'd be too busy to mope. Three . . . she couldn't really think of a third resolution, but they had to go in threes. Work very hard to get honours in the exams, and go waitressing in London next summer? Not the most exciting New Year's resolutions, but practical. Oh, and cut down on the chocolate, of course.

The water streamed off Maria in rivulets as she stood up and clambered out of the bath. She dried herself slowly, wanting to delay the moment when she would have to turn on the light and emerge. She caught a glimpse of herself in the mirror; how very unlike the average "Nude Bathing" canvas. Well, maybe a bony Cézanne. Maria let her palm linger on her stomach. It looked strange, a hand on a belly. A bit purposeless. What if it wasn't her hand, but somebody else's? Her face caught only a few wavelets of light from the street outside, just on the sharp tip of her nose and the bulge of her chin. It seemed completely blank; pleasant enough, but forgettable. She tried to imagine someone wanting it, memorising its lines, watching out for it in a crowd, rushing down a busy street after her like the nerd in the perfume ad. Someone putting a hand on her shoulder, then realising with embarrassment that she was the wrong girl. And she would accept the apology so graciously; "I am afraid," she mouthed in a French way at her foggy reflection, "we do not know each other."

"Maria," her youngest brother bawled indistinctly from the kitchen.

She opened the door a crack. The draught raised goose pimples all down her arms.

"Mam says did you know there's a pair of letters for you and they've been sitting under the teapot all day."

She was into her dressing gown and down the stairs in half a minute. Dublin postmarks under the brown stains.

In case you haven't glanced to the end yet, this is me, Ruth. Hello, my dear Maria.

This is a letter because face-to-face I'd get too emotional. And also because your fluffy scalp is hundreds of miles away in some godforsaken village I can't even visualise.

None of this is likely to make much sense as I haven't slept since the night before last.

It's sort of like a stir-fry, that's the only way I can think of to describe it, don't laugh. I thought you could chop up lots of different vegetables and mix them in and raise the heat, and they'd all make each other taste better. It never occurred to me that ginger and fennel might clash.

Here I am waffling on, and this was meant to be a brief note.

You see, I had this theory that among women, possessiveness and jealousy needn't exist, that women could sort of share themselves out and, to use my awkward analogy, make each other taste better. Like, for example, a flat of three friends, two of whom happened to be lovers.

Well, you must admit it was a good idea, if a little naive.

I overestimated my capacity not to mind. I overestimated all of us. Jael means no harm—well, not much—but she's like a kid, you know, she has to have a little bit of whatever's going. The pull between us two is still there, but I think it might be going to smash us right through each other. Not that I'm blaming you, Maria. I realise now that you had no idea where we were heading. I should probably have done something at the start, offered some kind of earthquake warning, but what could I have said? I was afraid of seeming paranoid, one of these ghastly wifey types who goes into fits if her girlfriend even glances at anyone else.

Much the same kind of thing as I'm afraid of seeming in this let-ter! But things are a bit different now. Let's just say that I want to do the right thing—for everyone—it's just that I'm not sure what that is yet.

Will you be coming back to the flat? It's entirely up to you. I'm just so tired I couldn't give a shit.

What I mean is, Happy Christmas Maria.

Love (if you want it)

Ruth

Maria had sped through it too fast to take it all in; she was about to start again from the top when she remembered the second letter. It had no envelope, just a page folded up and stapled, postmarked the day after Ruth's.

M.

Apologies for ungentlemanlike behaviour. Stop. Have learned how to make Baked Alaska. Stop. Get your ass back here. Stop.

J.

🖪

The Dublin train was frantic on New Year's Eve; the burly man who sat beside Maria, gripping a bottle of champagne between his knees, had let it smash all over the floor of the carriage. He kept asking her did she think he'd have any chance of compensation because the driver had stopped the train so jerkily, or were they the crowd of crooks he'd always suspected?

Maria was noncommittal. She lifted her runners out of the fizzing puddle and turned her face into the corner of her seat.

A sojourn in Sea View Villa would be a wonderful rest; Yvonne's animated invitation over the crackling phone line had been exactly what she needed to hear. They could go clubbing tonight, then take it easy for a few days; stroll on the pebbled beach, bus into town for a look at the January sales. Her glam rags were all in the flat. Maybe she could slip in, to collect some clothes and books? Ruth would probably be over at her mother's, and Jael most likely out boozing. And if they were by any chance at home, well, she could manage a civil conversation, just "Happy New Year, see you round college next term, bye."

Maria couldn't have stuck another day at home, it was making her claustrophobic. Her mother had offered to teach her how to make choux pastry; she had to get away. At least Dublin was anonymous. She could avoid maudlin New Year's Eve thoughts by dancing herself numb in a strobe-lit nightclub.

"What would you say, carnations or chrysanthemums?"

She turned her head reluctantly.

The fretful man went on. "See, sorry to bother you, but I just wanted a female opinion. The blasted champagne was for proposing to her, my girlfriend, Frieda. I meant to do it tonight. But I don't have time now to get to an off-licence so I was thinking I could pick up some flowers at the station instead. They're not as romantic as champagne, but then, Frieda's not much of a drinker."

Maria was softened by his idiocy. "I'd go for white roses, if I were you. Just a few. That's if they have them."

The man was impressed. "I didn't even know they made white ones. Grew, I mean. So you think she'd prefer white to red?"

"I'm no expert," Maria assured him. She could just imagine some pragmatic Frieda turning up her nose at white roses. "I've never proposed to anyone."

"No, you wouldn't have—or only in a leap year," he said with a snigger. "It's us poor blokes who have to do the asking."

She shut her eyes and tried to concentrate on her plans again but lapsed into daydreams. Just imagine if somebody was waiting for her on the platform in Dublin with a bunch of white roses and a sheepish smile. "Name the day"—what a thrilling phrase, as if you could somehow stop time and tie a white satin bow around it, one day out of all the days in your life when a crowd of shiny faces would remind you how wonderful you were.

Maria shivered, wrapping her scarf more tightly round her throat. Even if she were happily married in five years' time, she thought, she still wouldn't feel a hundred percent normal. The flat's strangeness had rubbed off on her. She was branded.

⑤

Toiling up the last flight of stairs—Maria had forgotten how steep they were—she heard raucous laughter in the flat. A good sign; things must be patched up between them. Come on now, no chickening out. But as she slid her key into the front door and pushed it open, she heard a distinct "Oh, shit" from the kitchen. Jael hurried out, but when she saw who it was, her face lightened. "And it's the Virgin Maria in a rare appearance by public demand," she yelped.

Deciding not to be embarrassed, Maria carried her bag into the kitchen. The visitor, leaning against the table, was a thin woman with short black spiky hair; her tanned face warmed into a slight smile as she held up one hand in a gesture of welcome.

"Aren't you meant to say you've heard so much about her?" prompted Jael.

Making a face, "Must I?"

Jael, flurried, suddenly remembered her duties. "Oh, I forgot, Maria, this is Silk. She's just back from Greece."

"Are you the one who sent the postcard on Jael's birth-day?"

"I didn't know my communications were such big events," said Silk, looking up ironically at Jael, "but it's gratifying."

"Well, look," Jael began, and Silk moved toward the door, stretching her arms above her head as she pulled on her shabby black dinner jacket.

"Yes, I must be off," she said. "Mustn't risk running into her ladyship on the stairs. Listen, are you people partying tonight? ZZ's?"

"All depends on how persuadable Ruth is," said Jael doubtfully. "Keep an eye out for us anyway. It was good to see you."

"Been a while," Silk commented, and let herself out.

Left alone, they were suddenly awkward again. Maria launched into an apology: "I'm just picking up my stuff, I'm not actually staying. Yvonne's expecting me."

"Oh. Right."

"Well, I'd better—"

"Listen, about Silk, " interrupted Jael.

"Yes, by the way, where did she get her name?"

"I belive it was the pseudonym for a highly erotic haiku she got published in *The Pink Paper*."

"Mmm, that figures."

"What, that she's a dyke?"

"Well, not necessarily. Just that kind of person."

"What kind of person?"

"Oh, for god's sake," snapped Maria, "you know what I mean. I'm not labelling anybody, so don't get hot under the collar."

"I'm not getting hot under the collar." Jael stalked to the window and stared down at the street. "By the way, it might be as well if you didn't mention to Ruth that we had a visitor. They don't really get on."

"Why?" Maria was surprised at her own daring.

"Because I'm asking you not to. It would annoy her."

"No, but why don't they get on?"

"Because I've slept with them both." Jael turned, her voice iron. "OK? Is that what you wanted to hear? The prurient curiosity satisfied yet, Maria?"

She felt her face cave in. "I just wondered."

"You've been just wondering since you came into this flat three months ago," said Jael. "Do you think we haven't noticed the kind of games you've been playing? What do you think this is, feeding time at the zoo?"

"I have no idea what you're talking about." Maria's voice was shaking. "I think I'd better go," she added, moving toward the door.

Jael caught her by the elbow: "Don't act the fucking innocent." Her face was livid, six inches from Maria's. "If you want to know, ask."

"I don't want to know."

The grey crystal eyes were on the point of splintering. "Then why did you come back?"

"Not to take this kind of crap from you." Her own snarl astonished her.

Jael dropped her elbow.

"I came back to get my clothes. And to see Ruth. And to tell her I'm sorry if I've made her life any more difficult than you've already made it."

She let out a long breath. "I knew it. I had a feeling you'd overreact."

"What?"

"It was only a wee kiss. It's not like I raped you on the kitchen table, Maria. Mistletoe, you know? It's a tradition."

Maria's cheeks were scalding. "My reaction isn't the point."

"Well, Ruth's fine about it now, you know. She just pan-
icked a little at the time. It's been a sore spot, ever since Silk."

Anything to shift the spotlight from her own pinched lips.
"How did that happen?"

"We'd been friends for years; we just got a little carried
away one night in the summer when Ruth was in Majorca
with her mother."

"How did she find out?"

"I told her, of course," said Jael scornfully. "I may not be
the model monogamist, but I'm honest. And there was a
major brouhaha. And Silk told Patricia, who she'd been with
for five years, and they broke up."

"That's the Pat in the women's group?"

"You're catching on."

"Don't mock me," said Maria. "I understand enough."

"I doubt that." Jael was practically spitting. "You stand
there with your mouth all pursed up in disapproval of something you know fuck-all about."

"I just don't see why anyone would do a thing like that,"
said Maria wearily.

"What, a one-night stand? Don't knock it till you've tried
it. But then, maybe you're so sexless you wouldn't understand."

The front door was kicked open; Ruth stepped through the
curtain with a bale of turf briquettes and two brown-paper
bags of groceries. When she saw Maria she stopped short,
put everything down carefully and came over to give her a
hug. "Good to see you, pariah." They leaned into each other.

Jael swung out the door, muttering something about the
afternoon post.

When she heard the footsteps clatter down the stairs,
Maria gave Ruth a wan smile. "I'm only here to pack my
bags, I thought you'd both be out."

"Glad you're here."

Maria was disconcerted to feel tears behind her eyes. She picked up a bag of groceries to put away. After the baked beans and the orange juice, she was in control of her voice again. "Thanks for the letter; I didn't expect you to waste a stamp on me."

"Hey, don't start being soppy yet, we'll have enough of that at midnight."

"But I'm going clubbing with Yvonne."

"You're not!" Ruth giggled under her breath as she piled the fruit bowl high. "The social butterfly has got you in her clutches at last." Then, peering into the depths of the fridge, "You wouldn't consider staying with us tonight? You could ring Yvonne and explain."

Explain what, exactly? Playing for time, Maria straightened up the soup tins. "If you really wanted," she said at last.

"It doesn't matter what I want," said Ruth, folding the brown-paper bag and putting it in a drawer. She looked up and caught Maria rolling her eyes. "Sorry, did that sound rather masochistic?"

"Very."

"What I mean is, what I want depends on what you want. I think I need to ask now: Do you want to stay?"

Maria's hands went on picking spilled grapes out of the bottom of the bag. "What, here?" Surprised to find she knew the answer, she said in a rush, "I'd love to. If it were possible. If there were . . . room."

She could not read the expression in Ruth's brown eyes: amusement or disappointment or perhaps irony. The blurred look of a heavy sleeper when shaken awake on a winter morning. "Oh, there'll be plenty of room."

And the key rattled in the front door.

⑤

Over dinner, Maria recounted all the comic anecdotes she could wring out of her family Christmas. She even made up a few, in desperation; well, it would have been funny if that small cousin had thrown up all over her father's new cardigan.

Theirs had been quiet.

"Ruth spent Christmas Day with Mumsie," began Jael, "leaving me to douse my pudding in whisky all on my ownio. However, she did return to my bosom on Saint Stephen's Day, bearing a vegetarian 'turkey roll' that had all the texture and taste of an Aran jumper."

Ruth protested. "You stuffed your face with two thirds of the bloody thing."

"I did not," Jael informed her. "I chopped it into the sink-tidy while you were in the toilet."

Maria sneaked a glance at her watch; a quarter to ten. At this rate they'd never make it to midnight on speaking terms. "Listen, lads, I came up to go clubbing, so why don't we?"

Yvonne's number was engaged. "You can call her from a phone box on the way," said Jael brightly; she seemed determined to set off before Ruth could state any objection. In ten minutes they were dolled up and heading down the stairs.

"Where had you in mind?" asked Ruth, buttoning the cuff of her jacket as they halted at the bus stop.

Jael furrowed her forehead in concentration for a minute, then said, "What about, what was it called, ZZ's? It is still running, isn't it?"

A brief stare. "OK."

Maria's voice was uneasy. "Listen, what about me? I mean, I've no objections, but . . . "

"Don't worry," Ruth told her, "it's mixed. Lots of trendy straight couples go there too."

"Yeah, but I'm not a couple," said Maria coldly.

"We'll find you a nice boy to take home," Jael reassured her.

"I just don't want to feel totally out of place, that's all."

"Trust me, kid." Jael put on her Bogart voice. "I'll protect you from the big bad butches."

⑤

"Hello, who's calling, please?"

"Yvonne, can you hear me? It's Maria. Sorry, the music's deafening."

"If you don't mind my asking, where the hell are you?"

"I don't remember the name of it. I tried ringing you earlier, I'm terribly sorry."

"I was expecting you hours ago. My mother made Chicken Kiev."

"I'm so sorry. I dropped into the flat, and Jael and Ruth asked me to come out with them; apparently I'd arranged it before but I forgot. I can't let them down."

"Right."

"Yvonne? Don't hang up. Listen, can't you go on without me?"

"Who with?"

"Aren't you and Pete—"

"No."

"But I thought there was a crowd going. You said you knew the doorman at the Purple Snail."

"He's in Mexico. Oh, forget it. I don't care about tonight, there's a party I can gate-crash. It's just your attitude, Maria."

"What attitude?"

"You seem obsessed with these, these bloody flatmates of yours. And nobody else matters. Are normal people just too boring for you nowadays, is that it?"

"Yvonne, sorry to butt in, but I'm on my last twopence. Look, I'll ring you tomorrow, OK? OK?"

⑤

Jael clung to a lamppost, weeping with laughter. "So what did you say to her then?"

"Stop making fun of me. All I said was, 'Sorry, I don't have the time.'"

Jael leaned on a car and pounded the bonnet softly in time with her paroxyms. "That has to be the all-time conversation killer. A verbal chastity belt."

Ruth was walking ahead of them, but she glanced back and called "Get away from that car before you set the alarm off."

Ignoring the remark, Jael staggered after Maria. "'I don't have the time,' you told her. Jesus H. Christ!"

"Well, how the hell was I meant to know she was asking me to dance?" demanded Maria. "It's not every day of the week that strange women proposition me, you know."

"Me neither," said Jael regretfully.

"Yeah, well, I couldn't hear her properly, the music was far too loud. And she had no right to just presume I was that way inclined. You told me it was a mixed club."

"The only way she wanted you inclined was horizontally," shrieked Jael.

Maria gave her a shove and she tripped into the gutter, but it only brought on a fresh spasm of mirth. "The poor girl. The blank look on her face when you said you hadn't got the time . . . Not a bad looker either. Good ass."

"Just wish I'd never got that haircut," muttered Maria as they rounded the corner into Beldam Square.

Jael cast her a sly glance. "Nobody forced you."

Ruth had reached their building already and was fumbling with her keys. "Yoohoo, Valium," Jael carolled from halfway down the street. She ran along, doing figure-eights around parked cars, till she got to the door.

Maria came panting up behind. "What time is it now?" she asked hoarsely.

Ruth didn't answer, but Jael grabbed her wrist and read

aloud, "One-thirteen or thereabouts." Ruth twisted her arm away and headed up the stairs without turning on the light.

"She's cross because I called her Valium," explained Jael in a breathless whisper. "But it's the perfect name for her—she sends me to sleep and she's easy to take orally."

Maria gave her a cold stare. "One more dig like that," she whispered as they climbed, "and I swear I'll kick you down the stairs." As she caught up with Ruth her voice came back to normal. "So we missed the bells," she remarked regretfully. "I think I was in the toilet when they played 'Auld Lang Syne.'"

"They didn't play it," panted Jael from behind. "We got to shamble round in a chain to 'Aga-do-do-do' instead; there's modern Ireland for you."

By the time they reached their door, Maria was painfully aware of Ruth's silence. She scanned her mind for something to say that would make them all relax. "What are your New Year's resolutions, ladies?" she inquired.

Jael flung herself into the rocking chair and reached down for her whisky bottle. "I'm giving up women," she announced. "They're too fucking complicated. And what about you, light of my life?" she asked, turning, but Ruth had already disappeared down the corridor. Jael tucked her feet under her and began to rock the chair.

Maria avoided her glance. Then, summoning courage, she asked in a low voice, "Why are you being like this?"

"It don' matter how ah be." Jael accompanied her twang on an imaginary banjo.

"Would you stop play-acting for one minute."

"The bag is packed. It's beyond mattering how I behave."

Maria looked at her warily. "What bag?"

Jael's mouth spoke from between her hands. "Mrs. Johnson's hand-me-down leather suitcase. It's half full and hidden in the back of the wardrobe."

A long silence. "Maybe if you—"

"I'm damned," Jael told her distinctly, "if I'm going to play at being nice for an evening to beg her back."

Maria's exasperation boiled over. "I've never met anyone so full of herself. Listen, you wouldn't have to be nice—we could hardly expect that of you. All you'd have to do is tell her how you really feel."

"Shit, that's how I feel. Absolute scum." Jael splashed more whisky into her glass.

"I don't mean how you're feeling, I mean how you love her."

No answer. Jael looked at her over the top of the glass. Finally: "What if I can't remember how I feel?"

She forced her fury into a whisper. "It's such . . . waste. I don't believe you're about to lose the best thing in your life because you can't humble yourself enough to say three words."

"Ah, Maria." Jael's voice was oddly compassionate. "We're gone a bit beyond that now."

Maria slashed through the bead curtain. Ruth's door was shut. She stood outside, her fingers against the wood, waiting for the right words to come. Not a sound from behind the door. What was she expecting—a sob, breaking glass, the snapping strings of a guitar?

Her thoughts were interrupted by a flush, and suddenly Ruth was behind her, toothbrush in hand.

"Hi," said Maria, her back to the door.

"Did you want something?" Ruth's voice was barely audible.

Light caught the wet bristle of the toothbrush. Maria stared at it stupidly. "Just to say good night."

"Sweet dreams, Maria." Ruth shut the door behind her.

Maria lay in bed awhile, vaguely aware of the strains of "Auld Lang Syne" leaking from the kitchen in Jael's hoarse contralto. The night was safe at last. Probably. All those sharp words would evaporate with the dew, and she would make her flatmates pancakes for breakfast. Out of the corner of her eye she noticed her Dietrich poster hanging awry from one drawing pin; the whites of the eyes glimmered in the street light.

By the time she woke again the house was silent. Maria lay inert, flexing her stiff neck. When her door creaked open slowly, she blinked, then squeezed her eyes shut. It was Ruth; she had made out her silhouette in the dark. Nothing happened for a full minute. Maria knew she was being looked at and let her mouth hang slightly open. Finally Ruth's voice came out of the black. "Are you awake?"

Go away. Maria was dead. She was limp like a tracker who didn't want to be eaten by the bear. Go away.

After a few seconds she heard the rustle of paper, then a murmur of words that she could not distinguish; it could have been "Good luck." The door closed. She waited till the front door thudded shut too, then sat up; maybe there would be a note. But it was a brown-paper bag, propped on the end of the bed. Inside was nothing but the black cap, no message. Maria slid down in bed and pulled it over her face. The worn velvet was warm and utterly dark.

8

SERVING

Maria was woken at half seven by the sensation of a boulder on her chest. She sat up and took a deep, ragged breath. The night before began to run, image by image, through her head. She lay down flat again.

Reading *The Radio Times Special Seasonal Edition* cover to cover killed a couple of hours. At around ten her stomach began to protest in a series of creaks she was sure could be heard through the walls. Besides, skulking in bed was an adolescent strategy. She pulled on her jeans and limpest jumper and plodded down to the kitchen.

Jael was ensconced on the sofa in her duvet. Surely people only slept on the sofa in Hollywood comedies? But then again, Jael was capable of any histrionic gesture. Unless it was Ruth who put the duvet over her. Was she still asleep? Yes, snoring prettily, and just look at the ashtray full of crushed butts beside her. Back on the fags; Ruth must be gone for good, so. Maria decided not to think about that yet. She leaned over the sleeping face; the soft lines around Jael's eyes and mouth were beginning to show her age. Without the vitality she had when awake, her face looked slack, nearly vulnerable.

After a civilised breakfast of juice and granola, Maria still felt empty. To hell with civilisation. The furious hiss of a frying pan woke Jael; she sat up, sneezed twice, pulled on her orange kimono, and asked for a sausage. They ate wordlessly, swapping sections of last Sunday's newspaper. Over the washing up, Maria remarked that she had better head over to Yvonne's.

"Thought you had a bust-up on the phone last night."

"Lord, yes, I'd forgotten all about it. I could ring and grovel, I suppose."

"Is it worth it?" Jael's mouth was curved ironically.

"No," said Maria, suddenly decisive. "Well, I'll give Thelma a ring then."

Jael flicked through the last pages of the sports supplement. "I gather you're looking for a new abode?"

"I'd better." Maria willed her embarrassment away.

"You'd do as well to hang on here for a few days, you know, till you find somewhere. Unless you want to go home again."

"No way." She felt cornered. "Well, I suppose if the next rent isn't due till, what is it, the fifth?"

Jael looked up, her eyes grey as feathers. "Maria, the rent doesn't matter; stay as long as you want."

"Thank you," said Maria stiffly. Then, repentant—hadn't the woman lost enough?—she offered to do a sketch of Jael in her kimono. They lit the fire because it was such a cold, miserable morning and Jael thought firelight might hide her double chin.

"Let's have a peek?" she kept asking, till Maria threatened to tear it up.

"I warn you, it'll be no good. I've only got lined paper, and the pencil's too soft."

"Never mind. Use your imagination. Give me bigger tits."

Maria ignored her, concentrating on the proportion of

limbs. It felt like a Sunday; slightly too warm, with the smell of sausages fading from the air. After ten minutes Jael complained of being bored, so Maria dumped *Don Quixote* and a fresh pack of cigarettes into her lap. She sketched on, wanting to catch the likeness, but the drawing got more and more heavy, latticed with pencil strokes.

The flat was silent except for the lick of the flames. Jael dropped a casual comment about Maria's hair getting curly, but Maria spent so long wondering whether it was a criticism or a compliment that she forgot to respond.

Finally she handed the sketch over with a regretful grimace. Jael was impressed: "Ugly as sin, but very like me."

"Really? People don't usually see their own likeness."

Jael considered, turning it to one side, then upside down. "All I can say is, it looks just like me in the mirror after a hard night's carousing."

"You can keep it if you like."

"Don't you want it?"

Maria tripped over the words. "Well, yes, if you don't, but if you do, I don't."

Jael smiled like a cat. "We can photocopy it." She tossed it back, but a draught caught it and nearly sucked it into the fire. Maria whipped out her hand, then put it back in her lap. Laughing under her breath, Jael rescued it with the tongs, only one corner singed.

⑤

Lulled by the tug of the train, thin winter light in her eyes, she felt as if last night had never happened. She looked across at Jael and could not turn her bruised sense of loss into angry words. It was almost impossible to hold Jael responsible for anything; the redheaded child drawing faces on the dusty window seemed to have nothing in common with the virago of the night before.

Jael wiped her finger on her sleeve and shivered vigorously. "I could get hypothermia," she remarked, chafing her ankles. "What a way to go, eh?"

"Take your muddy boots off the seat."

"Yes, Mammy."

"You've done nothing but whinge since we left home; this outing was your idea, remember?"

Jael stuck her lower lip out. "Didn't realise Dublin Transport was using its passengers as guinea pigs for refrigeration technology, that's all. Are we nearly there?"

"Two more stops, then it's Bray," said Maria. "There's the sea out the other window."

"Looks wicked. Grey and hungry."

"Shut up."

They had walked halfway down the blue peeling promenade when a wave lurched over the stones and soaked them to the shins. "I'm cold and wet and I want a bag of chips," announced Jael. "Steaming hot with lashings of vinegar."

"Bad for your digestion."

"The stress of doing without would be infinitely worse for it."

Ten minutes later they were following the cobbled path up the hill. "You been up Bray Head before, Maria?" said Jael rather muffledly.

"Never."

"It's the most piddling of mountains, but the view over Dublin is good." She tossed a chip to a low-swooping gull, who caught it. "I came here first on a Girl Guide mystery hike at the age of eleven."

"Was it fun?'"

"Up to the point where I gave Angela Cowley a playful shove and she rolled down the hill and broke her collarbone."

"You're taking the piss."

"I am not. I was suspended from Guides for six weeks for

unladylike violence." Jael bit a chip neatly in half.

Shaking her head, Maria led the way up through the bracken. Her breathing grew harsher; after five minutes she leaned her back against a head-high boulder and looked out over the bay. "What's that kidney-shaped island?"

"Haven't a clue," said Jael, scrunching the greasy paper bag into a ball and rolling it down the rock.

"Litterbug! Ruth'll—" She stopped herself, and the wind carried off her words.

"Mind yourself here, the pine needles are slippy." Jael, one arm around a tree, offered Maria the other hand. They pulled themselves up through the steep wood, lunging from one tree to the next.

"Is it far?" asked Maria glumly. "I think I've got a splinter in my palm."

"Just the big cairn to go now. See the cross?"

They scrambled on all fours over the hillock of rounded boulders and landed on the granite base of the huge stone cross. Maria took a painful gulp of the pineapple juice, then passed it over.

Jael retained her hand and turned it upward. "That's not a splinter, it's just a scratch. Should I kiss it better?"

Suddenly chilly, Maria pulled her hand back. She craned upward. "Why is there a U2 T-shirt on the top of the cross?"

"In case God gets cold," said Jael succinctly, biting into her apple.

The sun edged out from behind a muddy cloud, and the hill began to glint violet and copper. Maria glanced at Jael, pale-faced and eyes closed, leaning back against the granite. She leaned closer. "Is that a scar there, just on your hairline?"

Jael rubbed her left temple with her thumb. "Have you never noticed my fractured skull before?"

"Yer wha'?"

"I was knocked off my bike when I was nine."

Maria was impressed. "I hope you sued the driver."

A reminiscent grin spread over Jael's face. "My parents settled out of court for a hundred and fifty, which was megabucks at the time. I spent the money later on a portable television." She started to chuckle and went on: "What none of them knew was that my brakes were cut."

"What do you mean, cut?"

"It was a sort of game. I was spending the summer with my gran in Killiney, and on the first day of my holidays I cut my brake cords with the garden scissors. Every now and then I'd dare myself to ride down Killiney Hill."

Maria was not smiling. "You maniac. You could have been killed."

"That was the fun of it."

"Did nobody check your brakes after the accident?"

Jael shook her shining fringe out of her face. "I remember when I woke up from my coma—"

"You were in a coma?"

"Well, state of unconsciousness, whatever, anyway I woke up with a blinding headache, and the first thought that struck me was, they'll have found the brakes cut and I'm going to get lynched. But luckily the poor guy's car had flattened my bike, so I got nothing but sympathy."

"And cash. You're a fundamentally dishonest person, do you know that?"

"That's me." Jael nibbled her apple.

Maria was watching the sky. "Is that a hang-glider, that red thing? I'd like to do that once before I die."

"Better get moving then."

"No, seriously. I dream about it all the time. Only I'd never have the nerve."

"How can you tell?" Jael stretched her arm back and hurled her apple butt over the cross.

"I know myself. When the time came for jumping off the

mountain, I'd start crying and beg to be untied."

"You underestimate yourself." Jael stood up, tall against the skyline, flapping her hands to restore circulation. "Hey, let's go back along the cliff path. I love watching the trains rumble past two hundred feet below."

"It looks a bit crumbly," Maria mentioned as they waded through deep heather to the barely visible path.

"Just a little." They flattened themselves to the rock to let a party of German backpackers go by.

"Jael, you promise you won't even threaten to give me one of your playful shoves?"

She turned with a look of injured innocence. "Would I do a thing like that?"

🔲

"What's for dinner?" Jael stretched her feet toward the fire, yawning.

Maria looked blank. "Are you hungry already? Suppose we could heat up something out of a tin." The flat smelt empty already, and Ruth was gone only a day.

"Why don't I nip down for a takeaway?" Jael shot off, refusing to let Maria look for her purse.

Six o'clock, and already the night was closing in. The window was a black square; not a star in sight, the smog blotted them all out. She would lie flat on her bed for twenty minutes. What was the yogic formula Ruth was always quoting? Ten minutes of deep relaxation was equivalent to three hours' sleep. Maria peered down at her toes, wondering if they were deeply relaxed; she couldn't feel them, but that might be the cold. She felt an itch on her sole and sat up to scratch it.

In the bathroom the fluorescent bulb was flickering; she turned it off and splashed her face with cold water. The white outlines in the mirror looked lopsided. The front door slammed.

"Maria? Where are you?" came the call, almost plaintive. For god's sake, she thought, where could she be hidden in a four-room flat? Rummaging in the cupboard for the hand cream, she knocked over a clutter of bottles and cursed softly. Snapping on the light again, she stooped to pick them up, and her eyes were caught by a label. "Jael?"

"What?"

"Whose is the henna?"

"Who the whatsit?" Her face appeared round the side of the door.

"Rich Russet Henna Highlights," Maria read out accusingly.

"Mine," said Jael placidly.

"You mean it's not real, your hair?"

"It's real, all right."

"No, I mean natural." Maria pursued her down the corridor.

"What's natural?" asked Jael, setting down plates on the rug beside the sleepy fire.

"I thought you were a real redhead." Maria's voice was stony.

Jael looked up from the cartons, wide-eyed. "Last year my hair was brown, this year it's red. Red's about as real as I come, Maria."

"Will I ever get a straight answer from you?"

"Eat your curry." Jael sat cross-legged and poured herself a tumbler of whisky. "Are you partaking?"

Maria settled herself. "Afraid not, I'm still unsophisticated enough to prefer tap water."

Jael shook her head in exasperation. "You've got such hang-ups!" she commented. "Like, what's with this sophistication business?"

"I don't want to be ultrasophis, like the kind of person it's hard to eat spaghetti in front of. Just sort of airily adult."

"Best ad for whisky I ever heard. Doesn't make me feel airily anything. More like earthily irresponsible." Then, after a minute, wonderingly, "I never found it hard to eat spaghetti in front of anyone, not even when I was seventeen."

"Maybe it's character, then, not age."

"You could lay off my age once in a while."

"I mean it as a compliment. What I need," said Maria through a mouthful of rice, "is for an experienced woman like yourself to write me out a little guide to life."

"You sure you want to end up like me? A lonely, middle-aged dyke, slugging unsophisticated whisky?"

Maria stared over her poised fork. "Are you lonely?"

"Not yet," Jael admitted, slightly sheepish, "but give me a few days."

"You should be." Maria let the words hang between them, without qualification.

They were silent, finishing off the curry. "But that sketch you did this morning," Jael remarked, as if continuing an unheard conversation, "it was actually good. You're lucky to be one of those people who can make things."

"What do you mean?" she asked, looking up from her plate.

"You're an achiever, a go-ahead person. Whereas I can only go other directions," said Jael with a faint smirk.

"What don't you achieve?"

"Ah, you know. Pictures, meals, college degrees, that sort of shit. I drift through existence just using things, never making any."

Maria was sceptical. "Since when have you passionately wanted any of those things?"

"Oh, I don't really. Just sometimes it seems a rather unproductive three decades." As Jael reached down the side of the sofa cushion to retrieve her lighter, a smile flickered across her face.

"What have you found, a half-eaten Yorkie?"

Jael brandished a fistful of crumpled black cards. "My tarot pack! You're in for it tonight."

"I don't think I want to know my future," said Maria doubtfully, but Jael was busy fishing cards out from under the cushion.

"Well, I do. Here," she ordered, splaying the deck to a broad fan on the hearth rug, "gimme three for your recent past, three for your present, and three for your recent future."

"How can a future be recent?"

"Oh, shut up, Maria. Short-term future, then."

She picked out nine cards, her hands shaking. "This is creepy. What if I get Death?"

"The death card only means a major trauma or loss," Jael reassured her. Snatching the thin pile from Maria, she laid them face up in three tiers and leaned over them, peering at the pictures. "OK, let's go."

"Hang on—"

Jael looked up in exasperation. "What is it now?"

"Surely they're a completely random selection?"

"Believe me, your subconscious was telling your hand which to pick. It's all fated. Now, which do you want, a lecture on occult theory or your own story?"

"My story."

Jael propped herself up on one elbow, perusing the cards. "OK. In the recent past we have the nine of swords, for guilt, nightmares, and a general heap o' shit. Beside it is the seven, which means secrecy and discretion, or quarrels with friends. Then the High Priestess—I love this card, look at the white flowers falling out of her dress."

"What does she stand for?" Maria picked the card up for a closer look.

"More secrets. She's Persephone, emerging with hidden knowledge from your psychic underworld."

Maria failed to stifle a snort. "So, cutting through the jargon, my recent past is about the exposure of a guilty secret. Mine or someone else's?"

Jael shrugged; "It doesn't say. Now your present: First is the Moon, for uncertainty and fickleness. See her three faces? She stands for someone you can't trust—again, maybe yourself. In the middle we have the Fool, which is about risk. The Fool has come out of the safe cave and is dancing on the cliff edge. Then—oh, I like this one—the Tower. That's about the breaking down of convention—a lightning bolt smashing your fortress. It can also mean punishment."

"Are you making this up off the top of your head?" Maria inquired.

Jael turned her face with a look of genuine hurt. "Why do you say that?"

"It's just that I was flicking through a book on the tarot in the college library the other day, and I distinctly remember that the Tower meant divine inspiration."

"They mean lots of things," said Jael coldly. "It's not a mathematical formula. I'm the reader, so I'm using my intuition to pick the interpretations that fit this pattern. And I don't think divine inspiration has a place in your story."

"Go on, I'm only slagging. So what's my present again?"

"You're uncertain about taking a risk," Jael summarised smoothly, "and it involves being unconventional, and maybe getting punished."

"And the future?"

"Well, this just covers the next few months . . . Aha, here's something spicy. Two of cups, the beginning of a relationship, blind young love." She put her head back to laugh. "And look what's beside it, the five of wands—marriage or alliance with a wealthy or powerful woman."

"What's that last one?" Maria picked up the Wheel of Fortune and looked at it from several angles.

"That's easy, read it yourself."

"I can't." She tossed it into Jael's lap.

"Just look at the little people tied to the rim, being spun round like ball bearings. Bet they feel nauseated."

"So that's what it means—nausea?"

"It's a change in your fortune—something big that just happens to you, and you feel you've no choice in the matter."

Maria yawned. "Well, the only wealthy woman I know is Yvonne's mother, and she's already hitched."

"Does the rest of the reading make any sense to you?"

"Bits," said Maria. She neatened the lines of the cards. Then a thought struck her. "Hey, hang on, didn't you deal them out from the top down? Then weren't the top three, not the bottom three, the ones I picked for my past?"

"Don't remember." Jael was building a house of cards.

Maria stared at her. "But that means the affair has already been and gone, and I'm in the uncertainty at the moment, so all the nightmares and secrets are yet to come?"

"You never know."

She glared. "You're after telling my story backward."

Jael nudged the bottom card to one side and watched the structure topple. "There's no one way to tell a story. You take all the elements and rearrange them to suit yourself; my version is as good as any." She began laying out the cards for a game of patience.

"You're a chancer, you know that?" Maria gave up and leaned back on the edge of the sofa. Her eyes were hypnotised by the fire, the room dwindling to a small red tongue. The coal was burning well; she wondered whether they had remembered to try out that new smokeless fuel over Christmas. She turned to Jael, who was motionless, staring back at her, a card between finger and thumb. They both drew breath, then stopped.

"Go ahead," said Jael.

"No, it was only something about coal," said Maria, then giggled, because it sounded such an unlikely topic of conversation. "No, seriously, it was nothing. What were you going to say?"

Jael tossed down the cards and squeezed out the words. "I think it's time to tell you—"

"No." The words moved before her brain did.

Faintly pink, Jael asked, "No what? Did I ask you a question?"

"Sorry. My mistake," said Maria.

"But what did you say no to?"

"I thought there was something you were going to ask," said Maria.

"Like what?" Jael's voice was innocent. "What would I have asked?"

"Can we drop the subject?"

"Too late for that."

"Oh, go on, then," said Maria testily. Please no, please let her have guessed wrong.

Jael made her wait. She poured herself another trickle of golden whisky. "What I wanted to say," she murmured at last, "is that I want you."

A great weariness came over Maria. She longed to lie down on the coach and sleep for a hundred years. "I thought it might be that," she said. Then, the silence stiffening between them, she added, "Since when?"

"Since now." Jael's eyes were glowing in the firelight.

Maria avoided them. Stirring herself to anger, she went on. "Twenty hours is your idea of a decent interval, is it?"

"I have been waiting quite a while," she said in her most gentle tone.

"It wouldn't be worth the wait," Maria protested.

Instead of the expected denial, Jael said bluntly, "I don't care what it's like, I just want you." To make matters worse, she slid over beside Maria and put her arm around her. Maria was furious to find herself dissolving into tears like the worst of Hollywood heroines, but it was unstoppable. No one had ever put a hand on the back of her neck like that. Gulping, she leaned against Jael's warm frame.

"Feeling better?" asked Jael gently when the sobs had lulled. She started running her fingers through Maria's feathery hair, cutting little jungle paths of sensation.

It would be so easy, thought Maria, to let her take over from here. For several long seconds she considered that option and let the sharp fingers bring her scalp alive. "No," she said at last, barely loud enough to hear. The fingers slowed. She cleared her throat and stared into the coals. "I wish I knew what you see in me to want. You're the first person who's ever looked at me like that, like I was worth looking at."

The fingers burrowed deeper, taking a warm hold of her head. "I'm sure there've been others you never noticed, because they were less crude and obvious."

Maria grinned sadly. "Well, I'm grateful. But the answer is still no. You should have realised that it couldn't happen," she hurried on, gaining conviction. "You know I'm not—"

Jael's voice was shaking with vehemence. "You don't know what you are."

"Don't patronise me." She shook her head free of Jael's hand.

"Maria, I've watched you for three months. You've changed under my eyes, you've come so far. You can't be too afraid to jump off the mountain."

"It's not fear, you stupid woman. I couldn't care less whether I turn out to be a lesbian or whatever." Maria blinked up at her in exasperation. "I just don't want to go to bed with you. This isn't the right mountain for me to jump off."

Jael's mouth twisted up at one corner. "I don't believe you feel nothing for me."

"I care about you. I don't trust you as far as I could throw you. Which wouldn't be far."

"So you don't actually want me at all?"

Jael's lips were so close, the sound reverberated in her ear, and the scorch of breath made her shiver. "Yes, a bit."

"Which bit?" Her lips met on Maria's cheekbone, then landed lightly an inch below and slid downward. Tiny hairs came alive as they passed. The lips paused, just to the side of her mouth.

"All right, quite a lot, to be honest." Maria's mouth was itching to turn into the kiss. All at once she angled her head away, so the lips brushed her ear and were gone. "But not enough," she told the hearth rug.

Jael sat back and crossed her legs.

Maria took this opportunity to fumble for a tissue and blow her nose. She hoped it would have the side effect of making her unkissable.

"You did come back to the flat," Jael remarked conversationally.

"Not for you."

"You stayed after Ruth went."

Maria tucked the folded tissue into her sleeve. "I was sort of sorry for you."

She had not meant to hurt, but when she looked up Jael's back was rigid.

"Sorry for me?"

"Because you'd lost her."

The stony eyes dissolved into puzzlement. "But Ruth left so that we could be together."

"She what?"

"She wanted to make room."

"Make room?" Maria's voice swelled to fill the space.

"You've lost the best of lovers, and you make her sound like a battery chicken?"

"It was obvious," retorted Jael. "She told me last night that she'd asked you whether you wanted to stay, and you said yes. So she left."

Maria swore more colourfully than Jael had ever heard her. After a moment, she gathered her wits. "Have you never a brain between the two of you? I didn't mean I wanted to stay and replace her. It won't hurt you to wash your own damn dishes for a while. How could she have thought that? I meant I wanted to stay in the flat with both of you, if I wouldn't be in the way. I may be only seventeen, but I can make up my own damn mind. Why didn't she ask me? Why didn't she stay?"

She put her head down on her knees and cried herself out. By the time she sat up, her face sodden, Jael had moved back to the rocking chair and was studying her whisky glass.

"I've been a bit of a gobshite, haven't I?" asked Jael.

Maria nodded.

"Don't bother forgiving me now, I'm sure you'll get around to it sometime. Listen, what do you want to do?"

Her mind was blank. She scrabbled for times, places, names. And then at once she knew exactly what to do. "I have to find Ruth."

"To tell her all this? You should know, she won't be coming back anyway."

"No, not to tell her. Just to find her."

Jael began speaking, then stopped herself, and realisation crept across her face. "I see. God, I hadn't even thought of that."

"Of what?" And then Maria stopped, because she knew.

"That makes sense of a lot of things."

They looked at each other in bewilderment. "It does, doesn't it," said Maria, mostly to herself.

Jael cleared her throat. "How come I never saw?"

"I didn't either, till now."

"She'll be at her mother's," said Jael automatically, breaking the silence.

"Oh. I'll be off, so," said Maria slowly.

"Do you have the address?"

Maria nodded abstractedly.

"Take the bus from the end of the road, and get off after the fancy bridge. Have you got enough change? They won't take notes anymore. You'll find change in the pocket of my jacket, on the back of the door."

Maria moved like a sleepwalker. Three minutes later she was packed and gloved, her pockets full of coins. The velvet cap was tucked into her coat pocket. She hovered by the fire. Jael got to her feet, rather unsteadily, and planted the lightest of kisses on her forehead.

The bus came at once; Maria knew it was a sign. She sat on the empty top deck, at the very front. The bus bucked and rolled on its speedy journey into the suburbs; it was like clinging to a sea monster. As she rode, Maria played through all the possibilities.

She would be unable to find the Johnsons' house; would wander and finally curl up on a park bench and be discovered dead of exposure by a gardener the next morning.

She would find the house, but Mrs. Johnson would refuse to admit any stranger with such a haircut and would whip her down the road with giant rosary beads.

She would find the house, but Ruth would not be there; would already have bussed to Kerry, shipped to Scotland, or flown to Lesbos.

She would find the house and wake Ruth with a pebble thrown against her bedroom window, and Ruth would appear in a white nightgown and say, get thee from me, foul fiend.

She would . . . The trill of the bell woke her from her possibilities. The bus swerved to a halt and let off three women with walking sticks. So far so quickly; Maria wondered whether she had been dozing. It was nearly her stop. She got to her feet and swayed down the top deck, touching the ceiling at times when she felt lightheaded. Glancing over her shoulder, she saw the bridge come into view and pulled at the frayed bellcord. The steps were deep, lurching as her feet reached for them. For the last few minutes of the journey she stood by the bus driver, balancing by bending at the knees, barely touching the pole with her palm.

He let her off on a patch of soft grass beyond the bus stop. "God bless," Maria told him, her face serious. She pushed her gloves into her pockets and set off walking along the grass verge. The first crossing she came to was, as she knew it would be, the right road. She counted the gates off one by one, patting their rough stone posts with her numb fingertips.

When she came to the house, the porch light was on. And it was Ruth who opened the door.